PRESCRIPTION FOR MURDER

I was alone at the streetcar stop in front of the historic inn, except for a man wearing what the young people call a "hoodie." He leaned against a building a dozen feet from where I stood, trying, in my opinion, to appear casual. When I looked in his direction, he turned away from me, dropped the cigarette he was smoking, crushed it with his sneaker, and walked away. I watched as he crossed Eighth Avenue and got into a car—a small silver sedan that looked like the one I'd noticed following us earlier in the day. The car quickly pulled away and sped past me, with the driver and the young man both looking straight ahead.

The streetcar arrived and, gripping the back of the seat in front of me, I slipped onto a bench. I was on edge. Ever since arriving in Tampa to meet up with Seth, I'd experienced this sort of unease—nothing tangible, no single incident to which I could point. Of course, witnessing Alvaro Vasquez's sudden death had played a part, but, as upsetting as that was, it couldn't explain the tension I'd felt before that awful event.

I was relieved when I reached the hotel. The first thing I did upon entering my room was call Seth. There was no answer, so I left a message. Strange, I thought, that he would have gone out without leaving word for me. I waited fifteen minutes and tried his room again. Still no answer.

Prescription for Murder

A *Murder, She Wrote* Mystery

A NOVEL BY

JESSICA FLETCHER & DONALD BAIN

Based on the Universal television series created by

Peter S. Fischer, Richard Levinson & William Link

AN OBSIDIAN MYSTERY

OBSIDIAN
Published by the Penguin Group
Penguin Group (USA) LLC, 375 Hudson Street,
New York, New York 10014

USA | Canada | UK | Ireland | Australia | New Zealand | India | South Africa | China
penguin.com
A Penguin Random House Company

Published by Obsidian, an imprint of New American Library, a division of Penguin Group (USA) LLC. Previously published in an Obsidian hardcover edition.

First Obsidian Mass Market Printing, March 2014

ISBN 978-0-451-46659-4

Printed in the United States of America
10 9 8 7 6 5 4 3

For dear friends James and Jeannette Vann, with whom we share a love of all things jazz, and who took us by the hand and showed us Tampa, Florida, their adopted city. Jimmy Vann is a superb neocubist artist who was named Tampa Artist of the Year in 2011, and two of his works proudly adorn the walls of our home. His murals celebrating life in Tampa, and particularly the contribution made to the city by its first black patrolmen, are must-sees when visiting Cigar City. Thank you, Jimmy and Jeannette, and happy fifty-fourth anniversary. (You can enjoy Jimmy's art and fanciful art-inspired items at www.jamesvannart.com.)

ACKNOWLEDGMENTS

Many thanks, of course, to our dedicatees, Jeannette and Jimmy Vann, who introduced us not only to Tampa, Florida, but also to most of the people mentioned below. We are grateful to the following, all of whom shared their time and love of Tampa, as well as a good deal of information, not all of which made it onto these pages: Charlie Miranda from District 6, chairman of the Tampa City Council; Major Gerald Honeywell, District 3 commander, Tampa Police Department; Captain Diane Hobley-Burney, Sector E commander, Tampa Police Department; Ronna J. Metcalf, executive director of the Life Enrichment Center; and Kathy Steele of the *Tampa Tribune*.

Thanks, too, to those we encountered along the way and who generously let us take advantage of their knowledge: neurologist Dr. Greg Scott, cigar fanciers Marilyn and Ed Dunn of Thonotosassa, and David Couzens of the Sandpearl Resort in Clearwater Beach.

We thank them all and remind readers that any errors are ours.

Chapter One

Vaughan Buckley's voice was full of enthusiasm. "Our marketing folks have set up an ambitious publicity blitz in Florida for your new book," my publisher told me. "Naturally, you're the centerpiece of it. We've got TV and newspaper interviews arranged, and a series of speaking and signing appearances. It kicks off on December first."

"Oh, my," I said.

"A problem?"

"I just prefer not to be traveling with the holidays coming up. There's always so much to do, and—"

"I understand," Vaughan said, "but the pub date is November fifteenth, perfect timing for people buying holiday gifts, and it's vitally important that we take advantage of every possible publicity opportunity. The fact that you've set the novel in Florida means that we'll be focusing our first marketing efforts there. I hate to pull you away from the Christmas season in Cabot Cove—I know how much it means to you—but I'll see to it that you're only gone a week."

The novel to which he was referring featured a recurring character I'd introduced in a previous book—a police sergeant from Boston who'd settled into what he assumed would be a relaxing retirement in the Sunshine State but soon found himself knee-deep in murder at his retirement resort. As much as I love my publisher and appreciate everything he's done for my career, I was poised to decline. But because I consider myself a professional, I decided on the spot that I had an obligation to help sell my new book. As the writer, I was part of the publishing team, and that meant doing what was expected of me.

"Back in a week?" I said lightly. "That's a promise?"

"My hand is over my heart as I say it," Vaughan replied with a chuckle.

"Okay," I said. "You'll send me the itinerary?"

"I'll e-mail it first thing in the morning."

The itinerary arrived as promised. The promotional tour was scheduled to kick off in the Miami area, move up the coast to Fort Lauderdale and Palm Beach, and end in Tampa.

As I reviewed it, I made a call to my dear friend and Cabot Cove's favorite physician, Seth Hazlitt, whose recent travels had frequently found him in Florida. "Looks like I'm headed to Tampa first week in December," I said, and explained the nature of the trip and the schedule.

"Is that so?" he said.

"Just thought you'd want to know, since Tampa

seems to have become your home away from home recently."

"I wouldn't go that far," Seth said, "but as it happens, your call is very timely."

"Why?"

"I just got off the phone with Susan Shevlin, booked a flight and hotel the second week of December in Tampa."

"That's wonderful," I said. "You really know your way around that city by now. Maybe if our paths cross there you can show me the sights."

"And introduce you to Al."

"Dr. Vasquez?"

"Ayuh. I've told him a lot about you already, Jessica. He'll be delighted to meet a real-live bestselling author."

"Even if she writes about murder?"

"*Especially* because she writes about murder. We'll coordinate our trips."

Dr. Alvaro Vasquez had been one of Cuba's leading medical researchers studying Alzheimer's disease. Seth had met him on a trip to the island nation, having traveled to Havana with a group of U.S. physicians under a new policy established by the current administration in Washington to open up travel to Cuba for select groups, including medical practitioners, artists, religious organizations, and journalists. I was surprised when he'd announced his decision to join the physician group and make the trip. He certainly was no fan of Castro's regime, and I'd heard him speak fondly of the day when the Cuban people would be free. Seth was also critical of what he considered the United States' ironfisted embargo against Cuba: "All this pigheaded embargo of Cuba accomplishes is to give Mr. Castro an excuse for why Cuba is in such desperate straits. He blames us and the embargo, and nobody challenges him, at least publicly."

But Cuba had proven a siren song for my old friend, and he'd visited there again and again, returning each time to wax poetic about his new friend Dr. Vasquez.

Then, about a year ago, newspapers and TV newscasts announced that Dr. Alvaro Vasquez, one of Cuba's leading medical researchers, had defected. His stature within its medical community had become world famous, and to have someone of his importance elect to leave was obviously a blow to Castro and his regime. According to the news reports, Dr. Vasquez and his wife had attended a medical conference in Bern, Switzerland. Rather than returning home, they'd flown to Washington and asked for asylum. Their application was under review, but no one doubted that someone of Vasquez's stature would be approved.

Naturally, Seth was excited about the news and was especially pleased when Vasquez called him a few weeks after arriving in the States. "Al is anxious to get together with me," he proudly told me after the call.

"You two have really bonded," I said.

"Ayuh, that we have. We get along because he appreciates straight talk from me. Lots of people he works with fawn all over him, tell him what he wants to hear. That's not me."

"No, it certainly isn't," I agreed lightly. "Have you made plans to visit him?"

"No, but I will. He and Ivelisse have decided to live

in Tampa, Florida. I'll wait until they're settled in before setting up a visit." Seth had since made several visits south to see his friend, and now the opportunity had arrived when we were both going to be in the city at the same time.

Seth gave me his itinerary and said, "Mind a suggestion, Jessica?"

"Of course not."

"You'll be coming off your book tour and needin' some rest and relaxation, R and R, as they say in the military. I think you should plan to rest up in Tampa while I'm there, enjoy some downtime. The long-term forecast for early December here in Cabot Cove is for snow and more snow and subzero temperatures. Be nice to bask in some sunshine and enjoy fancy drinks with little umbrellas in 'em."

"Sounds appealing," I said. "I'll think about it."

"You do that. If you decide to stay in Tampa, call Susan. She'll book you into the same hotel I'm staying at. Should give the tongues of the rumormongers here something to wag about. Got to run. Let me know what you decide."

I thought about what he'd suggested for the next couple of days before making the decision to extend my Florida trip for a week. It meant cutting into my pre-Christmas activities, but the contemplation of some rest in a more favorable climate became overwhelmingly appealing. I'd also become increasingly interested in Seth's friend and was eager to meet Dr. Alvaro Vasquez. I'd Googled him a bit and was impressed with his expertise and standing among his fellow physicians.

According to what I'd read, his quest for a cure for Alzheimer's disease was admired by his peers, although there seemed to be some sort of mystery surrounding his work, a sense that there were those in the medical research community who questioned his methods. He was known to be extremely secretive about his work, something that other Alzheimer's researchers found arrogant. One even went as far as to brand Vasquez a "grandstander" more eager for fame and fortune than in contributing to science.

Seth had dismissed the harsh views when I'd pointed them out to him. "Medical research is a highly competitive field, Jessica. I'd bet my last nickel this came from a jealous colleague."

"But, Seth, isn't it important for researchers to share important developments in their work so faster progress can be made toward effective treatments?"

He shrugged. "In a perfect world, perhaps. But medical research is every bit as big a business as any other," he said. "If Al gave away his findings, his company might lose the edge they have. Then funding could be compromised and the research delayed, or worse. No, Jessica, I think Al has it just right. Once he's found the results he thinks will be effective, and has them patented or protected in some other way, that's the time to lay his cards on the table, but not yet."

The idea of a medical company patenting its results didn't sit well with me—although I understood that the efforts to come up with treatments or even a cure for any disease deserved to be rewarded—but perhaps I'm naïve when it comes to my expectations for medical research. I didn't argue with Seth, reserving my judgment until I'd met this paragon of Alzheimer's research he was so thrilled with.

I dragged out some of my warm-weather clothing and packed for the trip, although I read that portions of Florida were experiencing record-breaking cold temperatures. Jed Richardson, who owned a small fleet of Cessnas based in Cabot Cove's airfield, flew me to Hartford, Connecticut, where I caught a plane to Miami. Two members of Vaughan Buckley's publicity staff met my flight, and we set off on a whirlwind tour that occupied every minute of the day, and evenings, too.

Coral Gables was gloriously sunny, if a bit cool, and the line of book buyers snaked around the corner from the stop we made at Books & Books. Even though I love staying home surrounded by my friends and the familiar routines of my daily life in Cabot Cove—and leave reluctantly when travel is planned at particularly busy times—I always find myself energized when I'm on the road. Staying in new places or even ones I've visited before is stimulating. There are new sights to see, new foods to taste, and, best of all, new people to meet.

In Miami, I was delighted by the obvious contributions to the city made by its Latin American community and was able to steal some time from the book tour to spend an afternoon in a section called Little Havana, with its colorful art galleries, theaters, restaurants, and cigar stores. I even picked up a set of Cuban dominoes as a souvenir.

Everywhere we went we met crowds of enthusiastic readers, whether they bought their books in a store, borrowed them from the library, or downloaded e-books. I especially enjoy meeting readers. Hearing about their reactions to my novels, what they liked and, occasionally, what they didn't, is helpful to this writer, when so much of my time is spent alone at the computer. All writers need to get out in the world to see what's going on. After all, it's our experiences away from the keyboard that make up the foundation of our stories.

We ended up in Tampa, as scheduled, where the weather was indeed chilly, and I was glad that I'd included a couple of sweaters and a fleece jacket in my suitcase. As we'd seen at each of my stops, fans came out to meet me, and I gave a talk and signed books for several hundred buyers at a large Barnes & Noble. A reporter, Kathy Steele, interviewed me for the *Tampa Tribune*, resulting in a lengthy front-page article accompanied by photographs, and I did two TV interviews and a radio call-in program. My final appearance was at the Tampa Life Enrichment Center, where I spent an hour with men and women taking a class in creative writing, an enriching experience for me, and I hoped for them.

"You're a real trouper, Jessica," Vaughan Buckley's publicist said in the hotel lobby as he and his colleague prepared to head for the airport for a flight back to New York. "Vaughan said to thank you for accommodating his marketing plan."

"It was wonderful," I said, "but I admit I'm ready for some downtime here in Tampa."

"With that colorful character Dr. Hazlitt? We've heard about him."

My publisher had met Seth on a few occasions when he'd traveled to Cabot Cove to confer with me about my books, and apparently he'd shared his views of my good friend.

I laughed. "I never think of Seth as a 'colorful character,' but I suppose in his own way, he is. He's certainly been behaving in unexpected ways lately." I checked my watch. "Five o'clock," I said. "I'd better get to my room and freshen up. Seth and I are meeting at six."

"Vaughan said to send him his best."

"I'll do that," I said, wondering what new surprises my old friend might have in store.

Chapter Two

The hotel's dining room was small and intimate, with crisp white napery, heavy flatware, and a vase of pink roses on each of the fifteen tables. Seth, who had arrived before me, chatted with a waitress by a small bar meant more for fulfilling drink orders than for directly serving customers.

"She says our table will be ready in a few minutes," he told me in greeting. "You don't look any worse for wear after your book tour."

"It went well," I said. "No hitches, and the people I met were lovely. You look well yourself."

"There you go again, Jessica, trying to kid a kidder. The last week back home was busy. Seems that everybody in Cabot Cove decided to come down with the flu at the same time. Tough strain this year. I even had a few patients end up in the hospital. Had me running around like a headless chicken, but they're all on the mend now. Good thing, too. We got a real cold snap, lots of snow. There's something to be said for those snowbird folks who escape cold winters and head south."

"It's pretty chilly here in Florida, too," I said.

Which was true. Temperatures had dipped to near freezing every night since I'd arrived, threatening the citrus crop and causing Floridians to walk around bundled in heavy coats and sweaters.

"I'd call the weather here pleasant," was Seth's reply.

I decided to change the subject. "Have you seen your friend Dr. Vasquez?"

"Only briefly. He's been occupied with his research lab."

"A research lab must cost a lot of money," I said.

"Doesn't seem to be a problem. Al has funding from K-Dex, a pharmaceutical company in Tampa. He introduced me to K-Dex's founder and CEO, a nice chap named Peters, Bernard Peters, a real go-getter who has great faith that Al is making important strides in coming up with a definitive treatment of the disease."

"If he succeeds, it could be worth millions, even billions," I commented.

"It takes millions to find cures for diseases," was Seth's response.

It occurred to me that since Al had defected to Tampa, the Cuban government had not only lost a distinguished citizen, but stood to lose bragging rights for pioneering a medical breakthrough, to say nothing of the money that it could generate for the island and its people. I expressed my thoughts to Seth.

"Ayuh, Al is very aware of what it means to the Castro regime to have a breakthrough in Alzheimer's research happen here in the States after so much of the initial research was done in Cuba," Seth replied. "I had a long talk with him about that very subject. Al's philosophy is that it shouldn't matter where the breakthrough occurs, just as long as it happens."

"I imagine the Cuban government isn't happy that he's defected," I offered.

"No, I imagine they're not," Seth said.

"How do you feel about it?" I asked. "If Dr. Vasquez did most of his research in Cuba, shouldn't the Cuban people share in the rewards of his work?"

I didn't ask it to put my friend on the spot, but he reacted as though I did. He muttered something about it being premature to think about such things, then said, "Are you finished with your third degree, Mrs. Fletcher?"

I laughed. "I didn't realize I was interrogating you."

"Well, you were."

"In that case, what do you say, sir? Ready to take our table? I'm famished."

He motioned for the hostess, who came to us. "I reserved a table for four," Seth said. "Hazlitt."

I looked at him quizzically.

"I took the liberty of inviting two others to join us," he said, "to slowly introduce you to the local cast of characters. Hope that's all right with you."

"Of course it is," I said as we were led to a window table. "Who are they?"

"A couple of folks I've met on my previous trips to Tampa. Oona—that's Oona Mendez, a terrific young lady. She works for the Cuban American Freedom Foundation, some kind of organization that lobbies the State Department. They've just started flights directly from Tampa to Havana, and that was one of their projects. Bright as a newly minted penny, and pretty, too. She's got herself a boyfriend—I suppose that's what you'd call him—a fella named Karl Westerkoch. He's older than Oona, a bit of a stuffed shirt. Not sure what she sees in him, but that's not my business. He's got a German name but talks with a British accent. Hard fella to figure out."

"What does this Mr. Westerkoch do?" I asked as our waitress filled our water goblets.

"Never did find out," Seth said. "Looks like he might be some sort of diplomat, dresses that way, very high in the collar, if you get my drift, doesn't say much, and when he does talk, he mumbles."

"Sounds lovely."

"Not sure I'd use that word," said Seth. "But she's lovely. Let's check the menu. I'm starvin'."

We'd no sooner begun to peruse our menus when Seth's guests arrived. He had been right: Oona Mendez was indeed a pretty woman—and a tall one, skirting six feet with the high heels she wore. She'd donned a form-fitting green-and-yellow silk dress, the narrow waist of which made her substantial hips and bosom seem larger. Her hair was jet-black and worn long, her café au lait face skillfully, albeit heavily, made-up.

Mr. Westerkoch, her companion, was slightly taller than Ms. Mendez. He was a foppish sort, graying hair worn long on the sides and cascading down over the collar of his blue button-down shirt. His paisley bow tie drooped fashionably. His blue blazer was double-breasted and hung loosely on his pencil-thin frame. He didn't look like a diplomat to me, but I was beginning to learn that Seth and I saw more things differently than I'd realized before. What I noticed most about Mr. Westerkoch at that initial meeting was his posture and mouth. He perpetually leaned forward as though being propelled in that direction, and there was a curl to his lip that could be taken as a physical trait or an editorial comment. It would take a while for me to decide.

After we'd finished with introductions and they'd been seated, Oona said, "I've been looking forward to meeting you, Mrs. Fletcher. Dr. Hazlitt tells me that you're quite famous as an author."

"Thank you," I said. "I've been fortunate in my career."

"That's very self-effacing," she said.

"One attribute Jessica doesn't have is an inflated ego," Seth said.

"That's refreshing in this day and age," Westerkoch said through his crooked lip.

"You know who I am," I said, "but I'd like to know more about you, Ms. Mendez."

"Please, it's Oona."

"And I'm Jessica."

I glanced at Westerkoch, who didn't offer his first name.

Seth jumped into the conversation. "Oona is a close friend of Al's," he said.

"Dr. Vasquez," I said.

"A dear, sweet man," Oona said, "speaking of self-effacing. As a Cuban American, I'm very proud of Alvaro and the work he's doing in medical research." She paused and then continued. "He is extremely pleased that Dr. Hazlitt has taken such an interest in his work. You've become one of his most trusted friends, Seth."

"I do seem to enjoy Al's confidence. He's not only a fine gentleman; I believe that he's onto a very important medical breakthrough." Perhaps to stave off more questions from me, Seth abruptly changed the subject and suggested that we order a bottle of wine.

"And so secretive," Oona added, winking at me.

"Who?" I asked.

"Alvaro, of course," she replied. She wagged her red-tipped index finger at Seth. "I really believe that only you and his lab assistant know what's really going on behind that fortress of a lab that Alvaro has built."

Seth seemed flustered at the comment, turned, and waved our waitress to the table. We gave her our dinner choices from the menu. "We'd like a bottle of wine," Seth said. "What do you recommend?"

"Is there Cuban wine?" I asked.

Westerkoch, who hadn't said anything, rolled his lip into an even more pronounced snarl and said in a low voice, "Cuban wine is dreadful."

"It is not!" Oona said.

"Did you have Cuban wine when you were in Havana?" I asked Seth.

"Ayuh. Didn't think much of it, but . . ."

"But what?" I said.

"Well," he said, "Al knows this physician from Cuba, a neurosurgeon, I believe, who left Cuba years ago, settled in Oregon, and has a winery that produces what he calls Cuban wine."

"How can it be Cuban wine if it's produced in Oregon?" I asked logically.

"Cuba's climate is bad for the grapes," Westerkoch said, waving a hand in front of his face as if to dissipate a bad odor. "It's too hot there. Grapes need cool winters with cold rain. It only rains in Cuba in the summer."

"I suppose because the doctor was Cuban, he can claim it's Cuban wine," Oona offered as an answer to my question.

Seth asked our waitress, "What wine would you recommend to go with the food we've ordered?"

She smiled and said, "We have a Cuban pinot noir that some folks say goes nicely with the paella, but you can't prove it by me. It does have a pretty label, though."

Seth ordered a California wine.

The conversation during dinner spanned a variety of subjects, the Tampa professional sports teams taking center stage. Westerkoch seemed to come to life when discussing the relative prospects of baseball's Rays and the National Football League's Tampa Bay Buccaneers. He also held a heated debate with Oona about whether restaurants in Havana have improved; and, of course, Cuba itself was a hot topic, and Fidel Castro, who in 2008 had ceded control to his brother Raúl. I listened with great interest as Oona, who was into our second bottle of wine, railed against the Castro brothers and the destruction they'd brought to her beloved homeland.

"They took what was a thriving economy and turned it into a Communist slum," she said.

"It wasn't any paradise before Castro came," Westerkoch said in a tone that did not invite debate. "It was a sinner's paradise when Batista was in power, nothing but gambling dens and brothels run by the bloody U.S. mafia."

"He's such a hypocrite," Oona said, referring to Fidel Castro. "He complains about the food in Cuba, but when *paladares* are allowed to open he complains that the owners are being enriched."

"Paladares?" I said.

"Private restaurants in homes," Oona explained, "where the best food is served. They were illegal until 1994, but the government charges them so many fees, as much as six hundred U.S. dollars every month, the owners can barely survive."

"Cuban food is pretty good here in Tampa," Seth said.

This prompted Westerkoch to mutter, "They put salami on Cuban sandwiches here in Tampa. Real Cuban sandwiches don't have salami."

And so went the rest of the table talk. Westerkoch's frequent and barely stifled yawns heralded the end of the evening for our two dinner guests. As Seth examined the check to determine how much of a tip to include, Oona said to me, "I hope you're up to par tomorrow, Jessica."

"I expect to feel fine," I said.

"No, no," she said, laughing, "on the golf course. I understand that you have plans to play golf tomorrow with Alvaro, our Dr. Vasquez, and your charming friend Dr. Hazlitt."

I looked at Seth, who smiled and said, "Forgot to mention it to you, Jessica. Al is a big golfer, got serious about it after coming to the States. I thought a morning on the course was a perfect way for you to get to know each other."

"But I—"

"We'll discuss it later," Seth said as we walked with the others outside where Westerkoch's car was parked.

Oona gave me a big hug and said that she looked forward to spending time together. "At Alvaro's house tomorrow night," she added.

Another event that Seth had "forgotten" to tell me about.

After they left, Seth and I repaired to the lounge, where he ordered a mojito and a glass of club soda with lime for me.

"Golf?" I said. "You know I don't play golf, and I wasn't aware that you did either."

"Another thing you don't know about me, Jessica. True, I haven't played in years, at least not in Cabot Cove. But I did play when I was a teenager and young med student—was pretty decent, as a matter of fact. Al persuaded me when I met him in Havana to play a round with him, and I did pretty darn good considering how many years it was since I last held a golf club. I've been playing with Al whenever I visit him here in Tampa."

"So much for your golfing history," I said. "The last time I played was in—let me see—it was at least fifteen years ago. I hated it."

Seth laughed, tasted his mojito, and complimented the bartender on the drink. "As good as they make in Cuba," he said. He turned to me. "You'll love it out on the course, Jessica, fresh air, sunshine, good conversation. All you have to do is keep your eye on the ball and swing the club smoothly. You'll be fine, a regular Babe Zaharias."

"What will I wear?"

"Slacks, a sweater, what you have on right now. The country club'll provide you with golf shoes. Trust me. It will be a nice informal get-together. The perfect way for you to meet Al."

"What about this event at Dr. Vasquez's house tomorrow night?" I asked.

"A party to honor *you*, Jessica."

"I thought I was staying an extra week in Tampa for R and R."

"Can't think of a better way to rest and relax than bask in the spotlight at a party welcoming you."

I sat back, cocked my head, and said, "Something has come over you, Dr. Hazlitt."

"Oh? What might that be?"

"Ever since you befriended Dr. Vasquez, you've— well, you've changed."

"Still my usual charming self," he said, smiling broadly.

I returned the smile. The fact was that Seth *had* changed. There was a twinkle in his eye that hadn't been there before, the sort of twinkle that you see in Santa Claus at Christmas. Whatever was behind it— and it certainly wasn't off-putting—my extended week in Tampa was shaping up to be unusual, to say the least.

Chapter Three

Golf!

The last time I'd been on a golf course was during a charity tournament to benefit Cabot Cove's fire department—and more than fifteen years ago, as I'd told Seth earlier. I'd actually enjoyed the experience because we did more talking than playing, and I even managed to hit that little white ball straight a few times, although not very far. As I recalled, Sam Watson, a local financial planner and accountant, won the match, which surprised no one. He and his wife were avid golfers who played even in winter when the course wasn't covered with snow. For some the game is that much of an obsession.

I had, however, played many rounds at our local miniature golf course and had always done quite nicely.

As I settled in a chair by my hotel room window to

read a few chapters in a novel before going to bed, I had visions of swinging a golf club and completely missing the ball, or managing to make contact and sending it into someone's head, causing massive brain injury leading to death. Would I be liable for manslaughter? Then I wondered whether a skilled golfer who deliberately aimed at an intended victim would be guilty of murder, one of those "what if?" moments.

Those bizarre thoughts got in the way of the novel, and I closed the book's cover, sighed, and tried to conjure reasons for begging off the golf date. I didn't come up with anything plausible. Sprained ankle? Carpal tunnel syndrome from working too much at my computer? A terminal case of prickly heat? None of the above. I decided I'd be a good soldier and go along with the plans for the day, wishing that my initial meeting with Dr. Vasquez took place at his house party rather than on a golf course.

After showering and dressing the following morning, I spent a few minutes in front of a full-length mirror swinging an imaginary golf club at an imaginary golf ball. I tried to remember the few tips Sam Watson had given me during my earlier foray on the golf course but came up blank. Keep my left arm straight? Or was it my right arm? Keep my eye on the ball, or focus on where I wanted it to go? It was a hopeless exercise, and I abandoned it to go down to the restaurant where Seth was to meet me for an early breakfast. As usual he was there before me.

"Al is sending his driver for us at eight," he told me as we perused the buffet.

"Your friend Al obviously has plenty of money," I

said as I scooped scrambled eggs on my plate and used tongs to pick up a single strip of bacon.

"Let's just say that he lives comfortably," Seth said.

"You told me that this fellow who heads a pharmaceutical company is bankrolling him."

"Ayuh."

"He must have great faith in Dr. Vasquez and his research."

"It appears that he does. You'll get to meet him at dinner tonight. In the meantime, I assume that you've been practicing your golf swing." There was mirth in his voice.

"Yes," I said in the same light tone. "I played eighteen holes before breakfast. You do realize, Seth, that I'll be embarrassing you."

He looked at me quizzically.

"Playing golf for real," I explained.

"Nonsense, Jessica. Nobody expects you to write bestselling novels *and* be a pro golfer. Al loves the game, but to be honest he isn't all that good at it. He's new to it, of course, and he can't seem to get enough of it. He's that sort of personality, throws himself totally into everything he does. Anyway, you might even beat him."

I laughed away that suggestion and looked out the window. It was an overcast day with low-hanging gray clouds. A stiff breeze sent palm trees into motion and kicked up dust in the parking lot.

"Looks like rain," I said idly.

"Wishful thinking, Jessica," said Seth. "You'd like our golf date to be washed out, called on account of rain like a baseball game."

He'd read my mind.

We waited in front of the hotel until precisely eight, when a long black Mercedes with tinted windows pulled up and a man emerged from the rear.

"Hello, Al," Seth said as the man closed the gap between us, shook Seth's hand, and took one of my hands in both of his.

"And you, of course, are the famous Jessica Fletcher," he said through a dazzling smile.

I'd envisioned Dr. Vasquez to be a smaller, older man than the person standing in front of me; the one photo I'd seen of him in the newspaper after he'd defected had been blurry, and he'd been in the background. Instead he was tall and movie-star handsome, his dusky complexion a perfect scrim against which very white teeth and deep brown eyes sparkled. Black hair streaked with silver lay close to his temples, not a strand out of place. A thin black mustache curved perfectly over his upper lip. He wore white slacks, a teal polo shirt, white sneakers, and a tan sweater casually draped over his shoulders, the sleeves tied on his chest. I could see him as a tennis pro with whom his female students fell madly in love, or a luxury cruise ship captain holding forth at the dinner table reserved for special passengers. He was, as my friend Mara back in Cabot Cove would say, "a hunk." The famous, and infamous, actor Errol Flynn came to mind.

"It's a pleasure," I said. "Seth speaks of you so often."

"Positively, I hope."

"Of course."

He turned to Seth and slapped him on the shoulder. "The good Dr. Hazlitt here keeps me honest."

Seth's laugh sounded a tad uncomfortable to my ears. "But not on the golf course. Al shaves a stroke or two off his score now and then."

Vasquez adopted a shocked expression. "Nothing is sacred with your straight-talking doctor friend," he said. He looked up into the menacing sky. "Shall we? I've reserved an eight thirty tee time. From the looks of things, we'll be lucky to get in only nine holes."

I kept my smile to myself.

I noticed as we prepared to enter the car that there was a second man in the front seat next to the driver. Neither man paid us any attention, looking straight ahead as we got in. I sat between Dr. Vasquez and Seth. The air-conditioning was running full blast despite it being a chilly morning; it felt like entering an igloo. The driver pulled away from the hotel without instruction from his boss and we joined the flow of traffic.

"Where are we going?" I asked.

"My club," Vasquez replied. "Hunter's Green Country Club. Excellent course, one of the best in the area."

"You've played them all, I assume?" Seth teased.

"When I've had time, which never seems to be the case." Vasquez's words were tinged with his Cuban heritage. "Life was more leisurely in Cuba," he said somewhat wistfully. "Not as good as here in the United States, of course, but more—leisurely."

"Did you get to play much golf in Cuba?" I asked.

"Unfortunately, no. We have a splendid course, the Varadero, built on property once owned by your du Pont family, but I never had the chance to use it. Their mansion, Xanadu, is now the clubhouse."

"Is Fidel Castro a golfer?" I asked.

Vasquez's smile was wide. "Hardly. He considers it a wasteful pastime of the rich, which I suppose it is for some." He laughed gently. "For me it is a way to escape the laboratory and to try to conquer something that is easier than finding a cure for Alzheimer's."

He sounded melancholy, and I wondered if his transplanted research program was not proceeding as successfully in the U.S. as he had expected.

"I wouldn't say becoming good at golf is easier than *anything*," Seth said.

"Sometimes I think you are right, my friend," Vasquez said. "But I keep trying."

I decided to go on the record before we arrived that golf was not something that I knew anything about, and that I would likely slow down everyone's game.

Vasquez patted my hand, then squeezed it. "Nonsense, Mrs. Fletcher. I have a feeling that you are being too modest. Surely hitting a tiny white ball is considerably easier than writing a bestselling mystery novel. You must tell me how you do that. I'm afraid that if anyone asked me to write a book, I would be at a complete loss."

"Now who's being too modest?" Seth said as the driver pulled into the entrance to the golf club. "When you finally come up with a cure for Alzheimer's disease, publishers will be clamoring for a book from you."

Vasquez laughed. "If that is so, perhaps Mrs. Fletcher will collaborate with me."

"But only if you call me Jessica," I said.

"And I am Al. Very American, yes?"

A security guard examined the ID card the driver

presented and waved us through. Now that we'd arrived, I felt my heart racing a little faster. It had never occurred to me when I agreed to spend a week in Tampa with Seth that it would involve playing golf. If he had suggested a fishing expedition, I would have enthusiastically agreed. I do a fair amount of trout and salmon fishing back home. I enjoy tying a fly to my line and wading into the myriad cold, crystal clear streams and rivers that are within minutes of downtown. Even if angling in Tampa meant deep-sea fishing, it would be something with which I was familiar.

But golf?

As we entered the clubhouse, Vasquez stopped a young woman, introduced me and Seth to her, and said, "These fine people are my guests today. Mrs. Fletcher will need a proper pair of golf shoes. I'll take care of Dr. Hazlitt."

She escorted me to the women's locker room, where I was fitted for a pair of splendid-looking white shoes and assigned a locker. A few minutes later she took me to a covered area near the first tee. Vasquez and Seth were standing there waiting for me, along with a short, rotund, pink-cheeked man decked out in golf attire.

"Jessica," said Vasquez, "may I introduce you to my good friend Bernard Peters."

I recognized the name; Seth had told me Peters was the CEO of K-Dex, the pharmaceutical firm that was financially supporting Dr. Vasquez's research. I hadn't expected to meet him until that evening.

"A real pleasure," Peters said. "My wife's a big fan of your books."

"I'm delighted to hear that."

"I think she has every one of them. She has a stand-ing order at our local bookstore for your books when they're released."

"What every writer needs," I said.

Vasquez motioned for a middle-aged man sitting in a golf cart to pull up to us.

"This is Harry, the best caddie at Hunter's Green," Vasquez said. "Let's get started. Jessica, you and I will team up against these two old duffers."

"Oh, no," I said. "Why don't you and Mr. Peters be partners? I'd rather drive Seth crazy with my ineptitude."

"I wouldn't think of it," said Vasquez. "I'm sure you'll do me proud."

I tried my best to justify his optimism. I completely missed the ball on my first swing, but hit it on my sec-ond, sending it in a fairly straight line that traveled about thirty yards. After many other swings—some suc-cessful, some not—we reached the first hole, and to my amazement my first putt went in, which brought forth a round of applause from the others. Buoyed with that success, I proudly moved on to the second hole and the third, my confidence waxing and waning depending on the accuracy—or lack thereof—of my shots. Bernard Pe-ters, who certainly didn't appear to be athletic, proved to be an excellent golfer, as well as a good sport with the slow pace I set. He didn't say much but had a ready smile and encouraged me each time it was my turn to play.

As we progressed, a certain tension developed with

Seth. I know him well enough to pick up on subtle clues when he's annoyed, and it happened on the second hole. Vasquez took it upon himself to give me a golf lesson as I prepared to putt. He came around behind me and placed his hands on mine as they clutched the shaft of my club. Having him press into me from behind was discomforting, and I glanced over at Seth, whose expression was disapproving.

"I think I've got it," I said, creating space between me and Vasquez.

"Yes, I agree," he said. "You certainly do have it, Jessica, in more ways than one."

He did the same at the third hole, but my body language and unwillingness to allow him to get that close sent a message that he obviously received. Seth's displeased expression was gone, and we continued with the game.

Despite my early better-than-expected performance, I kept my eye on the heavens and my fingers mentally crossed. I must admit that having the match canceled due to rain was a pleasant contemplation. The sky appeared to cooperate, turning increasingly dark, almost black at times, and the chilly wind seemed to swell with every step we took. I was about to putt on the fourth hole when jagged flashes of bright white lightning lit up the horizon, followed by a deafening clap of thunder. I looked around at my companions. Peters frowned up at the sky, but Vasquez waved off the weather. "It'll clear up," he said. "These things don't last very long. Go ahead, Jessica. Just don't let the noise throw you off."

I'd experienced plenty of thunderstorms before, but nothing like the heavenly show that was about to take place. The cloud-to-ground brilliant white streaks came in rapid succession, followed by thunder that shook the earth around us. The lightning illuminated the dark sky as though it were created by a mad theatrical producer pulling switches. All was black; then the next bolt came, and the next.

"Let's go," Harry, the caddie, said. "This looks like a bad one."

"We can wait it out," insisted Vasquez. "Look! It's clearing up over there."

"C'mon, Al," Peters said, shoving his club into his golf bag. "It's not like this is the last game you're ever going to play."

The caddie collected the remaining clubs, and no sooner had we squeezed into the golf cart than the rain came pouring down, set in motion by the increasing winds. The light plastic poncho that the caddie handed each of us offered minimum protection. The cart jounced along the track that skirted the course. Each rumble of thunder caused me to wince, and I gripped the sides of my seat to keep from sliding off when we hit a bump on the path. I was greatly relieved when we reached safety beneath the clubhouse's overhang, where other golfers and their caddies had also sought cover.

"My apologies for not providing better weather," Vasquez said as we shed our makeshift rain gear and went inside.

"Saved by the bell," I murmured to Seth, "or in this

case, Mother Nature." Aloud to the group, I said, "I'm afraid that golf will never be my game."

"You did splendidly," Vasquez said, and Seth, bless him, reinforced the compliment.

"Quite a storm," Seth commented as we filed into the clubhouse restaurant. Vasquez insisted that we join him for breakfast even though it was a second one for both of us.

Peters begged off: "I have a meeting to get ready for," he said. "See you all tonight. A pleasure to meet you, Jessica."

"What a nice fellow," I said as the maître d' held my chair.

"Peters? Yes, he's a fine fellow," Vasquez agreed, but there was something in his expression and tone that butted heads with his words. I glanced at Seth, but he didn't seem to have picked up on the contradiction.

Our table afforded us a panoramic view of the golf course, and we watched the theatrical majesty of the storm play out as a waitress took our order. After the bouncy ride to the clubhouse, I didn't think my system would stomach anything stronger than an English muffin and a cup of tea, but my male companions seemed to be energized by the squall and ordered accordingly.

"I've never seen a storm quite this violent," I said. "Does it happen often in Tampa?"

"Tampa's the lightning capital of the world," Seth answered. "I've read that as many as fifty people are struck here every year."

"True," said Vasquez. "I've learned since coming to

Tampa that when a lightning storm erupts, it's best to seek cover—immediately. Storms here are not to be taken lightly."

I thought that we'd moved rather slowly to leave the course once the storm hit, but didn't express it.

"Look," I said. "The sun is out."

Although it continued to rain, sunlight cut through, creating a pretty pattern on the ground outside.

"I told you they don't last long. Typical of the weather here," Vasquez said. "It can change by the hour. Time for my morning cigar. Join me?"

I looked to Seth, who seemed ambivalent.

"Your doctor friend still hasn't adopted the habit of a good cigar after a meal," Vasquez said, "but I'm working on him."

"Too early for me," Seth said, as though discussing an alcoholic drink.

We accompanied Vasquez outside, where he lit up a very long black cigar, using a lighter that was more of a small blowtorch to ignite the cigar's tip.

"A Hoyo de Monterrey Double Corona," Seth said.

"I believe I gave you one, Seth."

"Ayuh, that you did, Al. I'm saving it for a special occasion."

"Every occasion is a special one for a fine cigar," Vasquez said as he sat back in a webbed chair under the overhang, drew deeply on the cigar, slowly blew its blue smoke into the air, and sighed with contentment. He turned to me and said, "I suppose you find it strange that a medical doctor would indulge in such an unhealthy habit."

"It crossed my mind," I said.

He laughed. "Everything in moderation," he said. "Right, Seth?"

"That's my creed," Seth said.

Fortunately the breeze, which had died down along with the storm, blew in a direction that carried the smoke away from me.

After twenty minutes of watching Vasquez indulge his love affair with his cigar, we returned to the car, where the driver and his front-seat companion awaited our arrival. They were beefy men in black suits, white shirts, and skinny black ties, bodyguards right out of central casting.

"I enjoyed our little round of golf even though it was abbreviated," Vasquez said, displaying his wide smile, as the car pulled in front of our hotel.

"And I enjoyed it, although I was sure I wouldn't," I said, not adding that I'd been silently gleeful when the rain came.

"I have a special musical treat for my guests tonight," said Vasquez, helping me from the car. "And authentic Cuban food."

"Seth has been raving about the food ever since he came back from Cuba," I said.

"And for good reason. It will be a pleasure to introduce you to the delights of my native country. But before the party, I would like you, and Seth of course, to be my guests this afternoon at my laboratory. I will give you a personal tour."

"I'd like that very much," I said.

"Good. The car will pick you up here at two. There isn't that much to see, just the usual laboratory paraphernalia, but I think you might find it of interest."

"I know I did," Seth said. He nodded in my direction. "You know, Al doesn't allow many people into his inner sanctum, Jessica. This is quite an honor for you."

"Then I'm grateful to be among the chosen," I said.

"Splendid!" Vasquez said, taking my hand. "I look forward to seeing you. Until then . . ." He raised my hand to his lips, kissed my fingers, and got back into the car.

"Charming fellow, isn't he?" Seth said as the car pulled away and we walked into the hotel.

"Hmm," I said, not exactly agreeing.

Charming certainly would be an apt description of Dr. Alvaro Vasquez, although there was a certain slickness that accompanied that adjective for me, which I kept to myself. It represented an unfair judgment, I knew, based on such a preliminary meeting, but initial impressions are often the most lasting ones.

I told Seth that I needed a little break to freshen up before we went to the lab. "You go rest for a bit," he said. "Meet you in the restaurant at twelve thirty for lunch."

Lunch! Hadn't we just had two breakfasts?

My friend of many years walked to the elevators and disappeared into one. It struck me that he'd fallen under the spell of Dr. Vasquez, which in itself was certainly understandable. Although Seth was a general practitioner back home—a family doctor who practiced medicine in the broadest of senses—he'd always been keenly interested in the more esoteric disciplines of medicine, which stood him in good stead when having to refer patients to specialists. Seth kept up on the latest in medical research, constantly reading and attending conferences when time permitted. That he was vitally interested in Alzheimer's disease didn't surprise me, not only from an intellectual standpoint but because he had patients who'd fallen victim to the progressive, debilitating illness.

But he seemed to be unusually deferential to Vasquez, a side of Seth that I'd seldom seen in our many years of friendship.

I pondered that as I made my way to the covered patio off the restaurant, took a table, and ordered an iced tea. It had turned into a lovely morning, the sun bright, the gentle breeze bracing. The deck was on a canal in which a number of expensive yachts were secured to floating docks, and I enjoyed watching the passing of a variety of small crafts as I sipped my tea.

Reflections on our golf outing soon gave way to thoughts of Dr. Vasquez and Seth's involvement with him, and I found myself becoming a little uncomfortable. Don't ask me to explain my feelings, because I'd be unable to point to anything tangible. Maybe it was Vasquez's defection from his homeland that added an unusual dimension to the situation. I also wondered about the relationship between Vasquez and Bernard Peters, CEO of K-Dex, the company financing Vasquez's research. The amount of money being put up was obviously substantial. Of course medical research is expensive, and probably as speculative as the stock market for those investing in it. But clearly Vasquez was living the high life, presumably on Mr. Peters's dime, as the saying goes, and I'd detected a certain disdain on Vasquez's part when referring to his benefactor.

Stop questioning everything, Jessica, I chided myself.

You're in Tampa for a week of relaxation, a peaceful respite before returning to Cabot Cove and the hectic pace of the holiday season.

Relax!

Stop looking for intrigue.

Just sit back and enjoy this trouble-free week.

Chapter Four

The same two gentlemen in black suits picked us up in the limo to deliver us to Dr. Vasquez's laboratory. As in the morning, they said nothing, simply nodded as we approached the car, held open the door, closed it, and drove off. While they weren't what you would call discourteous, their demeanor was disconcerting, and I wondered what their role in Vasquez's life was. Were they simply from a service hired for the occasion of Seth's and my visit? Or were they employees of our host or of his benefactor, on permanent duty at the disposal of Dr. Vasquez? The few words I'd heard them speak were in Spanish. It would be interesting if their lineage was Cuban, since they worked for a Cuban American physician. But there were many Hispanic citizens in Tampa, from an array of countries. *And why would it be significant if they were Cuban?* I asked myself.

My musings were interrupted by our arrival at the laboratory, a nondescript pale blue one-story building not far from an airport (the sounds of planes taking off and landing confirmed that). While one of the limo drivers opened the car door for us, the other went to the building and punched a code into a box next to the heavy white metal door. A male voice was heard through a tiny speaker. The man in black responded in Spanish. Moments later the sound of some sort of security bars being disengaged could be heard before the door opened and a young man wearing a white lab coat over street clothes stood in the entryway.

"Hello," he said as we approached. He looked at Seth and said, "Welcome back, Dr. Hazlitt."

"Hello, Dr. Sardina," Seth said.

"And you are Mrs. Fletcher," the young man said.

"Yes."

"I'm Pedro Sardina, Dr. Vasquez's assistant. He's waiting for you." Pedro Sardina looked as if he'd spent all of his life inside the laboratory. Of medium height, with a pale complexion, he had prematurely thinning black hair and wore large, thick glasses. The pockets of his lab coat were bulging with items he'd stuffed there and probably forgotten. And a plastic protector in his breast pocket appeared to have been an afterthought, since faint ink stains were visible along the bottom seam.

Once we were inside, Dr. Sardina secured heavy metal bars across the door and reactivated the security system by coding in numbers on a panel.

I said the first thing that came to mind: "It certainly is well protected here."

Sardina smirked. "Security is important," he said as he indicated that we were to follow him down a short corridor. The hum of a motor grew louder as we approached the door at the end of the hallway, where he again entered a code.

"Pedro?" Vasquez's voice asked through the speaker.

"Yes."

The now familiar sound of a bar being raised was heard, and the door opened.

"Ah, I am so pleased you've arrived," Vasquez said, beaming. He, too, wore a white lab coat, over a blue shirt and tie and gray slacks. "Come in, come in."

I don't know what it was that I expected, but somehow the lab didn't match my vision. It was modern, certainly, but rather small. On one wall, white cabinetry was topped with a long green glass counter on which sat a few machines, their functions unknown to me. Above, a stainless-steel shelf held colorful bottles of fluids, which I assumed were chemicals; they were unlabeled. Also on the shelf were boxes of latex gloves, cotton face masks, and containers of antibacterial wipes. On the opposite wall, a bank of three computers, each on a rolling stand, sat next to another cart holding an elaborate maze of interconnected wires snaking out from what looked like an oversized microwave oven. A sanitary hood—at least that's what I think it's called—was tucked in a corner. The hum we'd heard in the hall, which must have been some kind of ventilation system, was close to a roar in the lab. Since there were no windows or skylights—no natural light at all—overhead fixtures gave the room an eerie glow. Could a cure for Alzheimer's disease actu-

ally come out of this modest facility? Evidently Vasquez
and his backers at K-Dex thought it could.

Sardina closed the door and lowered the bar behind
us, its clang jarring in the confined space.

"Like Fort Knox," Seth said with a chuckle.

"A necessary precaution," said Vasquez.

"Why is so much security necessary?" I asked.

"Jessica," Seth said in a disapproving tone. Clearly
he didn't want me to challenge Dr. Vasquez in any way.

"No, no, my friend," Vasquez said to Seth. "She may
ask whatever questions she likes, although"—he
wagged a finger at me—"I may not always answer." He
led us around a large table to where Dr. Sardina had
settled on a high stool and was peering into a powerful
microscope.

"Security is necessary because I have, unfortunately,
made enemies in my defection from Cuba, enemies
who would like nothing more than to discredit my research and to find a way to contaminate my results. By
restricting access to the lab, we know who has been
here and we can account for their time and actions. I
am assuming my work is safe in your hands, señora, is
it not?"

"Absolutely!" Seth inserted.

"Of course," I said, smiling. I cocked my head at his
assistant. "What is Dr. Sardina looking at?" I asked,
hoping I wasn't being unduly intrusive.

"The latest result of an experiment we've been con-
ducting for the past month," Vasquez responded. "Tell
me, Jessica, what crops do you immediately think of
when I mention Cuba?"

I hadn't expected to be quizzed, and I laughed.

"Well," I said, "since Seth has visited Cuba, I think of cigars. Tobacco. And . . . well, sugar, I suppose."

"*Excelente,*" Vasquez said, reverting to his native language. "Yes, sugar, Cuba's most famous and lucrative crop. Sugar thrives in Cuba as in no other place in the world. Its soil is limestone and goes deep into the ground, as deep as seven meters, ideal for growing sugar; as much as eight million tons are produced each year. The sugar harvest, the *zafra,* from November through June, is a cause for celebration in Cuba. The *macheteros,* the harvesters with their machetes, work round the clock to feed the world's love affair with sweetness. Of course, tobacco, as you point out, is also important to my country's well-being. Enough tobacco to make eighty million cigars is harvested each year. Impressive, yes?"

"I suppose so," I said, "but what do sugar and tobacco have to do with your research on Alzheimer's disease?"

Vasquez looked to Seth and said, "Your lovely friend asks many good questions."

"Ayuh, that she does," Seth concurred happily.

"Sugar," Vasquez said as though pondering the meaning of it. "Glucose. I don't wish to bore you with a lot of big medical words, Jessica, but glucose—sugar—plays a vital part in not only our entire body, but is especially important to the brain. It is widely known that people with diabetes have a greater propensity to develop Alzheimer's. It is also known that the brain is the primary consumer of glucose—as much as two-thirds of all glucose circulating in the body goes to the brain. Glucose is the major fuel for our cells, including those in the brain. As our bodies ingest glucose from the foods we eat, insulin must be released from the pancreas to keep the glucose level in check. But many, including diabetics, become what is called 'insulin resistant,' which means, of course, that the glucose is allowed to build up. The result? Diabetes. And, I am convinced, Alzheimer's disease." He laughed. "Am I becoming too technical for you?"

"Not at all," I said, "although I'm sure your research delves into the subject at far greater depth."

"Yes, of course. There is much more to it. Let me just say that the role that glucose plays in how brain cells use sugar and produce energy might well be at the root of Alzheimer's, especially in how it enables the development of beta-amyloid peptides, and protein strands called 'tau,' or tangles that are common with Alzheimer's patients."

"Now you've lost me," I said.

Vasquez turned to Seth and tapped him on the shoulder. "My colleague here knows what I am talking about."

Seth nodded. "Course, I'm not nearly as knowledgeable as Al is, but I do understand the underlying theory of what he's trying to accomplish. If he can establish a direct link between glucose—simple sugar—and the development of plaque in the brain that's synonymous with Alzheimer's disease, and can come up with a way to counter insulin resistance, it could lead to a cure."

I asked the obvious next question. "How close are you to accomplishing those things?"

"That, my dear lady, must remain a secret known

only to me until I am ready to announce it to the world."

I immediately thought of Bernard Peters of K-Dex, the man and the company investing in Vasquez's work. Did Vasquez keep from Peters the progress he'd made—or hadn't made?

As I debated asking that question, Vasquez said, "My dear friend Bernie Peters is always asking me for an update on how the research is going, but he knew from the first day that I would not provide him or anyone else with regular progress reports. He expresses his unhappiness with this arrangement, but . . . Well, let me just say that he must live with it."

I thought to myself that were I Peters, I, too, would be unhappy being deprived of regular progress reports. How much was Vasquez's research costing Peters and K-Dex? It had to be in the millions. It was also obvious that K-Dex's money was not only going to supporting the lab and the research; it was fueling a lavish lifestyle for the researcher.

Vasquez commented while laughing, "Of course, I give Bernie an update now and then just to keep him happy and to keep the funds coming."

Sardina looked up from the microscope and winced, an expression that clearly said that he did not share in Vasquez's humor.

Vasquez took us on a tour of two other rooms in the laboratory complex. In one, an empty animal cage sat on the counter.

"We are anticipating a delivery of SCID mice—mice specially bred for medical research," he said.

I said nothing, but privately I thought, *I'm glad*

they're not here now. There was no way I would get into a debate on the merits of animal research—I had neither the experience nor the expertise to take up the cudgels in that argument—but personally I hated to see any animal, specially bred or not, made to suffer even if humankind benefited as a whole. Seth would disagree, I knew, but I couldn't help my feelings.

"Are you the only tenant of this building?" I asked.

"Yes. Bernie leased it in its entirety for me. I insisted that be the case when I agreed to continue my research here in the States. It's a small building, as you can see, but it is adequate to the task. Once we are to the level that demands a larger, more sophisticated space, we'll deal with it then."

We ended our tour in a small office at the rear of the building permeated by the odor of cigar smoke.

"Join me?" Vasquez asked as he removed one of his large black cigars from an elaborately decorated case he drew from his shirt pocket. He cocked his head and said, "It is not unheard of for ladies to partake in cigars, you know."

Seth, bless him, sensed my unease and said, "I think we'd better be getting back, Al."

"As you wish. The evening is shaping up nicely at the house. Ivelisse has things under control, although she has plenty of help."

Sardina showed us out, and we were driven back to the hotel, where a tea service was under way. "I'd love a cup," I said with a sigh as I sank into an upholstered wing chair near a window overlooking a tropical garden.

"Well, Jessica. You've been keeping me guessing.

What did you think?" Seth asked as we were served tiny tea sandwiches, pastries, and a steaming pot of tea.

"About Dr. Vasquez?"

"Of course about Dr. Vasquez. Who have we been spending the last few hours with?"

"And most of the day," I murmured to myself, taking a sip of my tea.

"C'mon, woman. What are you dillying about?"

"Well," I said, "I find him to be charming, dynamic, and good-looking, but maybe a little too much of each."

Seth's expression mirrored his surprise at my comment.

"He's too good-looking? Never heard anyone complain about that."

"Don't get me wrong," I said. "He's a perfectly wonderful host, and I certainly admire the work he's doing. If he succeeds in helping conquer Alzheimer's disease, it will be a monumentally important gift to mankind, and womankind, too. He'll probably receive a Nobel Prize."

"My thoughts exactly," said Seth, popping a salmon sandwich into his mouth. "I feel privileged to have been taken into his confidence."

"It doesn't surprise me," I said. "You share his obvious love of medicine and medical research, and as he says, you level with him."

"Try to."

"So let me ask you, is he as far along in his research as he wants others to believe? I'm referring specifically to Mr. Peters at K-Dex."

"You sound suspicious, Jessica."

"Nothing of the sort. It's just that I have trouble getting my head around his extreme secrecy, especially with the man who is making it all possible by funding the research."

Seth shrugged, bit down on a tiny cucumber sandwich, and took a sip of tea before responding. "He told you why he needs the security. You know it must be very embarrassing to the Castro regime to have lost such a shining light in medical research to the U.S. It wouldn't surprise me in the least if they made efforts to break into the lab and steal his work," he said. "As for K-Dex, I understand the company was struggling before hooking up with Al. It had a series of setbacks, promising drugs failing to pass FDA muster, the sort of situations that plague all pharmaceuticals. From what I've been able to glean, Al's work generated a fresh influx of investors and could make the difference between K-Dex surviving or going under."

"And so Mr. Peters is desperate enough to allow Dr. Vasquez to proceed on his own terms."

Seth hesitated before saying, "I suppose you could put it that way."

"From what you've told me, Dr. Vasquez's work in Cuba was pretty far along."

"Call him Al. He prefers it. I'd say that your assessment of his work in Cuba is accurate, at least based upon what he's shared with me."

I chose a salmon sandwich.

"I was surprised at how small the lab is and that Al has only one assistant," I said. "It seems to me that research on something as daunting as Alzheimer's would—well, would demand a much larger lab and staff."

"It's the size of the man's brain, Jessica, not the size of his laboratory that counts," Seth said rather sharply.

I fell silent for a time and concentrated on what was left of the sandwiches and pastries.

"Something bothering you?" Seth asked.

"Oh, no," I said. "I guess I'm accustomed to you being more skeptical. It's one of your curmudgeonly traits I most admire. But here you seem to have what might be termed blind faith in what Al is doing, the way Mr. Peters must or seems to."

I checked his face for a sign of annoyance. Instead, he appeared to be hurt. I quickly added, "I don't mean to disparage your belief in him, Seth, but—well, it's not like you to accept on the surface whatever someone tells you."

Which was true. For as long as I've known Seth Hazlitt, he's been a man who seldom takes others at face value. Not that he's unduly suspicious or dismissive of what others say, but he's quick to cast a critical eye on claims without confirming backup.

He sat back and gazed out the window, as though peering into another world that only he could see. When he finally turned back to me he asked, "Have you ever wanted to be someone else, Jessica?"

I pondered the question. "I don't think so," I said. "There are plenty of people that I admire, but wanting to be them? No, I can't think of anyone at the moment."

"I admire that," he said.

"Why?"

"Because it means you're supremely contented with who you are and what you've done with your life."

"Yes," I said, "I believe I am." I paused before adding, "Aren't you?"

"I suppose I am for the most part, but when I was a young man coming out of medical school, I had visions of making a big breakthrough in science, dreamt of coming up with a cure for cancer or heart disease, doing something monumental to benefit society."

"And that's exactly what you do," I said. "How many people in Cabot Cove owe their lives to you? How many mothers have healthy children because Dr. Seth Hazlitt was there to deliver their babies and see them through illness?"

He held up his hand. "I get the point, Jessica, and I won't argue with you. But Al's work is historic. It could mean better lives for millions of men and women. That he's allowed me into his world, considers me a colleague, is . . . How can I put it without sounding shallow? It's flattering; that's what it is. To be close to a man who had to escape a brutal dictatorship in order to find the freedom to pursue his passion gives me a sense of . . . a sense of *importance*."

I didn't know how to respond. I understood what he was saying, and tapped into the emotions behind it, but I was surprised that this dedicated physician who meant so much to so many in our town would feel the need to rub shoulders with someone else to achieve a sense of worth.

"Sounds silly, right?" he said as he finished off a tiny cream puff and what was left of his tea. "Forget we ever had this conversation. Just a foolish old man talking. This aging sawbones is feeling his age, needs a good nap before the festivities this evening. You'll excuse me?"

"Of course. But, Seth, I—"

My words trailed behind him as he walked slowly from the restaurant and disappeared into the lobby.

A wave of sadness swept over me. I'd rarely heard him talk that way about his life and unfulfilled aspirations. Yes, he was getting older, as we all were, and age can generate a tendency to look back at what might have been. But Seth was shortchanging himself. He'd had a wonderful, meaningful career—and still did.

As the sadness abated, a feeling of resentment toward Dr. Vasquez took its place. Why? I couldn't explain it and willed it from my thoughts. I was reading too much into what Seth had said and the hold that Vasquez seemed to have over him at that point in his life.

"More tea?" the waitress asked.

"What? Oh, no, thank you. Please put the charge on my room."

As I sat in a red-and-gold wing chair in my suite, I felt a chill that had nothing to do with the room's temperature. A sense of foreboding had settled in, and I found myself dreading the dinner party at Vasquez's home.

I wished I were back home in Cabot Cove.

Chapter Five

Seth had been downbeat when he left the restaurant that afternoon, and I expected his mood not to have changed. But there he was in the lobby, nattily dressed in a blue blazer, white shirt, and red bow tie, and looking every inch like the Seth Hazlitt I knew and loved. He was absolutely ebullient as he greeted me, took my arm, and guided me outside, where we would be picked up. The weather didn't match his upbeat mood, however. Dark, low-flying clouds heralded the approach of another storm, and I hoped the party wasn't planned as an outdoor event.

"You look splendid," I said.

"And you, Jessica, will turn every man's eye at the party. I have one request."

"Which is?"

"That you ignore my maudlin conversation this afternoon. Don't know what got into me. You'd think I was one of those morose drunks cryin' in his beer, but all I had was tea."

"As you wish, sir," I said as the black Mercedes pulled up, manned by our usual escorts.

"Did you get a good nap in?" I asked after we were settled in the back and on our way to the party.

"Never took one," he replied. "Perked up the minute I got in the room. Anxious for you to see Al's house. It's really nice, backs right onto the water on Davis Island. He's got his own dock and boat there, gave me a little tour of the bay last time I was in Tampa."

"Have you met others who'll be there tonight?"

"Ayuh, a few. Oona Mendez and her disagreeable companion will show, I suppose; probably Al's son, Xavier—nice young chap, doesn't say much, a bit of a brooder, if you get my drift, like so many young men these days—and Al's assistant, Dr. Sardina, I imagine. Oh, and Bernie Peters mentioned on the golf course that he and his wife were invited. I should let you know that Al's wife, Ivelisse, comes off a little strange now and then."

"Strange?"

"Lovely woman, very gracious, but sometimes she can be, well, 'scattered' might be the right term."

"Thanks for the warning."

Alzheimer's naturally crossed my mind, although I didn't ask. Becoming forgetful isn't necessarily caused by a disease. How many times lately had I forgotten why I went to another room, or drawn a blank on someone's name, someone I knew well? I believe it's called "aging." Still, my writer's mind almost always creates scenarios even when none exist. Dr. Vasquez was doing research on Alzheimer's disease. His wife, according to Seth, was forgetful. Did her husband suspect that his wife might be falling prey to the very illness he was trying to conquer?

Stop it, Jessica! You're not creating a plot for a book now.

Seth's contagious, upbeat mood continued throughout the drive.

"That's Al's home there," he said enthusiastically as we turned onto a street called Adalia. We approached an imposing two-story white house with a balcony that ran the length of the second level, and a set of large glass doors leading into the first. As we pulled into the circular driveway, the sound of music with a Latin beat could be heard over the crunch of our tires on the gravel. The car's door was held open for us as we exited, and we went up a short set of concrete steps to where a large man, also dressed in a black suit, white shirt, and black tie, stood. He recognized Seth and greeted him.

"This is Mrs. Fletcher," Seth said.

"*Sí,*" the man said. "She is on the list. The guest of honor, in fact." He gestured at the doors. "Please go in."

My mind immediately conjured disturbing reasons for why a party would generate a formal guest list, or need someone to be standing guard at the front door, but I forced the thoughts away, and we went inside. Dr. Vasquez, dressed in a white guayabera trimmed with layers of lace, and a woman I assumed was his wife, Ivelisse, stood in a sizable foyer that was decorated with white-and-black tiles on the floor and a series of vividly colored abstract paintings on the walls. A massive modern chandelier constructed of a maze of burnished brass pipes and a hundred small bulbs was suspended from the ceiling by a thin metal tube. *I'd hate to be under it if it fell*, I thought.

Vasquez smiled and stretched out his arms. "Ah, my guest of honor," he said. "Welcome." He turned to his wife, a stunning woman with closely cropped white hair who was wearing a silver metallic sleeveless top over tight black pants. "My dear, this is Jessica Fletcher, our honored guest for the evening, and you know Dr. Hazlitt."

Mrs. Vasquez smiled sweetly and extended her hand. "It is such a pleasure to have you in our home, Mrs. Fletcher."

"I'm honored to be here," I said, "and please call me Jessica." I cocked my head in the direction of the music, which was louder now. "That music is wonderful."

Vasquez laughed and moved his feet to the rhythm. "Ah, they play a *guaracha*. Cuban musicians," he said, "very good ones. They did as I did—came to America to get away from Castro and his fascist regime, which frowned on the Creole forms of our popular music. Here, they may play what they like—and what we like. Come, the party has already started." He took my hand and led us from the foyer into a spacious living room, where the festivities were under way. I took note of large French doors leading out onto a long deck landscaped with flowering plants and potted palm trees, and ending in a dock, where a cabin cruiser could be seen bobbing in the water. Inside, most of the furniture in the living room had been pushed back or removed to accommodate the party, but oversized cubist oil paintings added color to the few spaces along the walls that weren't covered with floor-to-ceiling book-cases.

The source of the upbeat tunes was a group of five musicians dressed in colorful flowered shirts earnestly playing the composition I'd heard from the foyer. Two dozen other guests were in the room—stylishly dressed women, and men in what might be called business-casual attire. A couple danced, and others cheered them on, clapping hands and occasionally shouting "Olé" as though witnessing a bullfight. The atmosphere was captivating, and I felt myself swaying to the infectious rhythm. I don't consider myself much of a ballroom dancer, although I do enjoy a turn around a dance floor now and then. My late husband, Frank, was a better dancer than I am and gave me the confidence to try new steps, sometimes successfully, sometimes not, but always enjoyable.

Vasquez pulled me across the room to where an el-derly gentleman sat at a small wooden desk, rolling tobacco into cigars. "This is Adelmo, one of the finest cigar makers in Tampa."

"How do you do?" I said.

The old man rapped his knife on the table but didn't reply.

"We bring him here both to entertain our guests and to provide a welcome gift." Vasquez plucked two of the completed cigars from a box on the desk with a smile. "You will excuse me, Jessica, will you not?"

"Of course," I said.

"Please take one for Seth," he said and went through the French doors to the deck, where he was immedi-ately joined by his lab assistant, Dr. Sardina.

I picked up a cigar but then put it back. If Seth wanted to smoke a cigar, he could come get one himself. I would not encourage a new habit.

Adelmo looked up at me curiously. Not wanting to appear rude, I asked him, "Are you using Cuban tobacco?"

"No, señora. One cannot bring Cuban tobacco into this country. But this is very fine Dominican tobacco, and the wrappers are from Connecticut. Perhaps you know this state?"

My eyebrows rose. "Connecticut? I had no idea tobacco was grown in New England."

"Shade tobacco," he replied, "very much like the Cuban leaf."

"Ah, yes, shade tobacco," said a stout gentleman who joined us at the desk. "Grown in a shed to mimic the Cuban tropical climate," he said to me. "And how are you tonight, Adelmo?"

Their conversation allowed me to make a graceful exit, and I rejoined Seth, who was standing with Mrs. Vasquez, her arm linked in his.

"Do you dance, Dr. Hazlitt?" Ivelisse asked.

"Not one of my talents," he replied. "I heard a band like this when I was in Havana. Somebody said it was salsa, but I wouldn't know one sorta music from another. I thought salsa was something to eat."

"I think you are too modest," she said, and turned to me. "Don't you agree, señora?"

"That Seth is modest? Yes, I certainly agree with that."

As we stood in the group enjoying the dancers, Oona Mendez, whom I'd met at dinner with her companion Karl Westerkoch, joined us. "Wonderful to see you again," she said.

"Likewise. We're enjoying the music and the dancers."

"Cuban music," she said reverentially. "It is so full of spirit, so joyous, so—so sensual."

"Does what they're playing have a name?" I asked.

"*Son*. It means 'sound' in Spanish. It is the basis for all Cuban music, the *danzón*, the habanera, the mambo, and of course salsa."

"All I know is that it sounds wonderful," I said. "Is Mr. Westerkoch here this evening?"

She pointed across the room, where he stood leaning against a bookcase, a drink in hand, his dour expression testifying to his mood, which was decidedly not a party one.

A uniformed waiter approached carrying a tray of hors d'oeuvres—tiny crab and chicken croquettes accompanied by a silver bowl of hot sauce, sweet peppers filled with mushrooms and ham, and lobster meat on small pieces of flatbread drizzled with pepper aioli.

"I hope you like things spicy," Oona said, spearing a croquette with a toothpick.

"As a matter of fact, I do," I said, "as long as it isn't too hot." I tried a flatbread with lobster and assorted spices. "Hmmm," I said, "just right. Delicious."

Ivelisse Vasquez excused herself to greet Bernard Peters and his wife in the foyer. They say that people tend to marry those who look somewhat similar, and that theory held up when it came to Mr. and Mrs. Peters. They were both short and round, her ruddy cheeks matched his, and they were dressed in clothing of the same color. Ivelisse escorted them into the main room and I was introduced to Frances Peters. She greeted Seth with a kiss on the cheek; he'd certainly gotten around and met people during his previous stays in Tampa.

Mrs. Peters was a cheerful lady who punctuated everything she said with a laugh. Her husband had been good-humored, too, on the golf course, but that certainly wasn't his demeanor this evening. He gave me a cursory hello and headed straight for the bar, behind which a uniformed gentleman plied his craft.

"Are you ready for a drink Ju—ah, Jan—Señora Fletcher?" Ivelisse asked.

"Please call me Jessica," I said.

"Thank you, Jessica. We're serving authentic Cuban mojitos and"—she paused and screwed up her face in thought—"oh, yes, authentic daiquiris."

"Daiquiris were Ernest Hemingway's favorite cocktail. Maybe if I have one, it will help me write like him."

Alvaro Vasquez, who'd returned inside, caught the end of the conversation. "Another of your American authors, Norman Mailer, once scolded JFK after the Bay of Pigs disaster. He supposedly told your president that the mistake he'd made was invading a country without understanding its music."

"I hadn't heard that," I said.

"Or without understanding one of its favorite cocktails. Come. Enjoy a daiquiri."

With that he led me by the hand to the bar, where Westerkoch was getting a refill.

"Good evening," I said.

He mumbled something in return, took his glass from the bartender, and walked away.

What a strange egg, I thought as Vasquez ordered a daiquiri for me. "Make it especially good for our guest of honor," he instructed.

I tasted my drink. It was delicious, although I had the feeling that it would go down too easily and reminded myself to nurse it throughout the evening.

"I want you to meet someone, Jessica," Vasquez said, leading me to where a handsome young man stood talking to Pedro Sardina and a lady I would learn was his wife, Ofelia, an attractive, slender young woman with an oval face and sad brown eyes.

Vasquez didn't wait for a pause. He cut into their conversation and made the introductions. "And this is my son, Xavier," he said proudly.

Xavier, a relatively short man compared to his father and mother, frowned at the interruption but managed a smile for me. "My father has told me a lot about you," he said.

"I'm afraid our initial meeting wasn't an ideal place for me to make a good impression," I said. "I'm not much of a golfer."

"Nonsense," Dr. Vasquez said. "Give her a few days of practice and she'll win all the tournaments."

"I don't play golf at all," Xavier said. "It's a stupid game."

I wasn't sure that I agreed with his assessment, but I didn't question it. Nor did his father, who forced a smile.

"I understand that you live in Tampa," I said, changing the subject.

"That's right, when I'm not in Key West."

"Oh? You go there often?"

"Xavier has a lady friend in Key West," his father said, "conveniently far away from his parents. Fortunately he has a plane that he can fly to see her."

Xavier glared at his father.

"A plane?" I said. "You're a pilot?"

"Yes," he said, never lowering his gaze from his father.

"What sort of plane do you fly?" I asked, hoping to move the conversation into a neutral area.

"A Cessna one-seventy-two, a later model, four-seater."

"I ask because I have a private pilot's license," I said a bit self-consciously, "although I'm afraid I don't get to fly very much." I smiled at the Sardinas, whom Vasquez had completely ignored.

"That's a shame," Xavier replied, his attention back on me. "You'll excuse me, please," he said, bowing slightly and nodding at the Sardinas. "It was a pleasure."

He walked away and I saw dismay on his father's face.

"What a handsome young man," I said to break the tension.

"He takes after his mother," Vasquez said.

An awkward silence ensued.

"I met your husband at the lab today," I said to Ofelia. "I'm impressed with the work he and Dr. Vasquez are doing to find a cure for Alzheimer's disease."

"Pedro doesn't talk much about his work," she said

in a voice so soft that I had to lean closer to hear what she'd said.

Vasquez laughed. "The best kind of assistant," he said, nodding at Sardina. "Less talk and more research."

"The daiquiri is delicious," I said, taking a small sip.

"Don Casimiro classic silver rum," he said. "Only the best."

As the band launched into its next tune, Vasquez once again left my side and strode to where Bernard Peters was engaged in conversation with Oona Mendez.

"C'mon," Sardina said to his wife. "I want another drink."

"A pleasure meeting you," I said to Ofelia Sardina.

She smiled and they walked away.

Left to my own devices, I sipped my daiquiri and glanced around at the other guests. Despite the pulsating, joyous music, the couples dancing, and the tasty canapés, there was a palpable tension in the room, and it was more than the father-son contretemps. My gaze fell on Ivelisse Vasquez, who stood alone in an alcove and seemed to be in a world apart. Her son, Xavier, had disappeared altogether, and I wondered whether he'd decided that the party, like golf, was "stupid." I watched as our host escorted a frowning Bernard Peters onto the deck.

The hors d'oeuvres became more plentiful, enough so that it was necessary to balance plates and glasses while using utensils that were passed with the food. Westerkoch had commandeered a small, tall glass-topped table on which to rest his plate, and I placed my plate there, too.

"Lovely party," I said.

"Like other parties the doctor hosts. Frankly, I don't care for the music. It's too loud, and there's a tribal aspect to it, people jumping up and down like savages."

"I, ah . . . Are you involved in medical research, Mr. Westerkoch?" I asked.

"No."

"I just thought that—"

"I'm a consultant."

A friend once told me that when someone says he or she is a consultant, it means they're out of work, but of course I didn't verbalize that cynicism. Instead I asked, "What sort of consulting do you do?"

"Government basically. You ask a lot of questions, Mrs. Fletcher."

I didn't take his comment as a challenge and laughed. "I suppose that's because I'm a writer."

"How convenient. I understand that you and your doctor friend visited Vasquez's lab this afternoon."

"That's right. I was pleased to be invited."

"Your friend seems to have successfully invaded Vasquez's inner circle."

"Has he? Invaded? That's rather an odd way to put it. All I know is that he feels a camaraderie with Dr. Vasquez."

"I get the feeling that it's more than that. What does your friend tell you about Vasquez's research?"

"Very little. Dr. Vasquez explained it to me in the simplest of terms. You and he are obviously acquainted. What has he told *you* about his research?"

"As little as possible." He turned toward the French doors, through which threatening weather could be seen in the distance. "I need some fresh air before the sky opens up."

I seem to be repelling all comers, I thought as Westerkoch abandoned the table we shared. But the next half hour gave the lie to that thought. Guests to whom I hadn't been introduced invited me into their conversational circles, and I began to thoroughly enjoy myself. Seth, who'd spent much of the night with others, eventually wandered to where I was listening to a joke told by the gentleman I'd encountered at Adelmo's cigar-rolling desk. Carlos Cespedes owned a cigar shop and factory in Ybor City, the Cuban section of Tampa. ". . . and so Fidel Castro, he has trouble sleeping and goes to his doctor. 'I have insomnia,' he says. 'What should I do?' And the doctor says, 'Try reading some of your speeches.'"

We all laughed at this dig at Castro's famous, impossibly long speeches. Cespedes was about to launch into another tale when Seth guided me away from the group and toward the French doors, through which Vasquez and Bernard Peters could be seen on the deck. From their body language and the movement of their arms and hands, it seemed an argument was in progress.

"Is there a problem?" I asked Seth.

"Appears that way, doesn't it?"

We had only a few seconds to witness the confrontation; then Peters threw up his hands, came through the doors, and stomped across the room in the direction of his wife. On the deck, Vasquez pulled a cigar from his elaborately decorated case and held it up to his nose, inhaling the scent of the tobacco leaves.

"Let's keep him company," I said.

When Vasquez saw us, he substituted his gregarious side for the upset he'd just experienced and said, "Good, good, I need someone to share a good smoke with. Please," he said, offering Seth his cigar. "It was a gift from someone special. It's Cuban."

"Not for me, Al, but thanks."

Vasquez raised his eyebrows questioningly at me.

"No, thank you, sir," I said. "I just thought some fresh air would be nice."

"You can't blame my cigars for the stuffy air inside, Jessica. Ivelisse and I have an understanding. I can smoke to my heart's content, but only outside, or in my office at the other end of the house. I had a professional air cleaner installed in it, like ones in restaurants. I am an agreeable husband, yes?"

"It certainly sounds that way."

He fired up his lighter and went through the elaborate ritual of lighting his cigar, blowing a stream of smoke into the air with a satisfied smile. "Come. Let me show you my latest gadget on the boat," Vasquez said. "Jessica, you haven't seen my new toy."

"Uh-oh," I said as a drop of rain landed on my nose. I looked up into the black sky. "Better get back inside," I said.

"Nonsense," said Vasquez, "just a few raindrops. I can't waste this good cigar." He drew deeply on it and watched the blue smoke curl up into the air.

"Sorry," I said, "but I don't have a cigar to save." With that I made for the French doors and stepped inside. I looked back to where Seth and Vasquez continued to stand together, Vasquez smoking, Seth saying something that I couldn't hear. As I watched them, shadows emerged from behind a shed farther along on the deck. I squinted until I could make out Westerkoch and Oona Mendez. They approached Seth and Vasquez, stopped for a moment to say something, and came inside.

"A storm's brewing," Oona said.

"So I see," I said.

A sudden shaft of lightning illuminated where the two men stood, followed by a low rumble of thunder.

"They should come in," I said. "They told me that lightning here in Tampa is particularly dangerous."

Seth slapped Vasquez on his back and headed inside.

"Why is he staying outside?" I asked.

"He wants to finish that cigar," Seth replied with a laugh, brushing a few raindrops from the sleeve of his jacket.

More lightning bolts turned the deck brilliantly white, as if giant klieg lights had been turned on. The light show drew others to the French doors, Westerkoch, Oona, and Ivelisse Vasquez.

"Hello," Ivelisse said, smiling at me. "I'm Ivelisse Vasquez. Have we met?"

Her comment startled me, as much as a clap of thunder that made me jump.

Outside, Vasquez looked up as though surveying the heavens. He took another deep drag on his cigar and raised it, seemingly offering it to the gods. As he did, the brightest and most menacing of lightning bolts carved a jagged path from the sky to where the deck met the water. In its harsh light Vasquez looked like a Shakespearean thespian portraying Hamlet, a spotlight establishing his stage presence. Then, as we watched in horror, Dr. Alvaro Vasquez doubled over and dropped to his knees, the cigar flying from his hand. He pitched forward and lay still as the sky opened up and the rain came down in sheets.

Chapter Six

Oona Mendez shrieked.

Karl Westerkoch said, "Damn," and pushed the door open a crack, allowing the sound of the pelting rain to reach inside.

Ivelisse Vasquez stood motionless, her face blank.

Seth wrenched open the door and ran out into the downpour. I followed.

He knelt over Vasquez and placed his fingertips against his neck. "Get an ambulance," he shouted to no one in particular. "Call nine-one-one!" With that, he straddled Vasquez and began administering CPR.

I looked back in the hope that someone would bring an umbrella, but no one moved until Xavier appeared carrying a tan raincoat. Seth climbed off, and Xavier spread the coat over his father, including his face. Seth pulled it back and again tried to discern a pulse in the neck. He shook his head and continued pressing on

Vasquez's chest with rhythmic thumps. "Come on, Al. Don't give up," he told his patient. "Where's the ambulance?" he called out.

"Did you call for an ambulance?" I asked Xavier.

He ran back inside the house.

One of the waitstaff who'd passed hors d'oeuvres came to where Seth labored over the still lifeless body. She popped open a large black umbrella, which provided some protection from the elements, and passed it to me.

"Is he dead?" I asked Seth.

"I can't get a pulse, but I'm going to keep trying." Seth's face was red from the exertion, but he refused to stop his lifesaving efforts, even when another guest offered to take over.

"Come on, Al, breathe," Seth exhorted. "You can't die. You have too much important work to do. The world needs you. Ivelisse needs you. Xavier needs you. Pedro Sardina can't do it alone. Breathe, man, breathe."

"Another umbrella," I shouted at those standing at the French doors.

One of the security men heeded the call and brought a second one; between the two of us, we managed to shield Seth and the still unresponsive Vasquez from becoming further drenched.

Seth looked up at me. "Get inside, Jessica. No point in you getting soaked, too. Nothing you can do here. Where is that ambulance?"

I glanced behind me. The party guests were grouped around the glass panels watching the drama on the deck. Then Ivelisse prodded one of the waitstaff, who pushed opened a door. The waitress took a tentative step on the wet deck and then darted forward to retrieve the cigar Vasquez had tossed aside when he'd been struck down. She placed the cigar butt on a plate and returned inside.

A moment later, the second security man emerged from inside. "The ambulance is on its way."

"Thank goodness," I said, handing him my umbrella. "Please keep them as dry as possible," I said.

Someone opened a door for me and I entered the house, sopping wet and shivering against the clammy feeling of my clothes on my skin. People moved back away from the doors and gathered in small knots, speaking in low tones. I looked around for Ivelisse but didn't see her.

"What happened, Mrs. Fletcher?" a guest asked.

"I'm not certain, but he may have been hit by lightning."

"Is he—?"

"I'm afraid I don't know. Dr. Hazlitt is doing everything he can. Tell me, do you know which way the kitchen is?"

He pointed and I followed his direction down a short hallway until I reached an ultramodern kitchen with a wall of identical cabinets with invisible pulls. A large marble-topped island dominated the center of the room, and I spotted the plate with the cigar butt sitting next to a stack of dishes waiting to be washed. Several of the waitstaff—those who weren't still in the living room—huddled around the island, apparently not sure what they should be doing. One fellow, seeing my doused state, jumped forward with a roll of paper towels. "Can I get you something else, madam?"

"Not unless you have a spare uniform I can put on in place of these wet clothes," I said.

"I'm sure we can find something for you," he said. "Beatriz," he called to a waitress, who hurried to a large case left on the side of the room.

I tore off two of the paper towels, wiped my face, and when no one was looking, swiftly folded the sheets over the cigar, wrapping it up carefully.

Beatriz offered me a white jacket, apologizing profusely that they didn't have a complete uniform to provide, but I was grateful for anything that was going to allow me to shed my wet blouse. I changed swiftly in an adjacent bathroom, dabbing myself dry with paper towels. I deposited my shirt, the remaining towels, and the paper-wrapped cigar in a plastic bag Beatriz had provided.

I thanked the kitchen staff and returned to the party room, wandering among the guests, searching for a familiar face. No one paid any attention to me, and I realized I was now partially incognito in my uniform jacket. I folded the plastic bag and tucked it on a lower shelf of a bookcase.

Xavier had returned to the party from a different part of the house. He was accompanied by a middle-aged woman wearing an apron. Ivelisse had retreated to her alcove but by this time seemed to have regained a sense of the moment and had started to cry. The woman in the apron put her arms about Ivelisse and gently led her from the room.

"She's the housekeeper," I overheard Oona say to Westerkoch.

"Does she even know what's going on?" he muttered.

"Who? The housekeeper?"

"No! His wife."

"Who can tell?"

"I heard that's why he stole the formula from Havana," Westerkoch said, "to speed up the process to find a treatment. It doesn't look like he succeeded."

"Shush! Someone will overhear you."

"Who cares?"

The band members had stopped playing and were packing up their instruments. Adelmo, the cigar roller, had left his desk. Another blinding lightning strike followed by a crash of thunder drew an audible gasp from the guests. It was succeeded by the sound of sirens coming from the front of the house. The security man who'd been at the door when we'd arrived opened it, and two uniformed EMTs rushed in.

"Where?" one of them asked.

I stepped forward and said, "Follow me." I led them out to the deck. Despite the recent celestial fireworks, the rain had stopped as suddenly as it had started. The EMTs knelt next to Seth and relieved him of his task. One of them used a stethoscope on Vasquez and attempted to find signs of life.

"You see what happened?" the other EMT asked Seth, helping him to his feet.

"There was a bolt of lightning," Seth said, breathing heavily, "but I'm not sure if it hit him."

"Are you okay, mister? Do you need to sit down?"

"Just winded," Seth managed to get out, sinking into

a chair someone pulled over for him. "I'm a doctor, been trying to revive him. Too late, I'm afraid."

"Looks that way, Doc. I'm sorry, but there's no pulse," the other EMT said.

"Are you all right, Seth?" I asked, kneeling at his side. I looked into his ravaged face. His jacket was soaked through and he was exhausted. I couldn't tell if the drops of water on his cheeks were from the rain or tears.

"I couldn't save him, Jessica," he said hoarsely, raising his trembling hands and wiping his eyes.

"If you couldn't, no one could," I said. "You were right there when it happened, Seth. You've been working on him all this time. There wasn't anything more you could do."

Seth shook his head sadly. "What a loss for humanity."

And what a loss for you, my dear friend, I thought.

The EMTs left, returning a few minutes later with a gurney. Seth and I watched them carefully lift Vasquez from the deck, place him on the gurney, cover him with a lightweight blue tarp, and roll him into the house, where everyone stepped back to give them a path to the front door. As one of the EMTs opened the door, two men wearing raincoats came through it. One of them put up his hand to stop the EMTs; the second man showed them a badge.

"What's going on here?" a guest demanded, his eyes on the gurney. "The man is dead. Let them through."

One of the newly arrived men, a heavyset fellow whose sparse hair had been plastered to his head by the rain, announced, "Police." He asked the crowd, "Who's in charge here?"

When no one stepped forward, Seth did. "The deceased is Dr. Alvaro Vasquez. This is his house. He was hosting a party, and—"

"We know who the deceased is," the portly detective said. "Are you a friend?"

"Yes, I am," Seth replied.

The second detective, a considerably younger man, asked everyone to sit. He turned to Seth and asked, "Has anyone left the party?"

Seth was obviously taken aback at being asked the question. He looked at me in bewilderment.

"We wouldn't know," I said. "We're from out of town. We don't know everyone who was invited, but a man at the door had a guest list."

His partner surveyed the others in the room. "Does anyone know whether any individual has left the party?"

Nervous looks were cast among the guests.

Seth spoke up. "I think we're all confused why the police have been summoned," he said. "I'm a physician. Mrs. Fletcher and I were—"

"Who's Mrs. Fletcher?"

"I am," I said. "Dr. Hazlitt and I saw what happened to Dr. Alvaro. He was—"

"I'd like you two to wait over there," the detective said, pointing to the bar area.

"I don't understand why—"

I cut Seth off and urged him to accompany me to where the detective had indicated.

We sat on the two barstools and watched and listened as the detectives obtained the guest list from the security guard and began asking questions of the others. They were interrupted by the arrival of an elderly man.

"Hi, Doc," one of the detectives greeted the new arrival, who ignored the detective and went to the side of the gurney, pulled back the tarp to reveal Vasquez's face, grunted, and covered him again. He waved his hand and the EMTs wheeled the body of Dr. Alvaro Vasquez outside.

The heavy detective guided the man called "Doc" to where Seth and I waited.

"I understand you're a physician," the older officer said to Seth.

"That's right. Seth Hazlitt, MD, of Cabot Cove, Maine. And this is Jessica Fletcher, the mystery writer. We—she and I—witnessed what happened to Dr. Vasquez. And I administered CPR, unsuccessfully, as you see, until the ambulance arrived. And you are?"

The police officer answered. "Detective Machado, Tampa PD. This is Dr. San Martín, Hillsborough County ME. We got the call that there was an emergency at Dr. Vasquez's home."

I suppose my puzzled expression asked the question, *Why would the police be called?*

Machado picked up on it and answered. "Dr. Vasquez is a well-known person in Tampa. We're always called in on cases like this."

Now I understood. The police aren't routinely called to the scene of what appears to be a death by natural causes or an act of nature. But when a leading citizen, particularly one who is newsworthy and perhaps controversial, is involved, the police naturally take an interest. So does the local medical examiner.

"We'll do an autopsy, of course," Dr. San Martín said. "Is the victim's wife here?"

"I believe that one of the household help took her away, probably to her bedroom," I said. "She was in shock, as you can imagine."

"His son, Xavier, is here," Seth added. He scanned the room. "But I don't see him at the moment. He's probably with his mother."

Dr. San Martín pulled a business card from his pocket and handed it to Seth. "I'm leaving with the body, but I would like to speak with you about what you saw. Will you be staying in Tampa?"

"Ayuh, at least for a few days."

"Maybe you'd be good enough to call me in the morning so that we can arrange a time to get together."

"I'll do that," Seth said.

The doctor started to leave, turned, and said to Seth, "One of the EMTs told me that you said the victim had been struck by lightning."

"Just an assumption on my part," Seth said. "We saw the bolt of lightning. It appeared that he had been hit, but I'm sure your autopsy will confirm or deny it."

"Yes, I'm sure it will," San Martín said. "Another lightning victim," he muttered more to himself than to us. "Welcome to Florida."

Chapter Seven

The two detectives asked everyone to provide their names and contact information before leaving. One guest protested. "This is an intrusion into our privacy," he proclaimed. "We're guests at a party where the host was unfortunately struck by lightning and died. You have no right to ask for personal information. You're treating us as though a crime has been committed."

Detective Machado politely explained that it was routine to collect information about the people who are present when an unusual death occurs. Although his demeanor was nonthreatening, his steely expression said something else. The man reluctantly gave his name, as well as his phone number, and left. The other guests followed suit.

While Machado's younger partner went outside to the deck and did a cursory examination of where

Vasquez had fallen, Machado returned to where Seth and I still sat at the small bar.

"The ME says he'll be speaking with you tomorrow," he told Seth.

"That's right," Seth said.

"Maybe you can tell me what you witnessed. It's *Dr. Hazlitt*, right?"

"That's right. Mrs. Fletcher here and I are from Maine. I'm here in Tampa visiting Dr. Vasquez, and Mrs. Fletcher decided to join me for a week. She'd been on a tour promoting her latest book."

"You're a writer?" he asked, eyeing my white uniform jacket. He must have assumed I was one of the staff serving the party.

"Yes. I write murder mysteries."

That brought a smile to his face. "You write about murders and I investigate them."

He and Seth talked for a few more minutes, and I took the time to sum up the homicide detective. I judged him to be in his mid- to late forties. He had a dusky complexion—I guessed that he might have a Hispanic background—and bore the remnants, albeit faint, of boyhood acne. He wasn't someone that I would term outgoing, but there was an openness that was appealing.

He eventually turned his attention to me. "Did you observe anything strange at the party, Mrs. Fletcher?"

"Strange? In what sense?"

"I'm not suggesting anything. However, when someone of Dr. Vasquez's stature dies suddenly, we need to cover all the bases."

"Of course," I said. "No, nothing strange happened at the party." I wondered whether the unsubstantiated tense feeling that I'd experienced was worth mentioning and decided it wasn't.

Seth looked past me and said, "Here's Dr. Vasquez's son, Xavier."

"How's your mother?" Seth asked when the young man reached us.

"Resting," he said.

"I'm so sorry for your loss," I said touching his arm.

He looked down at my hand, and I withdrew it immediately.

Detective Machado introduced himself and asked a few questions, which elicited nothing of interest as far as I could tell. When he asked Xavier the same question that he'd asked me—had he noticed anything strange that evening—the son replied, "It's always strange around here. If you don't have anything else to ask me, I'd like to get back to my mother."

"Sure," Machado said, and handed Xavier his card. He also handed one to Seth and said, "I doubt if I'll have anything else to ask you, Doctor, but give me a call if you think of something."

"Ayuh, I'll do that."

The departure of the body of Alvaro Vasquez, the EMTs, the ME, and the two detectives created a vacuum of sorts in the large room, like the air had been sucked out of it. Most of the guests had decamped, but Seth and I remained, together with Oona Mendez, Karl Westerkoch, Bernard Peters, and his wife, Frances. The band had finished packing up its instruments and departed. Two waitresses scurried about picking up plates and glasses, tossing anxious looks at the remaining guests as they ferried serving pieces to the kitchen.

Peters sat alone in a red leather wing chair, staring straight ahead, his hands outstretched as though asking for wisdom from an unseen source. His wife, Frances, stood next to him, her hand to her mouth—seemingly stifling a scream or a moan.

I leaned close to Seth and said, "I think we should go."

He nodded and stood.

We made the rounds of the remaining guests. Oona Mendez and Karl Westerkoch sat together on a couch. She said she hoped to see us again; he said nothing, simply nodded. I approached Bernard and Frances Peters. "This must be a dreadful shock to you," I said to him.

"Unbelievable," he said. "How could this have happened?"

I understood why he would be especially shaken by Vasquez's death. They'd not only been friends of sorts, but Peters and his company, K-Dex, had lost perhaps their only lifeline to solvency, based upon what Seth had told me of the company's shaky financial status.

"Will you be staying in Tampa?" Frances Peters asked.

"For a little while," I said.

Seth came up and offered his condolences. His arrival seemed to prompt Peters into a more animated state. He got up and said, "You were extremely close to Alvaro."

"I wouldn't say extremely close," Seth said, "but we did get along. I considered him a friend."

Peters led Seth a few feet away and said in a low

voice, but not so low that I couldn't hear him, "I would like very much to talk with you."

"Of course, whenever it's convenient for you," Seth replied.

"Tomorrow? At Alvaro's laboratory?"

Remembering his promise to meet with the medical examiner, Seth said, "I suspect that will be all right, only I might have another appointment. How about you call me at the hotel, and—"

Peters interrupted Seth with, "Dr. Sardina. He's gone?"

Seth shrugged.

"Have you see Dr. Sardina?" Peters asked me.

"Earlier in the evening," I said, "with his wife."

Peters's expression turned grim.

Seth repeated his suggestion that Peters call him at the hotel, and we went to the foyer, where the two men who'd driven us sat on a bench.

"We'd like to go back to the hotel," Seth said.

They slowly got up, and one opened the front door.

"Wait just a second," I said.

"What are you doing, Jessica?" Seth asked.

"Just be a moment," I said as I went back through the living room, pausing only to grab the plastic bag I'd stashed on the bookshelf. I opened it, checking to see that my blouse and the paper-wrapped cigar were still inside, and retraced my steps in the direction of the foyer, where Seth had observed what I'd done. He looked at me quizzically but said nothing until we were back at the hotel, where after changing into dry clothes, we settled in the lounge. Seth had a beer and I indulged in a glass of sherry. I'd barely touched my daiquiri at the party.

The upset of having just witnessed Dr. Vasquez's sudden death had set in, and we said little for a while, each of us immersed in our private thoughts. I ached for Seth at that moment. I knew how important his recently forged friendship with Vasquez was to him, and I wondered whether he would give vent to his emotions. Not that I expected it. He has a hard shell that he uses to mask his feelings, although they sometimes manage to slip through the cracks.

"I'd like to visit Ivelisse again while we're still here in Tampa," he said.

"I'm sure she'd appreciate that."

"I can't begin to imagine what this means for his research."

"I suppose it depends upon how far along he was and to what extent his assistant can carry on."

He grunted his agreement, took a sip of his beer, and said, "Hate to be nosy, Jessica, but what did you have in that plastic bag?"

"My wet blouse, for one thing," I said. "You didn't seem to have noticed that I was wearing a waitress's jacket. Tomorrow I should make arrangements to return it to the company."

"I noticed. Thought it was very clever of you to have found dry clothes. Anything else?"

I laid the paper-wrapped cigar on the table and unfolded it. "I know," I said, "it doesn't make sense, but I couldn't help myself."

"I've heard that from you before. But why? No need for you to go around pickin' up cigar butts. Happy to buy you a brand-new one."

"Oh, Seth, you know it's nothing like that. It's just

that . . . well . . . it was strange that the waitress came outside to retrieve it at Ivelisse's direction. Plus, it didn't look like the sort of cigar I'd seen Dr. Vasquez smoke earlier."

Seth examined it more closely. "Al didn't get to smoke much of it before he got hit," he said. "Just a few puffs."

"Look at the wrapper," I said. "I remember that you told me he'd given you a Hoyo something or other."

"Hoyo de Monterrey Double Corona," Seth said.

"Where did he get Cuban cigars?" I asked. "I thought buying Cuban cigars was illegal here in the States."

"Ayuh, that it is, but Al told me he had a source."

"Like knowing a drug dealer."

"Hardly the same, Jessica, but people who smoke Cuban cigars are very fussy. Know what President Kennedy did during the Cuban missile crisis?"

"No."

"The president enjoyed a certain brand of Cuban cigar and told his press secretary, Pierre Salinger, to go out and buy up as many of 'em as he could find. Mr. Salinger came back the next day and reported that he'd bought twelve hundred cigars, so Kennedy went ahead and signed the trade embargo with Cuba. He wasn't about to do that without his favorite stogies. Al always had a big supply of Hoyo de Monterrey Double Coronas on hand."

"But this one isn't that type," I said. "Look at the wrapper."

Seth took an even closer look. "Macanudo," he read from the soggy label.

"And it's not as fat or as black as the ones he usually smoked. At least I don't think it is."

"You're right about that," he said, "but I don't see why it would interest you. Must be a cigar that somebody gave Al as a gift."

"You're probably right," I said. "I was curious, that's all."

"Curiosity killed the cat," he said. "I suppose you know that."

"It seems I've heard it before from a certain physician friend of mine."

"Let me ask you a question, Jessica."

"Go ahead."

"Did you pick up that cigar butt because you question whether Al was killed by lightning?"

"No, I don't think so. Well, maybe. It just seems to me that—"

"That it's unlikely that lightning killed him? The autopsy will determine that, and maybe lightning *did* kill him. Al was in great shape. He'd had a physical just a few weeks ago and was told his heart and everything else about him was A-one. So if lightning *didn't* kill him, and it wasn't likely that he had a coronary, then what *did* kill him?"

Chapter Eight

I carried that morning's edition of the *Tampa Tribune* to the dining room, where I met Seth for breakfast.

"Already read it," he said when I handed it to him. "Not much of a story."

The article was only three paragraphs long and reported that EMTs had been called to the home of Dr. Alvaro Vasquez, a prominent Cuban American physician and medical researcher who'd defected from Cuba and who lived and worked in Tampa. It gave the cause of death as a possible lightning strike. It went on to say that the thunderstorm that likely killed Vasquez was one of the most violent in memory and that it was unusual for such a storm to develop in the winter months. The piece ended by saying that the Tampa medical examiner had also been called to the scene and that an autopsy would be performed.

"I called Dr. San Martín," Seth said. "We're meeting him at ten."

"We?"

"Ayuh. I told him that we both had witnessed Al's death and that you had superior powers of observation."

"You didn't."

"Of course I did. As long as you're here with me in Tampa, you might as well get involved. If you want to, that is. The doctor has already done the autopsy—did it last night. Eat your eggs before they get cold."

"And?"

"And what?"

"Did he say what the autopsy revealed?"

"No. He didn't say much of anything. He seemed anxious to get together, though."

As we talked, a tall young woman entered the dining room and came directly to the table. "Dr. Hazlitt?" she said.

Seth nodded.

"Sorry to interrupt your breakfast, Doctor, but the concierge pointed out to me who you were. I'm Peggy Lohman, *Tampa Tribune*."

"What can I do for you, Ms. Lohman?" Seth asked.

"Mind if I join you?" she said as she slipped onto a vacant chair.

"Seems that you already have."

She ignored his comment and said, "I'm doing a story on the death yesterday of Dr. Alvaro Vasquez. We ran a small piece in today's paper. We didn't have much to go on so we had to keep it short, but we're putting together a much longer piece today. I tried to get hold of someone in the family, but no one returns my calls. I can understand that they're upset, but this is a big story considering Dr. Vasquez's stature in the community, and I need quotes from people. I called the police—they were summoned to the house, which seems strange to me considering he died of a lightning strike—but they had nothing to say, which isn't unusual for them, at least in my experience. Anyway, I know that you and Dr. Vasquez were close friends and professional colleagues and—"

She spoke rapidly, the words tumbling from her mouth.

"Ms. Lohman," Seth said, "I know that you're looking for a story, but—"

The reporter turned to me. "You must be Jessica Fletcher," she said.

"That's right."

"I knew that you were traveling with Dr. Hazlitt."

"We're friends," I said.

"Of course. You were at the house when Dr. Vasquez was hit by lightning."

I started to respond, but she forged ahead.

"I think it's fascinating that you write murder mystery novels, and I know that you came to Florida to promote your latest book. I've always wanted to write a novel based on some of the cases I've covered, really juicy ones. I started a novel a few years ago but never seem to get back to it. Maybe you have some tips for me."

"I'm afraid I don't have any tips," I said, "but do you have a question for Dr. Hazlitt?"

If she was offended by my answer, she didn't show

it. She said to Seth, "Dr. Vasquez was working on medical research here in Tampa, something to do with Alzheimer's disease. Right?"

"Ayuh."

"Pardon?"

"That's Maine talk for 'yes,'" I said.

"You are correct," Seth said. "Al—Dr. Vasquez was doing research on the disease."

"Hadn't he been doing the same research in Cuba before he defected?"

"That's my understanding."

"How did you meet him?"

To my surprise, Seth settled into a comfortable conversation with her. I'd seen him handle the press before. He's never been a fan of reporters, although he's quick to point out that despite the media's excesses, it's the only true check and balance on government that we have in our society. What most upsets him is when reporters badger people after someone has died in the hope of coming up with a bit of sensationalism. Ordinarily he would have politely, but firmly, dissuaded the reporter from pressing him with questions. But here he was answering her queries, good-naturedly and even enthusiastically. He seemed to bask in having become close to Dr. Vasquez and wanted the reporter to know that he was. I kept silent during the interview.

When she stood to leave, she said to me, "I really enjoyed meeting you, Mrs. Fletcher. Maybe while you're here in Tampa we could get together and, you know, talk shop."

"Talk shop? Oh, about your novel. I'm not sure I'll

have the time—I plan to stay only a few days—but I do wish you all the best."

"Nice gal," Seth said after she was gone.

"You were certainly accommodating," I said.

"Just helping her do her job."

"I noticed that you couched your answers when she asked about Dr. Vasquez's research."

"Wouldn't be my place to talk about that. I'd better call Bernie Peters. He said he wanted to speak with us today."

"He wanted to speak with *you*, Seth."

"Seems it's up to me whether I bring you along. Course, if you really don't want to—"

"It's just that I was thinking of making plans to head back home."

"I'd really appreciate it if you'd stay awhile, Jessica. We were together when Al died, and I figure that we should stay together until his death gets sorted out."

The truth was that I wanted very much to hear what the medical examiner had to say, and to follow up on what Vasquez's death meant to Bernard Peters and his company. Call me inherently curious. I don't mind; I've been called worse many times over the years.

"I'll be happy to stay," I said.

Seth gave me an "I knew you would" smile. "Good. I'll call Bernie. Meet you in the lobby in a half hour."

My emotions were decidedly mixed at that moment. I had no official reason for staying in Tampa. All I'd done was witness someone's death by lightning. Seth's question about whether Vasquez had, indeed, died from a lightning strike seemed to me nothing more than idle speculation. Still . . .

As I considered this, I realized that my friendship with Seth had taken a new and interesting turn. I'd had the misfortune of becoming involved in a number of real-life murders over the years—I hate to acknowledge how many—and was usually the one who smelled a rat, as they say, when everyone else was pointing to natural causes in someone's passing. And it was always Seth who chided me about being overly inquisitive and suspicious.

But here he was, eager to meet with people involved in his friend's death, and even chatting with a newspaper reporter. I wasn't sure what to make of it, any more than I knew what had intrigued me about the fact that Vasquez had been smoking a cigar that wasn't his usual brand that night. But now that I'd determined to go along with Seth, at least in the short term, I would give it my best.

The office of the Hillsborough County medical examiner was located on North Forty-sixth Street. Dr. San Martín's secretary told us that he was in a meeting but would be free shortly. We read magazines for fifteen minutes, until he came through the door, apologized for keeping us waiting, and ushered us into his large, messy office. There were file folders, magazines, and large envelopes containing X-rays on every surface. Two piles of books leaned precariously in a corner. In another corner, a six-foot-tall classic wooden cigar store Indian cast its angry look over the room.

"I appreciate you finding time for me this morning," San Martín said as Seth and I settled in chairs across the desk from him.

"Hope I can be of help," said Seth.

San Martín's expression questioned my presence.

"I'm just along for the ride," I said. "Seth didn't think you'd mind."

"I don't, of course, but it is a little disconcerting to have a writer in our midst. I trust you aren't making notes for one of your novels."

"I assure you that I'm not," I said.

"Good, because some of what I say this morning isn't for public consumption."

He said it in a way that demanded a response.

"Count on it," Seth said, and I agreed.

"As I told you on the phone, Dr. Hazlitt, I did the autopsy last night. To be more accurate, I participated in the autopsy with a colleague of mine."

"Come to any conclusions?" Seth asked.

San Martín paused before replying. "Yes, I did, and my colleague concurs. Based upon a gross examination of the deceased, I do not believe that he was struck by lightning."

"That doesn't surprise me," said Seth.

"Oh?"

"I don't know a heckuva lot about lightning and what it does when it hits somebody—I've only had two patients who were hit by lightning."

"That's probably more than most doctors up north see," San Martín said.

"True. And in my cases, both survived, but one was left in pretty bad shape, had neuropsychiatric, vision, and hearing problems."

"You know more than you think," said San Martín.

"Appreciate that," Seth said. "The thing is, I got close to Dr. Vasquez right after he fell, tried CPR on him. I got a good look at his face and neck. From what little I do know, when someone gets hit by lightning, there're usually burns on the head and neck. There weren't any burns on Al—Dr. Vasquez—nothing on his clothing or on any exposed skin. I also remember reading that only twenty percent of folks hit by lightning die on the spot."

San Martín smiled. "Everything you say is correct, Dr. Hazlitt. The keraunopathologists would be impressed."

I tried to pronounce what he'd said and failed.

"Keraunopathologists," he repeated. "Specialists in the pathology of lightning. Not many of them. At any rate, your observations are correct. Usually when someone is struck by lightning, burn marks are visibly evident, especially at the entry and exit points. Most people don't realize that a lightning strike has about ten times the kilovolts as your typical industrial electrical shock. That sort of power burns a victim pretty bad. It immediately turns the victims' sweat into steam." He paused for effect. "There were no burn marks on Dr. Vasquez."

"So the fact that there was a lightning strike at the moment he died was a coincidence," I offered.

"I'd say that's a fair assumption," San Martín said.

"Your autopsy ruled out lightning as the cause of death," Seth said, "but did it give you any clue as to *why* he died? He'd told me that he'd had a physical exam a few weeks ago and everything was fine."

"Do you know who his doctor was?" San Martín asked.

"Can't say that I do."

"Easy enough to find out. I'd like his input. To answer your question, his heart looked fine. But there was a marked change in the muscles supplied by his cranial nerves, specifically his breathing muscles. It looks to me as though he died from sudden and total respiratory failure."

"What could cause that?" Seth asked, his expression skeptical. "Are we back to thinking it *was* lightning?"

"No," said San Martín. "I can't say I'm an expert with cases of lightning strikes—" He smiled at me. "Keraunopathy. But I have autopsied my fair share of lightning victims. This, after all, is Tampa. Florida has twice as many fatal lightning strikes as any other state. Even the name 'Tampa' is said to stem from a Native American word for 'sticks,' which many believe refers to lightning. Nationally, death by lightning is the third leading cause of weather-related deaths."

"But you don't believe Dr. Vasquez was struck by lightning," I said.

"No, I don't. Lightning can cause severe injury to the cardiopulmonary system, but that isn't the case with Dr. Vasquez. Something else affected his cranial nerves and respiratory system, and did it with incredible speed. His death was instantaneous. The toxicology report might give us some answers. I've put a rush on it. Did either of you notice anything unusual about his behavior that day? I understand he was hosting a party when he died."

"That's true," Seth said. He looked to me. "Did you see anything unusual, Jessica?"

"Since I barely knew the man, I wouldn't have picked up on changes in his behavior. He seemed healthy and happy, full of life and spirit. I did, however, wonder why he stayed on the deck after the storm hit. I remember him saying when we played golf that when a storm approached, you'd better get to cover fast."

Seth laughed. "He didn't want to waste that cigar he was enjoying. Al did love his cigars."

"Not unusual here in Tampa," San Martín said. "I personally can't stand them, but to each his own."

Seth asked me, "Do you still have that cigar that Al was smoking?"

"Yes, I do."

"When Al fell, the cigar went flying. Mrs. Fletcher retrieved it after the cleaning staff picked it up," Seth explained.

"Silly of me, I know," I said. "He'd mentioned that the cigar was a gift from a friend. Apparently it was different from what he was accustomed to smoking."

I dug in my purse and pulled out the cigar, which I'd placed in a small plastic bag I'd gotten from the hotel. I handed it to Dr. San Martín, who turned the bag so that he could see the cigar through both sides.

"It's a little squished," I said. "It was in a puddle when the waitress picked it up."

"Tampa used to be the cigar capital of the world," San Martín said as he dropped the bag on his desk. "That's how Ybor City came to be. Cigars! There used to be a hundred and fifty cigar manufacturers in that section of Tampa alone."

"I'm looking forward to visiting Ybor City while I'm here," I said. "I understand it's . . . well, that it's very colorful."

"That it is," San Martín said. He stood and stretched. "It was a late night and these old bones are feeling it. Thanks for stopping by and sharing what you know. There's more to doing an autopsy than examining the body. Everything surrounding a death has to be taken into account."

"I'd appreciate knowing if you come up with any other conclusions," Seth said as they shook hands. "I'm not only a doctor; I was Al Vasquez's friend."

"You'll hear from me," San Martín assured him. "Thank you for coming in with Dr. Hazlitt, Mrs. Fletcher. May I suggest that you take the trolley when you visit Ybor City? It's part of the experience."

Seth and I decided to take advantage of the warmer weather that day by walking back to the hotel rather than hailing a taxi. He'd arranged to meet with K-Dex's Bernard Peters at noon at Vasquez's lab, and for the three of us to have lunch following the appointment.

"Shakespeare wrote about lightning," I said as we walked slowly.

"Say again?"

"Shakespeare," I said. "I remember when I taught Shakespeare back when I was an English teacher. Let me see if I remember it. 'To stand against the deep dread-bolted thunder? In the most terrible and nimble stroke of quick, cross lightning?' It's from *King Lear*."

"He knew a lot, didn't he?"

"Shakespeare? He certainly did. Unless you meant Dr. San Martín. He's a lovely man."

Seth nodded his agreement. "Well," he said, "at least we know that Al didn't die of a lightning strike. I was pretty certain of that."

"A sudden respiratory attack, enough to kill him instantly," I said. "Have you ever seen that in a patient?"

"No, can't say that I have. It's not possible, as far as I'm concerned. There has to be some other explanation."

I stopped Seth and placed a hand on his shoulder as I raised a foot to shake out a pebble that had gotten into my shoe. As I did, I looked back from where we'd come and noticed a small silver vehicle driving very slowly. The driver had stopped when we did.

"Do you see that car?" I asked Seth.

"Which one?"

"The small silver one."

"What about it?"

"It was behind us when we took the taxi from the hotel."

"So?"

"Here it is again, driving slowly, as though trying to stay behind us."

"You feeling a little paranoid this morning, Jessica?"

I squinted at the car, trying to see if I recognized the driver through the tinted windshield. The car suddenly sped up, turned a corner, and was gone.

"Sorry," I said as we continued our walk.

"About what?"

"The car. Nothing unusual about a car being where we are twice in a day."

We'd almost reached the hotel when Seth said, "Did you see the driver of the car?"

"Not clearly. It was a man. He was alone, I think. Why?"

"No reason. Just asking."

As we entered the lobby, we were stopped by a desk clerk. "Someone came by and left you this, Dr. Hazlitt." He handed Seth an envelope on which his name was handwritten.

Seth opened it, frowned as he read the note that was inside, and handed it to me.

Dear Dr. Hazlitt,
     It is important that I speak with you. Please call me at my cell number as soon as possible.
                                        —Dr. Pedro Sardina

He included the number.

"Sounds important," I said, handing back the note.

"It does, doesn't it? I'll call from my room. Meet you back here in a half hour."

The message light was flashing on my room phone. It was a call from Oona Mendez.

I don't know what your schedule is like, today, Jessica, but I would like very much to meet with you at your convenience.

She, too, left a phone number.

I told Seth of Oona's message in the taxi on our way to the laboratory.

"Seems we're popular folks these days."

"It appears that way."

"I reached Dr. Sardina. He'll be at the lab when we're there with Bernie Peters, but he said he didn't want to talk with him around."

"I wonder why."

"I suspect there's going to be some tense times between Peters and Sardina," Seth said. "Sardina knows how far Al got with his research, and Bernie obviously wants to know, too."

"I can't fathom why a smart businessman like Bernard Peters would allow Dr. Vasquez to keep his research results under such close wraps. After all, Mr. Peters's company is paying for it."

"I don't understand it either, Jessica, but I intend to find out."

The conviction with which he said it startled me. I had no idea that he'd decided to seek answers to that question, or any question, for that matter. I knew that Vasquez's sudden death had had a tremendous impact on Seth. He'd kept his emotions in check, but it was obvious to me that he was struggling with them. Despite the little time they'd spent together, Alvaro Vasquez had become a treasured friend, something that few people I knew could claim. Yes, Seth Hazlitt had a world of friends back in Cabot Cove, but few were truly allowed entry into his inner circle, and I thankfully counted myself among them.

I decided to push him.

"Care to elaborate?" I asked.

"About what?"

"About wanting to find out the situation between Dr. Vasquez and Bernard Peters?"

"You sound as though I shouldn't."

"Not at all, Seth, but I didn't realize that you had issues to resolve aside from naturally grieving over your friend's death."

He thought before responding. "The way I see it," he said, "Al devoted his life to finding a cure for Alzheimer's. He pursued the cause despite interference from

Castro's totalitarian regime, and he showed guts when he and Ivelisse left Cuba and came here to continue his work. He was one hell of a fine man, and I want to make sure that his work gets the credit it deserves."

I started to say something, but he continued.

"There's more to it, though, Jessica. There's a real foul smell, the way he died. It wasn't lightning like everyone assumed. Sudden and complete respiratory collapse? Never heard of such a thing. Doesn't make sense."

It was my turn to think before speaking. When I did, I asked, "Are you suggesting there might have been foul play?"

"I'm not suggesting anything, Jessica. All I know is that something's rotten in Denmark, only it's here in Tampa, Florida, and I want to know what it is. I owe it to Al."

Chapter Nine

The guard who'd been at the door when we'd first visited the laboratory was on hand when we arrived to meet with Peters and Sardina. But this time the door to the building was open, and we weren't questioned as we approached. We entered and followed the narrow corridor back to where the lab itself was located. Peters and Sardina were there, and neither man looked happy.

"Good to see you," Peters said, shaking Seth's hand as we entered the lab. "Thanks for coming."

"No trouble at all," Seth said. He looked over at Vasquez's assistant. "Hello, Dr. Sardina," he said.

Sardina muttered what passed for a response and busied himself at one of the computers.

Peters indicated with a flip of his head that we should follow him outdoors, where he led us far enough away from the guard to ensure privacy.

"Hate to get personal," Seth said, "but I get the impression that you and Pedro Sardina were not havin' a pleasant chat about the weather."

Peters's tight lips and angry eyes confirmed that supposition.

"Anything I can do to help?" Seth asked.

"It's missing," Peters said flatly.

"What's missing?" Seth asked.

"Al's laptop computer, the one he used to chart the progress of his research."

"It can't just be missing," Seth said. "There's got to be a simple answer."

"You know the computer I'm referring to," Peters said. "I understand that Al shared some of the material on it with you."

"Ayuh, he did. I got to read some of the entries."

"That's more than he did for me," Peters said.

"Mr. Peters," I said, "I obviously have no knowledge of what transpired between you and Dr. Vasquez, but I have to ask a question that's been on my mind ever since I got here. Dr. Vasquez joked once that he kept progress reports from you. I can't help but wonder why you, as the source of Dr. Vasquez's funding, would be kept so much in the dark about his progress—and, I suppose, why you would put up with it."

Peters's smile was rueful. "Want a straight answer, Mrs. Fletcher?"

"Whatever answer you wish to give."

"I let Al get away with it because, frankly, I had no choice. His research was vitally important to me and to K-Dex. I'd known for years about his research in Cuba into the impact of sugar on the brain, and the role it might play in promoting the growth of beta-amyloids, a

chief component of the plaques that are a definite hall-
mark of brain abnormalities in Alzheimer's patients. The
same holds true of how glucose, and insulin resistance,
could influence the unusual growth of tau proteins, another provable aspect of the disease. To be honest, I was
taken in by Al's faith in his research. But who wouldn't
have been? Every report that leaked out of Cuba said he
was on the brink of a truly major medical breakthrough."

"And you believed those leaks?"

"I did. You might also have noticed that Alvaro
Vasquez was a charming, manipulative man."

"Charming? Yes," I said. "Manipulative? I wouldn't
know about that."

"Take my word for it," Peters said angrily. He made
a fist and rammed it into the palm of his other hand. "I
trusted him," he growled. "I had to. So much depended
upon his research providing a leap forward. If he'd
found a definite link between how glucose influenced
brain cells and Alzheimer's, and had come up with a
way to reverse it, it could have led to a cure, with K-Dex
leading the way. Think about what that would mean to
millions of people, Mrs. Fletcher. I never *stopped* thinking about it."

I thought for a moment that Peters might break into
tears.

"Let's get back to his laptop," Seth said. "Surely it
wasn't the only documentation of his research and the
progress he'd made."

"I've been led to believe that it was," Peters said rue-
fully.

"What about Dr. Sardina?" I asked. "Would he know
where it is?"

Peters's sad expression turned angry again. "I trust Dr. Sardina as far as I can throw him, the little weasel."

His harsh statement lingered in the air, and neither Seth nor I responded.

"I was questioning Sardina when you arrived. He's an arrogant young man, that's for sure. He claims that Vasquez kept him uninformed about how his work contributed to the big picture and that Al kept the overall progress reports to himself. Sardina would work on a specific project, give the results to Al, and that's the last he'd hear about it. When I asked him about the laptop, he told me that Al kept it under lock and key and took it home with him every night."

"Then that's probably where it is," I said.

"I can only hope, but I'm not sure I believe him. Of course, it might all be a moot point, depending upon how far along Al was. If he hadn't achieved the sort of results he was always promising, his progress reports won't be worth diddly."

There were other questions on my mind at that moment, all of them pertaining to why a businessman like Bernard Peters would enter into such a loose and problematic business arrangement with Vasquez. Of course, there undoubtedly were legal documents cementing Peters's interest in Vasquez's work. At least I hoped there were, for his sake.

"Have you gone to the house to see if the laptop is there?" I asked.

"I called and spoke to Al's daughter, Maritza."

"She's here?" Seth said.

"She just arrived from Cuba."

It had been in the back of my mind that the

Vasquezes' daughter had not accompanied her parents to Tampa. I remembered a conversation Seth and I had had shortly after we'd learned that Al had asked the United States for asylum.

"The newspaper said that both he and his wife defected," I'd said. "Do they have any children?"

"Oh, they do," Seth had replied, "a son and a daughter. I met them when I was in Cuba."

"They didn't defect?"

Seth had hesitated before answering, and I'd wondered why.

"It's a bone of contention with Al and his wife," he'd finally said. "Really none of my business. His son came to the States more than a year ago, which didn't sit well with his folks. The daughter is in medical school and refused to leave Havana. You know how families can be. Kids have minds of their own."

"Where does his son live?" I'd asked.

"In Tampa. He'd gone to Miami from Cuba, according to Al, but moved to Tampa not long after he arrived in the States. I imagine that played a role in Al's decision to settle there."

"So the parents and son are reunited," I'd said.

"Seems so," Seth had said. "I'm sure that pleases Al and his wife."

"I would imagine it does," I had replied at the time.

But the prickly relationship between father and son that I had witnessed at the party made me wonder whether Al had regretted moving to live near his offspring. Perhaps the decision had been made because Ivelisse was close to her son, but choosing to live near one child came at a cost. Her daughter had remained in

Cuba. The Vasquezes had never returned to their homeland. How long had it been since they'd seen Maritza?

"What did you say to Maritza?" I asked Peters.

"I expressed my condolences, of course, and I asked whether I could come to examine some of Al's belongings but didn't get anywhere. She said that her mother was in no condition to have visitors and that I should call back in a day or two."

Peters was obviously distraught, and I wasn't sure we should go through with plans to have lunch with him, but he settled it when he said, "Look, I have to cancel our lunch plans. I'm meeting with my attorneys to see if they can come up with a way to untangle this mess. If we can't, the company stands to go under. We'll do it another time."

"Of course," Seth said.

Peters went to his car and drove off, leaving us to decide what to do next.

"I suppose we should go back inside and talk to Dr. Sardina," I suggested.

Sardina was still at the computer when we walked in.

"Hope we're not disturbing anything important," Seth said.

Sardina looked up and shook his head.

"Mr. Peters has left," I said.

"Good," was Sardina's reply.

"We were talking about Dr. Vasquez's laptop computer, the one he used to keep track of progress," I said. "Did you help him input lab results?" I asked, already knowing the answer.

A rare laugh came from him. "Me? I think he would

have chopped off my arm if he'd seen me go near that laptop."

"He let me take a look a few times," Seth offered.

"I know," Sardina said. "He evidently trusted you more than he trusted me."

His bitterness was palpable.

"I'm sure he trusted you," I said. "After all, you worked side by side with him every day."

"Need to know," Sardina said. "That was his favorite saying, need to know. He told me just enough to keep me interested. I should have left ages ago."

His anger permeated the lab.

"Apparently, he didn't share any more information with Mr. Peters," I said. "He said if he can't find the laptop, the company will be ruined."

"Don't you worry about him," Sardina said sourly. "Bernie Peters ain't goin' to be missing any meals anytime soon," he said, putting on a southern accent.

"We understood the company invested millions of dollars in Dr. Vasquez's work and this laboratory," I said. "That's a lot to lose."

"And don't forget his home on Davis Island, and his boat, and all the other perks the great doctor received."

It was clear to me that Dr. Sardina had not been on the receiving end of any extra benefits and was resentful. "Don't you think those losses will affect K-Dex and Bernie Peters?"

"They would if they weren't well insured."

"What do you mean?" Seth put in.

"Peters had key-man insurance on Vasquez. Anything happens to him, the company recoups all its investments and Peters himself walks away with a tidy sum."

Seth pursed his lips and whistled. "Did Al know about this?"

"If I know, he knew," Sardina replied.

"Is this what you wanted to talk to me about?" Seth asked. "You called and said you wanted to get together."

Sardina pressed his lips together and stared at the computer screen. He then looked at me.

"Anything you want to say to me can be said with Mrs. Fletcher present," Seth said.

Sardina looked directly at Seth and said, "How much do you know about Alvaro's research?"

"Some," Seth said, "but from what he told me, he was about to reach a major advance, one that could lead to new pathways for drug trials."

Sardina's smile was small but said volumes.

"Tell you what, Dr. Hazlitt. You buy me a nice lunch and I'll tell you things about Dr. Alvaro Vasquez that I'm sure he never told you about himself."

Chapter Ten

Sardina drove us to a strip mall on the outskirts of Tampa and pulled in front of a restaurant whose sign promised an Asian buffet. "Hope you like Chinese food," he said as we entered the large, busy place and found an isolated table away from others. "I come here a lot. Good food, reasonable prices."

We took turns going through the multitude of hot and cold buffet lines, one of us staying behind to secure the table while the others filled their plates. Once we were all seated with our food, Sardina said, "I'll tell you right off the bat that I was no fan of Dr. Vasquez."

"I sorta gathered that," Seth said.

"Don't misunderstand," Sardina said. "I'm sorry that he's dead."

"Yes, I'm sure you are," I said. "How long had you worked for him?"

"A little over a year. I can't believe I stayed as long as I did."

"You indicated back at the lab that you wished you'd left a long time ago," Seth said.

"That's right." He tasted a few items on his plate before continuing. "Dr. Vasquez—he told everybody to call him Al, but not me; with me it was always Dr. Vasquez, very formal." He said the name again, this time with disgust. "Yes, I should have left long ago. No, I never should have gone to work for him in the first place."

"How did you meet him?" I asked.

"I knew him in Cuba, Mrs. Fletcher. We didn't work together there. He was into his research, and I—well, I'm not a medical doctor. I have a PhD in infectious diseases. We ran into each other now and then. Dr. Vasquez—" He grinned. "Now that he's gone, maybe I can call him Al like everyone else. Al was in favor with the Castro regime, got plenty of perks because of it. Ofelia and I were invited to a couple of parties at his house. Nice place—not what he has here, but a lot better than where we lived."

"I visited Al's home in Cuba, too," Seth said.

"He told me that you did." Sardina looked at Seth quizzically. "You and he really struck up a friendship, didn't you?"

"Pleased and honored to say that we did."

"He thought a lot of you."

Seth nodded, struggling to keep his emotions in check.

"How did both of you end up in Tampa?" I interjected, giving Seth a chance to compose himself.

Sardina turned his attention to me. "Ofelia and I left

a few months before Al and Ivelisse defected. We attended a conference in London and came here instead of returning home. That was before the government put a tourniquet on foreign travel. We were lucky to get out."

"If the government further tightened restrictions on travel after you left, how was Dr. Vasquez able to make his escape?"

"Al had connections," he said, and stopped.

I had the feeling that he wanted to say more but was editing himself. I asked a different question. "Why did you decide to come to work for Dr. Vasquez?"

"Necessity. I thought once we got to the States, I wouldn't have a problem finding work in my field. Well, I was wrong. As much as Cubans have assimilated into U.S. society, it doesn't mean we're welcomed with open arms. My degrees weren't recognized here, and all I could manage to find was a low-level job in a lab at a university. It didn't pay much, and I had a run-in with my supervisor, who knew less than half of what I know and refused to listen to my suggestions. It was around that time that Al called and asked if I wanted to work with him on his Alzheimer's research. I jumped at the chance. He was paying a lot more than the job I had. Besides, working on finding a cure for a major disease was really appealing. The reality turned out to be less so."

He seemed to be collecting his thoughts, and we ate in silence until he spoke again.

"Al—" He chuckled. "I can't get used to calling him that. Dr. Vasquez was—how can I put it?—he was not an honest man."

"In what way?" I asked.

"In every aspect of his life."

I could feel Seth, who was sitting next to me, stiffen. I put my hand on his arm to keep him from blowing up. "That's quite a condemnation," I said.

"And a truthful one, Mrs. Fletcher. Alvaro Vasquez was a smooth con man. I'm sure you saw that the few times you were with him. He lied to everybody—me, his wife, his kids, and especially Mr. Peters."

"Did he lie about how his research was going?" I asked, glancing at Seth to gauge his reaction to what Sardina was saying. Seth had had nothing but praise for Vasquez, personally and professionally, and I knew it must have hurt to hear his friend disparaged like this.

"I'm afraid so," was Sardina's reply.

"Now, hold on a second," Seth said, dropping his fork noisily onto his almost empty plate. "I'd like to know what you base that on."

Sardina, sensing Seth's pique, held up his hands in mock defense of himself. "Please don't misunderstand, Dr. Hazlitt," he said. "I know that you and he were friends."

"I'm not talking about our friendship," Seth said. "I'm talking about his research. Are you claiming that he wasn't honest about his research, that he lied about it?"

"Yes, sir, I am."

"But how could you know?" Seth paused and then continued. "You told us back at the lab that you weren't privy to how the research was progressing, that you only knew bits and pieces on, as you put it, a need-to-know basis."

"That's true," Sardina said, "but that doesn't mean that I was completely ignorant about the bigger picture. I hated the way Al strung Mr. Peters along, always asking for more money for a new phase of the research even when there wasn't a new phase. I was with him plenty of times when he did it. He'd get more money from Mr. Peters, and when he left, Al would laugh about it."

"I'm shocked to hear this," Seth said, and his face reflected his anguish. I wondered whether he was thinking the same thing I was, that what Sardina was saying didn't necessarily represent the truth. After all, Peters had said that he didn't trust the young researcher. We were hearing one side, and I've always believed in waiting to hear both sides before coming to a conclusion. Of course, the "other side" of the story was Dr. Vasquez, and he wasn't in any position to refute Sardina's claims.

I wondered whether there was more to Sardina's negative view of Vasquez, perhaps a personal motive. I decided to ask.

"What about Dr. Vasquez's personal life?"

The question came to mind because of what Dr. San Martín had told us about the circumstances of Vasquez's death. It certainly wasn't a new thought for me. It had been rattling around in my brain since our meeting with the medical examiner. If Vasquez hadn't died of a lightning strike, and since the autopsy had revealed what Seth considered an almost impossible circumstance—a sudden and total collapse of Vasquez's respiratory system—there was the possibility of foul play. I hated to even consider that option, but it couldn't be ruled out.

"What do you mean?" Sardina asked.

"He seemed to be a pleasant, well-liked man," I said. "Did he make enemies?"

"According to him, he had enemies from Cuba threatening to scuttle our work. That's why we were locked up tighter than a drum. Frankly, I think he just didn't want anyone else to discover what he was really about." Sardina motioned for a waitress to bring the check.

"Did he have personal enemies, as well? People without a nationalistic motive?"

Sardina snorted. "Let me just say that there wasn't a woman who was safe from his advances. I often think that his infatuation with Ofelia was why he hired me in the first place. He didn't make any bones about being attracted to her, and she's had to fend him off more than once. I imagine there were a lot of men who took a dislike to Alvaro Vasquez."

I thought back to the way Vasquez had tutored me on the golf course, pressing in close as he instructed me.

I grabbed the check when it was delivered by a pretty young Asian waitress, waving off Sardina's and Seth's offers to pay. "Let me," I said.

When we were in Sardina's car, he asked where he could drive us.

"Our hotel, if you don't mind," Seth said.

"Yes. That would be helpful," I said to Sardina. "I have a call to make," I reminded Seth, referring to the message Oona Mendez had left on the answering machine of the phone in my hotel room.

"I have some calls to make, too," Seth replied.

Sardina dropped us off in front of the hotel, but before he left, Seth leaned into the car through the open front window. "Mind a bit of advice?"

"Go ahead," Sardina said.

"I suggest that you keep your negative comments about Al to yourself. The man is dead and can't defend himself. He deserves your respect."

If Seth's harsh words impacted Sardina, he hid his reaction well. He simply said, "The truth is always hurtful, Dr. Hazlitt. I'm sorry if I've upset you."

Chapter Eleven

I called Oona Mendez when I got to my room and arranged to meet her at King Corona, a café in Ybor City on East Seventh Avenue. Before leaving, I called Seth and told him where I was going.

"Did she say what she wants?" he asked.

"I'll know soon enough. Have you had a chance to digest what we heard at lunch today?"

"If you mean the spareribs and fried rice, yes. As for what the young Dr. Sardina had to say, I'm still getting over it."

"He certainly had a litany of negative things to say about Dr. Vasquez. I wonder to what extent his claim that Vasquez made inappropriate advances to his wife colors his view."

"I wonder the same thing, Jessica."

"Care to come with me to meet Oona?"

"No, I think I'll catch me a nap."

"Sounds like a good idea," I said. "I'll check back in with you when I return."

I left plenty of time between leaving the hotel and meeting Ms. Mendez so I could take the historic Tampa streetcar to Ybor City as Dr. San Martín had suggested. Up to now, my plan for a week of R and R in Tampa following my hectic book tour had involved neither rest nor relaxation, and I was determined to change that. It was a lovely, crystal clear day in the city, and it felt good to be on my own, breathing in the fresh air and feeling the sun's warmth on my face. I picked up a map from the concierge and figured out where the closest streetcar stop was, only a few blocks from the hotel. I waited with a group of tourists until the next car came along, its bell clanging, the sound of its wheels on the rails and the brake the motorman applied reminding me of San Francisco's famed cable cars. I took one of the hardwood seats—whoever designed them did not have comfort in mind—and we lurched forward, passing the imposing Tampa Convention Center and the Tampa Bay History Center building, grinding to a halt at the Florida Aquarium, and then up to Ybor City, the Ybor Channel on the right, until reaching Eighth Avenue in the heart of this unique section of Tampa.

A brochure I took from the trolley told me that Ybor City was settled in 1886 by cigar makers Vicente Ybor and Ignacio Haya, who'd moved their thriving cigar-manufacturing business to Tampa from Key West. With a railroad, a port, and a climate that functioned as a natural humidor, cigar manufacturing flourished, turning Tampa and Ybor City into the cigar capital of the world. That lasted until the 1960s, when embargos against Cuban tobacco and declining cigar consumption sent the cigar-manufacturing industry into a steep decline.

Despite the hard benches of the streetcar, I thoroughly enjoyed the ride along the redbrick streets, taking in the large old-fashioned globe streetlamps and the period buildings with their wrought-iron balconies. I got off at a stop near the Don Vicente de Ybor Historic Inn and browsed this former real estate office that was built by Vicente Ybor in 1895. It became a health clinic until a businessman converted it into an inn in 1998. It was like stepping into an earlier era, and I could almost hear the voices of guests speaking Spanish and detect the scent of their cigars.

After that pleasant break, I walked a few blocks to the King Corona, where Oona was already waiting at an outdoor table. She was smoking a cigarette and had a large cup in front of her.

"Hope I'm not late," I said.

"Right on time," she said. "Tea? Coffee? A cold drink?"

"What are you having?"

"Tea, creamy vanilla rooibos tea, red tea, from Africa, a specialty here."

A waitress appeared, and I told her I'd have the same.

"King Corona's not fancy," Oona said, "but it's good, serves the real thing when it comes to simple Cuban food. Hungry? The Cuban cheese toast is always good."

"Oh, no, thank you, I just came from lunch."

"A good one?"

"Lunch?"

"Yes."

"Very good. Asian."

"You and Dr. Hazlitt?"

"Yes, and Dr. Sardina."

Uplifted eyebrows accompanied "Oh?"

"He seems like a nice young man," I said. "Naturally he's upset at Dr. Vasquez's sudden death. I think he must also be uncertain of his future."

"As we all are. Upset at Alvaro's death, that is. Your friend forged quite a friendship with Alvaro, didn't he?"

"Seth? Yes, he did. Dr. Vasquez's death has shaken him, as you can imagine."

"I find it interesting that Alvaro shared so much of his research with Dr. Hazlitt."

"Why? Seth is a medical doctor. It seems natural to me that they would be able to discuss complicated scientific investigations easily."

"It wasn't like Alvaro to be open about his work with anyone."

I smiled. "Seth has a way of inspiring trust in people. He's a wonderful physician and a fine gentleman. He's held in very high regard back home."

"Maine."

"Yes. Cabot Cove, Maine. Have you ever been up north to New England?"

"I can't say that I have. Jessica, you do know what my job is here in Tampa?"

"Only what you told me at dinner. Something to do with—"

"The Cuban American Freedom Foundation. Because the U.S. doesn't have formal diplomatic relations with Cuba, we represent Cubans in America and work to foster better Cuban American relations. Our main office is in Miami; there are more than nine hundred thousand Cubans living there. Tampa has the second-largest community. Our organization works closely with all branches of the U.S. government, including the Treasury."

"Sounds like an exciting job."

"Boring most of the time," she said, and laughed.

But her good humor faded quickly and her expression turned serious. "I'm still grappling with Alvaro's death. All I keep thinking is how ironic it is that he was killed by lightning. It's almost as though his charismatic personality acted like a target, inviting the lightning to strike him."

I wasn't sure that I agreed with her dramatic explanation of her friend's death but said nothing.

"He was a marvelous human being, Jessica."

She blinked back tears, and I thought of what Sardina had said, that no woman was safe from Vasquez's advances. Had Oona fallen for his obvious charms? Had he been her lover?

"I'm so sorry you've lost your friend," I said. "A sudden death is always difficult to comprehend. You have my sympathies."

"Thank you," she said, clearing her throat. She was composed when she added, "Alvaro's death brings with it certain complications."

I nodded, listening.

"It wouldn't surprise you, I'm sure, to know that the Cuban government would very much like his research returned to Cuba. His defection wasn't taken lightly by Castro and his cronies."

"So I've heard."

"Almost no one has been allowed to leave the country since then, certainly not any doctors or other medical personnel. The loss of Alvaro's research and the glory it would have brought the Cuban government was a terrible blow."

Did she know what Sardina knew, that Vasquez's laptop on which he was thought to have kept track of his research's progress was missing? Or was it?

I was about to ask when an old man, bent and limping, approached carrying a fistful of cigars. "Cigar?" he asked in a weak, singsong voice. "Best cigars. Robustos, Don Diegos. Cheap, too."

Oona waved him away.

It was my turn to smile. "Ybor City might not be the cigar capital of the world any longer," I said, "but they seem to be offered everywhere I look."

She ignored my observation and said, "I know that Dr. Hazlitt—what an absolutely charming man—was taken into Alvaro's inner circle, so to speak, and was privy to the status of his research."

I thought back to what Karl Westerkoch had asked me at the party about how much Seth knew. I had a feeling Oona was probing for the same information, and I was sorry Seth had decided not to accompany me.

"I really don't know the extent to which Seth was taken into Dr. Vasquez's confidence, Oona. I suppose you'd best ask him."

"Yes, of course, I should do that. Did Dr. Sardina

have anything to say at lunch about Alvaro's research and how far he'd progressed in finding a cure?"

I shifted in my chair and finished what was left in my cup. What had begun as a pleasant conversation about an unpleasant subject, Vasquez's death, was turning into a bit of an interrogation.

I fudged my answer. "He spoke about it, of course, but didn't say anything specific."

"What about Bernard Peters at K-Dex? Have you been in contact with him?"

I'm uncomfortable lying, always have been, and hate being put in a position where it might be necessary. Oona's questions were best answered by the people involved, Dr. Sardina and Bernard Peters among them.

"Seth and I had a brief chat with him this morning," I said and left it at that.

"He must be beside himself," Oona said. "It's my understanding that his company, K-Dex, has sunk millions into Alvaro's research."

"I really wouldn't know about that."

"But your friend Seth must be aware of it, considering how close he became with Alvaro."

I said nothing.

She must have sensed my growing unease with the questions, because she shifted subjects. She leaned closer to me and said, "There's more riding on Alvaro's research than money."

"Well, of course," I said. "If his research was successful, it would have a major impact on the lives of people with Alzheimer's and their families."

"That's not what I mean," she continued in the same

conspiratorial tone. "The disposition of his research could have serious ramifications with regard to the tenuous relationship we have with Castro's Cuba."

"I hadn't thought much about that," I said, which was true.

"I'm sure I'm not breaching any secrets," she said, "to tell you that the Castro regime has stepped up its efforts here in Tampa and Miami to sow discontent among Cuban Americans."

"I wasn't aware of that happening."

"Oh, yes. There are Cuban Americans in both cities whose sentiments are still with Castro. Well, that isn't strictly true. Some of them don't pledge an allegiance to anyone. They do it for the money. The bottom line is that the Cuban regime will pay almost anything to get its hands on the research. We can't let that happen."

"We?"

"Our government."

"Are steps being taken to ensure that Dr. Vasquez's research stays here and doesn't fall into Cuban hands?"

"Let me just say that the key is to find Alvaro's notes."

Did she know about the allegedly missing laptop? It seemed to me that she did.

"Is there a problem finding his reports?" I asked, this time doing the probing myself. Had Peters told her what he'd told Seth and me?

She paused before asking, "Do you know of a problem with that, Jessica?"

"How would I?"

"I just thought that your Dr. Hazlitt might have shared something with you."

The lame street peddler returned offering cigars and lighters. Oona again told him to leave, but I reached in my purse, withdrew a five-dollar bill, and handed it to him. He opened his almost toothless mouth into a smile and allowed me to take a lighter, a red one, from his hand.

"*Gracias,*" he said.

"*De nada,*" I replied.

I examined the lighter. It was similar to the one I'd seen Vasquez use to light his cigars, more like a blow-torch than any lighter I was accustomed to seeing.

"For cigars," Oona said. "It shoots out a flame."

I tried it and saw that it certainly did.

"Thinking of taking up cigar smoking?" she asked playfully.

"You never know," I said, dropping the lighter into my purse and getting up from my chair. "I really should be going."

"I'm glad you found time for me," she said, rising and shaking my hand.

"I'm sure we'll see each other again before I return home," I said.

She handed me a card on which her office contact information was listed. "Please call me if you hear anything that bears on what I've said."

"I can't imagine what that might be, but I certainly will stay in touch. By the way, I meant to ask you something about your friend Mr. Westerkoch."

"Yes?"

"He told me he was a consultant. What organization does he consult for?"

"Various agencies," she said with a small smile. "Thanks again for coming."

I watched her walk away and disappear around the corner.

Our conversation had raised more questions than it had answered.

That Dr. Vasquez's research would have political overtones had come as a surprise, although I suppose it shouldn't have. I could understand that laying claim to his research would be of considerable interest to the Cuban government, but it seemed to me that the ones with the most to lose were Bernard Peters and K-Dex, unless what Dr. Sardina had said about key-man insurance was true.

A chill in the air reminded me that it was time to get back to the hotel. I was eager to find out how Seth's afternoon had gone, and if other friends and acquaintances of Alvaro Vasquez were quizzing him. I left King Corona and retraced my steps to where I'd gotten off the streetcar. I hadn't realized how long Oona and I had talked, and it was starting to get dark. I was alone at the streetcar stop in front of the historic inn, except for a man wearing what the young people call a "hoodie." He leaned against a building a dozen feet from where I stood, trying, in my opinion, to appear casual. When I looked in his direction, he turned away from me, dropped a cigarette he was smoking, crushed it with his sneaker, and walked away. I watched as he crossed Eighth Avenue and got into a car—a small silver sedan that looked like the one I'd noticed earlier in the day. The car quickly pulled away and sped past me, the driver and young man looking straight ahead.

The streetcar arrived and I slipped onto a bench, gripping the back of the seat in front of me. I was on edge. Ever since arriving in Tampa to meet up with Seth, I'd experienced this sort of unease, nothing tangible, no single incident to which I could point. Of course, witnessing Alvaro Vasquez's sudden death had played a part, but as upsetting as that was, it couldn't explain the tension I'd felt before that awful event.

I was relieved when I reached the hotel. The first thing I did upon entering my room was to call Seth. There was no answer, so I left a message. Strange, I thought, that he would have gone out without leaving word for me. I waited fifteen minutes and tried his room again. Still no answer. He'd said he was going to take a nap. Was he still asleep? If he was, he would have awakened to the sound of the ringing phone. Seth was used to being called at odd hours by patients or the hospital and was a light sleeper. I made one more attempt before going downstairs. I poked my head in the bar and restaurant looking for him, before I approached the front desk.

"Did Dr. Hazlitt leave any messages for me?" I asked the young man.

"No, Mrs. Fletcher. Nothing here."

"I'm concerned about him," I said. "I've called his room three times with no response."

The young clerk smiled. "He probably stepped out for a while."

I shook my head. "He wouldn't do that without leaving me a message. Could we possibly go to his room and see if he's all right?"

A few minutes later the clerk arrived with an assistant manager, who accompanied me to Seth's room. We knocked, louder each time. No response. The manager looked at me for approval to use his master key to enter. I nodded.

He opened the door and stepped back to allow me to enter. I did so with trepidation. I'd conjured the dreadful scenario of walking into the room to find my dear friend dead of a heart attack or stroke and drew a deep breath of relief once I saw that he wasn't there.

"Looks like he decided to take a walk," said the manager.

"Yes," I said, "it does look that way. I'm sorry to have bothered you."

"Not a problem, Mrs. Fletcher. Better safe than sorry."

He stood at the door, and I realized he expected me to leave with him, which I understood. It wasn't my room; to have allowed me to stay would have been a breach of hotel security. I rode down the elevator with him, thanked him again, and went to the lounge. Although I'd peeked in there earlier, I was hoping Seth might have gone in while I was upstairs. I'd just come from the lounge when the concierge, who'd been absent from his post when I'd returned from Ybor City, greeted me. "Good evening, Mrs. Fletcher."

"Good evening. You haven't seen Dr. Hazlitt lately, have you?"

"As a matter of fact, I have. He left about a half hour ago."

Thank goodness, I thought with a sigh. "Was he alone?" I asked.

"No. He was with someone."

"Do you know the person he was with?"

He shook his head. "Afraid not."

"A gentleman?"

"Yes."

"Could you possibly describe him for me?"

"Regular-looking fellow, wore a suit. He was—I suppose you could say chubby."

"Thank you," I said, and headed for my room.

It had taken me time to get over the fear I'd felt when entering Seth's hotel room. I sat by the window in my suite and tried to imagine whom Seth might have left with, and why he didn't leave any message for me. The concierge's vague description had been no help. While I don't usually track down where Seth is— after all, he's entitled to his privacy and to make his own arrangements—I decided to call him on his cell phone. I retrieved my phone from my purse and discovered that it was turned off. When I activated it, the tinkle of little bells told me that I had a message. It was from Seth.

"You ought to get in the habit of leaving your phone on, Jessica," he said. "No sense havin' one if you don't keep it on. Anyway, I'm on my way out of the hotel, having a drink with Bernie Peters. He called me and said he had something important to talk about. Would have invited you, too, if you had your phone on. Speak with you later."

I called him back only to be connected to his message center. "I'm back in the hotel," I said. A minute later my phone rang.

"Hello, Seth."

"Jessica. You called?"

"Yes. I'm sorry my phone was off earlier. You're with Bernie Peters? I'm disappointed I missed you."

"Just about to leave. Should be back at the hotel in fifteen, twenty minutes."

"I'll be here," I said; then, as an afterthought, I added, "Seth, on your way back, please pay attention to your surroundings."

"Why do you say that?"

"Because I think we're being followed."

Chapter Twelve

"What's this about us being followed?" Seth asked after we'd been seated at a table in Bern's Steak House. We'd decided to treat ourselves to a leisurely early dinner, and the concierge had recommended Bern's, although he did caution that we'd have to dress up, which we did.

"That same silver sedan I noticed when we left the medical examiner's office was parked near where I was this afternoon in Ybor City," I explained. "There was a man in the front seat, and another lounging on the street, who I'm sure was observing me. When I looked his way, he got into the car and they drove off."

Seth looked at me over the top of his menu and raised his eyebrows. Actually, the menu was called the *programme du jour*, all eighteen pages of it.

"I know," I said, "you think I'm being paranoid."

"Not at all, Jessica," he said. "You know the old saying."

"Just because I'm paranoid doesn't mean I'm not being followed."

He smiled and returned to reading the bill of fare.

"Seth," I said, "I have this feeling of unease that I can't shake."

He lowered the menu to the table and placed a hand on mine. "We were witness to a shocking event, Jessica."

"It isn't Vasquez's sudden death that has me upset," I said, "although I know it must be a terrible time for you, grappling with the loss of a good friend."

"Thank you for understanding," he said. "I've been working hard to get on with life in a normal fashion. As a doctor, I should be accustomed to death—I've certainly been exposed to it enough times—but when it's someone you felt close to"—he paused for a moment to rein in his emotions—"well, then it's another story." Seth's eyes were moist. He coughed to clear his throat and took a sip of water before asking, "So if it's not Al's death upsetting you, what is it?"

"It's the people who are alive that concern me. Today, Oona Mendez kept pressing me about the research and how much *you* knew about it."

"What did you say?"

"I said she should ask you directly."

"Good for you. Not that I would necessarily share any information with her. Why would it be her business?"

"She said she's looking at it from a government

standpoint and told me that there are members of the Cuban American community here who are agents for the Castro regime."

"Wouldn't surprise me. Al felt the same way. That's why security was so tight at the lab. I'm a little annoyed that Peters and Sardina haven't kept that up. Careless of them. Probably why the laptop went missing. If Castro comes up with the research results, I blame those two."

"Even before Dr. Vasquez's death, Karl Westerkoch questioned me at the party, asking me how much you knew about the research. Bernard Peters, who was kept in the dark despite his and his company's support of Vasquez and the laboratory, is frantic to find the laptop to ensure the value of his investment. Pedro Sardina has nothing but bad things to say about Vasquez. And now we know that Al wasn't hit by a lightning strike. You say the way he died is highly unusual, almost medically impossible. I may be making too much of this, but it seems to me that all these things add up to good reason for me to be ill at ease."

"And there's that mysterious silver car you say is following you."

"Yes, that, too."

"Well," he said, "it's not as though I haven't been havin' some of the same feelings. I had an interesting time with Bernie Peters."

"That's right. I forgot to ask about it. I've been so busy with my own thoughts that everything else gets lost."

"It seems that Bernie and his lawyers are going to bring a suit against Al and the lab."

"Can they do that? He's dead. And what do they base the suit on?"

"They're demanding an accounting of the research and taking possession of it. Bernie leveled with me. He says he's invested every cent he has in Al's research, has almost bankrupted K-Dex, and has even mortgaged his home to keep the money flowing. He's a desperate man, Jessica."

"Then Sardina must be wrong about Peters covering his bets with insurance."

"Bernie says Sardina is not to be trusted. I'm of the same mind. I don't believe he told us the truth at lunch. I think he lied to us about Al to cover mistakes he made himself or to get back at a boss he didn't like. Bad-mouthing a man who's dead is pretty low."

"In that case, I can't imagine K-Dex would have any problem prevailing with a suit. Peters's company paid for the research. It belongs to them."

"Depends on how the agreement between Bernie and Al reads. Of course, chances are that the laptop is at the Vasquez house. Bernie says he's being stonewalled by Al's son, Xavier."

"Have you tried to arrange a visit? I have a feeling that because you were close to Alvaro, they might treat you differently."

"No, not yet, but I think it's time that I did. I'll call first thing in the morning."

"Any luck?" I asked when Seth joined me at breakfast.

"I got hold of Al's daughter, Maritza. She says her mother still isn't up to seeing visitors but that it was okay for you and me to come by."

"Both of us?"

"Ayuh. I said we'd be there in an hour. I think it's

time we rented a car. It's being delivered here at the hotel." He looked at the menu. "Too bad they don't have blueberry pancakes. I could go for a stack about now."

"They'd never be as good as Mara's," I said, referring to our favorite luncheonette in Cabot Cove, where the blueberry pancakes were a specialty.

"True. So I guess I'll go for an omelet. I'm hungry—always am after I have a big meal the night before. Let's eat and get moving."

Before getting into our rental car, I surveyed the parking lot in search of the silver sedan. Seth noticed what I was doing and asked, "Any sign of our tail? That's what they call it, don't they, a tail?"

"No sign of it, and yes, they call it a tail. Maybe I've been imagining things."

"Mebbe," he muttered as he got behind the wheel of our bright yellow Toyota and fumbled while looking for the ignition. "But you're usually pretty observant."

"If someone *is* following us," I said, "he'll never lose *this* car. Couldn't you find one a little less colorful?"

"Took what they gave me," he replied as he found where the key went and started the engine, and we headed off for the Vasquez house on Davis Island.

"I feel awkward coming to the house," I said.

"Why?"

"It's so soon after his death. You're sure his daughter said it was all right?"

"Not only said it was all right—she seemed to welcome a visit from us."

I sat back and took in the sights as we crossed the Hillsborough River on Kennedy Boulevard and eventually came to Davis Boulevard, which took us back across the water, Hillsborough Bay this time, and onto the island. As we pulled into the circular gravel driveway, I saw that one of the black-suited security men stood at the front door, arms folded across his large chest, a formidable gatekeeper. He grunted as we walked past, but he didn't stop us and looked on placidly as Seth rang the bell. We heard movement inside the house, and a few moments later a pretty young woman dressed in jeans and a pink T-shirt with sequins at the neckline opened the door.

"Dr. Hazlitt," she said without smiling. "It's good to see you again."

"Hello, Maritza," he said. "I'm sorry we get to meet again under such circumstances."

"Yes," she said solemnly and stepped back inside to allow us to enter. Although it was another unusually chilly day in Tampa, the air-conditioning was going full blast, the way it had been in the limo the other day. I had the macabre thought that a body could be preserved in the house for a very long time, but Maritza seemed comfortable in her T-shirt. I was glad that I'd worn a sweater.

We followed her into the living room, where I was surprised to see Ivelisse Vasquez sitting by a window, a red blanket wrapped around her, her attention directed at the outdoors.

"Mami, it's Dr. Hazlitt and his friend," Maritza said.

"Jessica Fletcher," I provided.

"And Jessica Fletcher," Maritza said.

Mrs. Vasquez turned slowly and appeared to be trying to focus on us. We approached, and Seth extended his hand, which she took.

"Hello, Mrs. Vasquez," I said, also taking her hand, which felt like holding a delicate bird.

"Thank you for coming," Ivelisse said, her voice weak. "Did you know my husband?"

Seth and I glanced at each other before Seth said, "Yes, we met in Cuba, and I've spent time with him here in Tampa."

"Oh, yes, of course," she said, returning her gaze out the window.

Seth gestured to a footstool next to Ivelisse, but I indicated that he should sit instead. I stood behind him, acutely aware that I was not a close family friend.

"He's gone, isn't he?" Ivelisse said absently.

"Al?" Seth said. "Yes, he's gone. Jessica and I are sorry for your loss."

Maritza, who'd remained at a distance, approached and said, "Time for some rest, Mami. You need to rest." She gently helped her mother stand. Seth stood, too, and secured the blanket, which had started to fall from Ivelisse's shoulders. Maritza led her mother from the room. "I'll be back in a minute," she said.

"I wonder if Xavier is here, too," Seth said, looking around.

"I don't suppose he's making funeral arrangements yet," I said. "The medical examiner will want to hold the body until the lab results come back."

Seth muttered something in response and pursed his lips.

"Do you think that the ME's finding that he wasn't killed by lightning has been reported to the family?" I asked.

He shrugged. "Under ordinary circumstances, it

would be, but since the ME doesn't have a definitive cause of death yet, he might hold up informing the family until he does."

Maritza reappeared.

"I don't think that my mother has accepted the reality of my father's death," she said.

"Sometimes it takes a very long time for that sort of reality to set in," I said. "I know it did when my husband, Frank, died."

"Has Mr. Peters come by?" Seth asked.

She made a sour face. "No, he hasn't," she said sharply.

"Is your brother here?" Seth asked.

"No. Xavier flew to Key West this morning. He had business to attend to there. He said he'll be back tomorrow."

"Would it be okay with you, Maritza, if I spent some time in your father's office?" Seth asked.

I wondered what her reaction would be to his directness. Would she find it an untoward request?

"Sure," she said. "I'll show you where it is."

"You don't have to bother," Seth said. "Your dad and I spent some time there together."

"No, I'll go with you," she said as she led us down a hallway past bedrooms to the rear of the house. "Papi thought so highly of you, Dr. Hazlitt."

"I'm flattered that he did. And he was very proud that you are following in his footsteps. Are your studies going well?"

Maritza stiffened. "I'm not following in his footsteps," she said. "My studies are in a completely different area." As we entered the office she asked, "Is there anything in particular you are looking for, Dr. Hazlitt?"

"No," Seth said, "I just wanted to think about your dad in this setting. He always seemed especially comfortable here."

"He always needed a retreat, as he called it, a place to escape, to get away from everything and everyone."

"Aside from your mother's shock at his death," Seth asked, "has she been all right otherwise?"

Maritza's raised eyebrows, and the stream of air that came from her lips, answered the question.

"Lately, she's seemed to be, well, a little forgetful," Seth said.

Maritza shook her head and straightened her shoulders, "Mami is fine, just fine," she said. "She has what you call 'senior moments,' that's all." She forced a laugh. "I guess it comes with getting older."

I knew what Seth was thinking—that in Ivelisse's case, age in itself didn't account for her slippages in memory, and that as a medical student Maritza would likely be attuned to her mother's symptoms. However, it was clear that she didn't want to believe her mother was failing, or in any case talk about it. "Was it difficult for you to get permission to leave Cuba?" I asked her.

"No. Despite what too many people think, the Cuban government respects when a family member dies, even when it's in another country. No, I got my card right away; I didn't have any trouble at all."

"I'm pleased to hear that," I said, a little surprised that it had been so easy for her to obtain a white card, allowing her to leave the country. From what I'd read, permission was routinely denied most people, no matter how valid their reasons for traveling out of Cuba.

"I have some things to do," Maritza said. "Make yourself at home. I'll be back in a moment."

"I didn't think she'd be so defensive about the Cuban government," I said after she was gone.

"I suppose she's right about what other people assume about Cuba," Seth said as he went behind Vasquez's massive desk, its edges inlaid with small, colorful tiles, and opened a drawer.

"Seth," I said, "I don't think you should be—"

He put his finger to his lips. "Just stand by the door and wave if you see her coming back."

It ran through my mind that I was aiding and abetting something, if not illegal, then certainly questionable. But I did as Seth suggested while he quickly opened and closed drawers in the desk. The last one he opened was the middle drawer. "What's this?" he said.

"What's what?"

"This envelope. It's addressed to me."

I went to him and looked at the envelope. The handwriting said, "Dr. Seth Hazlitt."

"It's Al's handwriting," he said as he slipped it into the inside pocket of his tweed sport jacket.

"Seth, I don't think you should do that."

"Why not? It's addressed to me, in Al's own hand. He obviously meant it for me, so I'll take it."

Seth got up from behind the desk and opened a closet, scanned what was in it, shook his head, closed it, and said, "Nothing." He returned to the desk and slumped in the large leather swivel chair behind it.

"What were you looking for?" I asked.

"Al's laptop, of course," he snapped.

"It's obviously not here," I said, "at least not in this office, but I'm not surprised. It's silly to think we could just come in here and find it waiting for us. We don't even know if he brought it here the day he died. Dr. Sardina said he took it home with him every night, but maybe he's exaggerating. Besides—and I don't mean to be critical, Seth—even if we do find the laptop, it doesn't belong to us. It would be the property of his estate, or belong to Bernie Peters."

Seth heaved a big sigh. "I know, I know. You're right, Jessica, and I wasn't intending to keep it. But if Al achieved some sorta breakthrough with his research, it has to be put in the right hands, people who can carry it further and put an end to Alzheimer's. Bernie Peters should have the results in his hands. He financed it. What bothers me is that if Al *did* bring the laptop here every night, then where is it?"

"One of his family members may have taken it," I offered.

"Makes sense," he said, "but what do *they* intend to do with it?"

Our conversation was interrupted when Maritza returned.

"I have a question, Maritza," Seth said.

"If I can answer it, I will."

"Your father used to bring his laptop home with him from the lab."

"Yes?"

"He showed me entries he'd made the last time I was here in Tampa."

"I don't understand the question," Maritza said.

"Well," Seth continued, "I was wondering whether you know where it is."

"Where what is?"

"His laptop computer."

"How would I know? I live in Cuba. I have no idea what my father did or how he ran his research. A laptop? I never heard anything about it."

Her denial of knowing anything about the laptop didn't ring true to me.

"Maybe Xavier would know where it is," Seth said.

She shrugged.

I was about to suggest that we leave when the doorbell sounded. Maritza jumped up to answer it. In her absence, I walked to a small table in a corner of the office where something had caught my attention. Idly, I picked up a thick brochure and unfolded it.

"What are you looking at?" Seth asked.

"This is an aeronautical chart," I said, "a sectional chart, actually."

Seth looked over my shoulder at the paper I held. "Pilots use these?" he asked.

"Yes. They give you everything you need to know about navigation, airports, radio frequencies to use, the height of obstacles like radio towers and mountains, all the essentials."

"Looks like a lot of gobbledygook to me," he said.

"They're not as confusing as they look once you become familiar with them."

"Maritza said that her brother was flying to Key West. Wouldn't he need them?"

I checked the date on the chart. "This one is out-of-date," I said. "I'm sure he has new ones."

I refolded the chart and laid it on the table. "Seth, I think it's time we left, don't you?"

"I do," he agreed, and we turned toward the office door.

"Wait a minute," I said, and returned to the table. "I just realized something."

"What?"

"This sectional is for Cuba."

"And?"

"I just wonder why he has a sectional chart for Cuba."

"You'll have to ask him when he gets back," Seth said, and led us down the hallway to the foyer, where Maritza stood at the front door talking to Dr. Sardina's wife, Ofelia.

"I just thought I'd stop in and see how Ivelisse is doing," Ofelia said.

"As well as can be expected," Maritza said. "She's resting now."

"I can wait." Ofelia walked past Maritza and settled in the living room.

"Ofelia," Maritza called after her, "is something wrong?"

"No, nothing's wrong. Did they—?"

Maritza nodded.

"I miss him already," Ofelia said.

"Has your husband gone away?" I asked.

"Can I get you a cold drink, Ofelia?" Maritza said quickly, and I had the feeling that she wanted to divert the conversation to a different topic.

"That would be nice," Ofelia replied.

When Maritza left the room to get Ofelia her drink,

I said to her, "We had a pleasant lunch with your husband. He took us to an Asian buffet restaurant and—"

"He told me," Ofelia said.

I wanted to ask about her husband's negative view of Vasquez, which I assumed he'd shared with her, but wasn't sure how to approach the subject. Instead, I said, "There seems to be some concern about Dr. Vasquez's research and how far he'd gotten with it. I imagine your husband will be asked about that many times in the coming days."

"Yes, I suppose he will," she said. She turned to Seth. "Did Pedro tell you much about the research, Dr. Hazlitt?"

"Can't say that he did," said Seth.

"But Dr. Vasquez did."

Seth thought before answering. "Yes, Al—Dr. Vasquez shared some of his results with me. Your husband was—how shall I say it?—your husband seemed to be disappointed in how little was shared with him."

"Oh, that's not true," Ofelia said, straightening as though to enhance her denial. "Alvaro always took Pedro into his confidence."

"I was mistaken, then," Seth said.

"Your husband's away?" I asked again, this time without Maritza interjecting herself.

"Just for a day. He'll be home soon."

"Business?"

"Ah, yes. He's on business."

"Having to do with the research?" I managed to ask before Maritza reappeared carrying a tall glass of what looked like lemonade.

"Oh, thank you so much," Ofelia said, taking the glass and sipping the drink. "This tastes like fresh lemons. I forget how good it can be with fresh lemons."

"I always use fresh lemons," Maritza said, taking a seat next to the other woman.

"We should be going," Seth said, taking my arm. "Please contact us at the hotel if there's anything we can do."

We got in the yellow rental car and pulled away.

"What do you think?" Seth asked.

"It's obvious that Maritza didn't want us asking questions about where Dr. Sardina has gone. It struck me that Xavier Vasquez and Sardina are both gone for the day. Do you think that—?"

"That Sardina went to Key West with Xavier? Certainly a possibility."

"Where are we going?"

"Back to the hotel, where I can read what's in that envelope Al left me."

We retraced our trip over the bay and onto the mainland. As we approached a stoplight, Seth swerved suddenly into the adjoining lane to avoid a pothole in the road, and stopped. A vehicle behind us also swerved but in the opposite direction, and ended up stopped at the light in the lane we'd previously occupied. I glanced over at the occupants of the dark blue car. I couldn't see the driver clearly, but the person in the front passenger seat was a young man wearing the same sort of gray hoodie that I'd seen on the man at the streetcar stop in Ybor City. He glanced at me for a second before turning away quickly so that his face was obscured.

"Seth," I said, "that's the same young fellow . . ."

The light changed and the blue car pulled away sharply and sped ahead of us.

"What say, Jessica?" Seth asked as we slowly moved forward.

"The passenger in the car next to us was the same young person I'd seen in Ybor City, the one who I was certain was eyeing me."

"Is that so?" Seth said, and accelerated.

I put my hand on his arm. "Please don't try to follow him, Seth. He's going much too fast."

"Not giving me a chance to be a real detective," Seth said, but he took my advice and slowed down.

We parked the car when we reached the hotel and settled on a sofa in the far end of the lobby. Seth pulled the envelope from his pocket, opened it, and unfolded the single sheet of paper it contained. His face was set in a hard scowl as he read, and even though we were in a public place, I wished he'd read aloud for my benefit. When he finished, he handed the paper to me. It was a typewritten letter to him from Dr. Vasquez.

My dear friend and brother-in-arms Seth:

It is my hope that you shall never read this letter, for if you do, it will mean that I am no longer alive. You see, my newfound best friend, I am surrounded by enemies, people on all sides of me, people who will not shed a tear should I meet with an unfortunate accident, or die from other than God's will. I can trust no one, not colleagues in the medical profession, not businesspeople, not even my own family.

As you know, my life has been devoted to

finding a cure for Alzheimer's disease. It wasn't always easy in Cuba. Funds were scarce, and I had to beg, borrow, and sometimes even steal to keep the research going. When I had a chance to leave Cuba and continue my work in the United States, I jumped at it, especially since the work I'd done in Cuba had enticed the pharmaceutical company K-Dex to commit to generous funding for me. Bernard Peters has been my lifeline, although I must say that his motives as well as his larcenous character have disappointed me greatly of late.

I have been meticulous in documenting my research in the hope that one day what is contained in my documentation will convince others to carry on when I am gone. But because of my distrust of others, I am placing a burden on you, Seth, as a man of character, and in whom I see a totally honest and straightforward human being. You would be excused for wondering why I would place such trust in a man with whom I have spent so little time. Call it instinct. Call it intuition. Call it what you will, my friend, but whatever it is, I trust it.

I have written this letter after our aborted golf outing with your beautiful and charming friend Jessica Fletcher, and intend to give it to you this evening at the end of what I trust will be an enjoyable evening of good music, good drinks, and good conversation. I will, of course, instruct you to not open it while I am alive. But should I die, I ask you to retrieve the copies I have made of what has been entered on my laptop regarding the progress in the laboratory. I have regularly copied my notes to these little devices—thumb drives—and have carefully stored them. They are located in Tampa Mini-Storage on S. MacDill Avenue. The code for my combination lock on unit number 61 is 7-2-9.

I know that you'll do the right thing, Seth. I am counting on it. Of course, I won't be around to thank you for taking on this weighty task, so I do it now, profusely.

Your friend,
Al

I finished reading and looked at Seth, who rubbed his eyes.

"This is remarkable," I said.

He nodded.

"To have generated such trust and respect in such a short time is—well, it is nothing short of—remarkable."

"I'm at a loss for words," he said.

"I understand," I said.

Neither of us said anything for a few moments. Finally, I said, "There's something to this beyond his obvious trust in you."

Seth cocked his head.

"Based upon this letter, I'd say that there's a strong chance that your friend Al was . . ." I hesitated.

"Yes?" Seth said.

I took a deep breath. "That he was murdered."

Chapter Thirteen

We made some wrong turns as we headed for the self-storage facility—by his own admission, Seth can be directionally challenged at times. Eventually we found South MacDill Avenue and drove along until arriving at a modern commercial building with a large red sign, TAMPA MINI-STORAGE.

"Do we have to check in with someone?" I asked as Seth found a parking space.

"Probably not. I've rented space in the storage facility outside Cabot Cove, and unless you want to use one of their carts, you just go to your unit. Should be the same here. Besides, it's not like we're breaking any laws. We have the combination to the lock. Just act like we belong here. They must have plenty of customers and can't remember what everybody looks like."

Buoyed by his confidence, we crossed an impressive, up-to-date lobby, gave a wave to two attractive uniformed people behind the desk, and headed straight for the area where the rental units were located. We walked down a long hallway with an immaculately clean floor. On either side of us, the walls were lined with shiny corrugated metal doors marking the storage lockers.

"Chilly in here," Seth said with a shiver as we searched the numbered doors until we reached unit sixty-one. We looked up and down the hall. We were alone. Seth took a slip of paper from his pocket on which he'd written the combination. He rotated the lock's dial, first all the way around, then to the right to the numeral seven, then left to two, and finally to the right again to nine. One end of the hasp pulled free of the lock. He slipped the lock off and opened the door. Lights had automatically come on when we entered the hallway, and an overhead light in the unit was also on.

The unit was large; the contents of a studio or small one-bedroom apartment would easily have fit. But the only thing in it was a small round table on which a smoked plastic box rested, like a featured piece of art in a museum. That was it. Nothing else was in the pristine space.

We heard footsteps in the corridor and I softly closed the door. Seth approached the table and ran his fingers over the top of the box. He glanced at me before lifting the lid and peering at what was inside. I stood next to him and shared his view. There were three black devices about an inch and a half long and three-quarters of an inch wide.

"What do you call these things?" Seth asked, picking one up.

"Flash drives," I said. "Or thumb drives. I use them all the time to back up my files."

"Thought you did that on those floppy disks."

"No one uses floppy disks anymore," I said. "Thumb drives are a lot easier to use and hold more data. Dr. Vasquez must have taken what was on his laptop and transferred the information to these."

"Can't believe those little things would hold all that much."

Seth's inherent interest in and understanding of the latest medical research doesn't translate to computers. He's always complaining about his computer and his inability to master even its most rudimentary processes. Fortunately, he has a local computer technician in Cabot Cove who's ready to rush to Seth's aid at a moment's notice, and a nurse in his office whose skills are better than his.

"What do you intend to do with them?" I asked.

"Take 'em with me, I guess."

"Maybe it's better to leave them here," I said.

He pondered my suggestion before saying, "I want to know what's on them."

"You'll need a computer for that."

"You didn't bring yours?"

"Of course I did. I always travel with my laptop. You can plug the thumb drives into my computer and store what's on them on my hard drive."

He took the three thumb drives and put them in the side pocket of his jacket.

"Why not take the box?" I asked.

"Don't see any use for it," he replied. "Let's go."

We peered out the door to be certain the corridor

was empty, then relocked the door and walked confidently through the lobby and to the car.

"Seth," I said.

"What?"

"Dr. Vasquez's letter to you. The police should know about it. He obviously feared for his life to have taken the time to write the letter and secure the thumb drives the way he did. We should tell Detective Machado."

"I don't know, Jessica. I wouldn't want anyone else to know that I have his research notes. Seems to me it's nobody's business except mine, until I decide what to do with them."

"I understand what you're saying, Seth, but you can't keep from the authorities that Vasquez was afraid that something would happen to him. It could be crucial to their investigation." What I didn't say was that if someone killed Alvaro Vasquez for the research notes, our lives could be in danger, too.

Seth drove faster than usual in the direction of the hotel.

"You know how to transfer information from one of these little thumb drives to another one?" he asked.

"Yes, it's easy. You plug one into my laptop, take the information that's on it and save it on my hard drive, then plug in a blank thumb drive and transfer the information back onto it."

"Tell you what," he said. "Let's stop and buy three new thumb drives, swing past the hotel, do what you say you can do, make me a second set, and then I won't mind sharing the letter with the police as long as I have a copy of Al's research notes."

Which is what we did. We purchased the drives from a Staples store we passed, went to my room at the hotel, transferred the material, and in less than an hour were back in the car with the originals in Seth's jacket pocket, the copies in his room's small safe.

We had as much trouble finding police headquarters as we did locating the self-storage facility but finally pulled into its parking lot and entered the building. A heavyset uniformed black man sat behind a Plexiglas shield. An open area beneath the shield allowed small items to be passed back and forth; it reminded me of a bank.

"Is Detective Machado in?" I asked.

"What's it about?" the officer said through a speaker in the Plexiglas.

"Dr. Alvaro Vasquez's death. I'm Jessica Fletcher, and this is Dr. Seth Hazlitt."

He picked up the phone and informed the detective who we were and that we wanted to see him. "Take a seat over there," he said, pointing to a wooden bench. "He'll be out in a minute."

Too nervous to sit, Seth and I perused various notices hanging on the walls. One sign proclaimed that the Tampa Police Department was able to translate English into thirty-eight other languages, including Yiddish, Polish, Haitian, Creole, Hindi, Serbian, Tagalog, Urdu, Dutch, Czech, Chamorro, Arabic, and Farsi.

"What in the world is Chamorro?" Seth mused aloud.

"I think it's a language spoken in the Pacific on places like Guam."

"You would know that," he said.

"Just don't ask me to speak it," I said.

Detective Machado appeared as we were admiring a large, colorful graphic of a speeding train cutting through a street map for District One, with the headline: CUTTING THROUGH CRIME. HAVE YOU GOT YOUR TICKET? Accompanying the detective was a man whose face was familiar, although I couldn't quite put a name to it.

"Mrs. Fletcher?" the man said.

"Yes. I know you from somewhere, but—"

"Carlos Cespedes," he said. "We met at Alvaro Vasquez's party."

"Yes, of course. You own a cigar factory. How are you?"

"My cigar factory isn't so big anymore. People smoke fewer cigars these days, more cigarettes. But this is a minor complaint." His already elongated face became more so. "How tragic," he said. "To think that our friend is no longer with us is—it is so unfortunate, so *triste*, sad."

"It certainly is," Seth said.

Machado said impatiently to Seth and me, "Is there something you want to talk to me about?" He looked fatigued.

Mr. Cespedes pulled a business card from his shirt pocket and handed it to me. "Please come visit me at my shop and factory," he said. He lowered his voice and added, "I must speak with you about Alvaro's death."

Cespedes went through the door, looking back nervously.

"You know him, huh?" Machado said.

"As he said, we met at Dr. Vasquez's party," I replied, wondering why he was at police headquarters conferring with the detective, and what he wanted to discuss with us about Vasquez's death.

"Come on in," Machado said. "Your timing is good. I intended to call you anyway."

He led us to an empty room that I assumed was used to question suspects. It had the requisite large window, which I was sure was a two-way mirror. The table was scarred and stained from countless wet cups, and probably cigarette burns from a time before smoking was banned indoors. The four wooden chairs were spindly. Seth and I sat on one side of the table; Machado took a chair opposite us.

"Tell you why I was going to call," he said. "I'm sorry to have to tell you that we're treating Dr. Vasquez's death as a possible homicide."

"Oh?"

"Looks like the victim wasn't struck by lightning after all, according to the ME."

Neither Seth nor I said anything. I knew that Seth was thinking what I was—that it might not go over well for the lead detective on the case to know that the medical examiner had told us that Vasquez wasn't hit by lightning before he'd been informed.

"Then what *did* kill him?" Seth finally asked.

Machado shrugged his large shoulders and rolled his fingertips on the table. "They're doing the toxicological studies as we speak. Of course, it could end up that he had a heart attack or a stroke, only the ME says he doesn't think that's the case. He told me that he had a conversation with you, Dr. Hazlitt."

"Ayuh, that's right, we did have a chat."

"Sometimes the ME and us here in law enforcement don't always connect the way we should. What'd he tell you?"

Seth was on the spot, and I wondered how he'd handle it.

"He didn't have too much to say," was Seth's reply. "We sorta had a medical conversation, you know, doctor to doctor." He smiled.

Machado did not. "I thought that because you were close to the victim, witnessed when he died, and are a physician, that Dr. San Martín might have told you things that he hasn't passed along to us yet."

I said, "Excuse me for injecting myself, Detective, but why would your medical examiner keep things from the police? That strikes me as highly unusual."

Machado, who wasn't a man for whom smiling came easily, managed one and said, "Doc San Martín sometimes gets his back up when it comes to passing on information. Doesn't like to be rushed. Plus, like any PD, we occasionally have somebody leak something to the press that shouldn't be leaked. The doc has raised holy hell about it more than once. For me, I think he's wrong to take it on himself to decide what to give us when and what to keep under his hat, but there's not a lot I can do about it." Seth started to respond, but Machado added, "And I'll tell you another thing. The PD isn't the only source of leaks. The ME's office has had its share, too." Machado's voice mirrored the fatigue on his round face. He sounded very much like a man under siege, someone in need of a vacation. I knew how he felt.

"This is all very interesting," Seth said, "but you said you intended to contact us about it. Why?"

"A couple of reasons. First off, Dr. Hazlitt, I'm told that you and the deceased were pretty chummy."

"Friends? Yes, we were," said Seth.

"Good enough that you made multiple trips to spend time with him."

"I don't know that I would call four trips over several years 'multiple.' I was simply visitin' a friend."

"Pretty expensive flying back and forth—to visit a friend."

"Not terribly expensive," Seth said. "Wouldn't you spend some money to enjoy time with a good friend?"

"Oh, sure, and don't get me wrong. I'm not accusing you of anything. It's just that because you and the victim were close, he might have told you things that would help me with my investigation."

It was the perfect time to bring up the letter that Vasquez had left for Seth, or at least to mention Vasquez's fear for his life. Seth picked up on the cue.

"Matter of fact, there is something you might find helpful."

Machado came forward in his chair and picked up a pen from his desk. "Shoot," he said.

"Al—Dr. Vasquez feared for his life."

"Whoa," Machado said. "When did he tell you that?"

"He, ah—well, to be honest with you, Detective, he wrote it to me in a letter."

I smiled at Seth. I was relieved that he'd decided to be completely honest and not to try to slant the story.

"When did he write you this letter?"

"A few days ago."

"And you knew about it the day he died and didn't come forward with it?"

"He wrote it a few days ago, but I didn't receive it until this morning."

Machado wrote something on a lined yellow pad before asking, "He mailed it to you here in Tampa? Where? Your hotel?"

"No, I—"

Obviously Seth didn't want to admit that he'd taken it from Vasquez's home office without permission, but he answered the question. "He left it for me at his house. Mrs. Fletcher and I were there this morning."

"Wait a minute," Machado said. "He dies a couple of days ago but leaves a letter for you at the house?"

"That's correct. He said that he intended to give it to me the night he died, after the party Mrs. Fletcher and I attended. Unfortunately he didn't live long enough to follow through."

"Okay," said the detective, "I think I understand. Where is the letter?"

"I have it right here," Seth said as he fished it from his inside jacket pocket and handed it across the desk.

Machado opened the envelope, placed a pair of half-glasses on the bridge of his nose, and read. When he was finished, he said, "He doesn't say who he thought might kill him. Did he give you any names?"

"No," Seth said. "This was the first I learned of his concern."

Machado said to me, "Where do you fit into all of this, Mrs. Fletcher?"

"I really don't fit in at all," I said, "aside from being Dr. Hazlitt's friend."

"You're more than that," Machado said.

"Meaning?"

"I Googled you. From what I read, you not only write big bestselling murder mysteries; you've been involved in more than a few real ones yourself—at least according to newspaper reports I got off the Internet, lots of stories about some of those cases."

"It's nothing I brag about," I said.

"Hey," he said, "I'm impressed. If you ever quit writing for a living, maybe you could become a cop."

"I think it's a little late for a change in career, Detective Machado."

"No offense," he said. "Look. If the ME is correct, that Dr. Vasquez might have been done in by someone else, I've got a real hot potato of a case on my hands. Vasquez was well-known in Tampa and controversial, too. My boss, Major Stacks, is already getting pressure from local Cuban American groups."

"Why?" I asked. "As far as the public knows, Dr. Vasquez was killed by a lightning strike."

"Tampa's no different from anyplace else," Machado said. "We've got our share of conspiracy buffs. Word gets around that some people think that maybe Vasquez wasn't killed by lightning and their paranoia shifts into high gear. Our liaison officers who work with the Cuban community tell us that some people are convinced that Vasquez was killed by our government to get his research and keep it out of Castro's hands. We've also got pressure from the feds."

"The FBI?"

"Right. So my boss tells me in no uncertain terms to wrap this up."

"Why would the FBI be interested in a local death?" I asked, hoping I wasn't sounding too naïve.

"Because of who the victim was, Mrs. Fletcher. Vasquez defected from Cuba. It made all the papers. He supposedly was sitting on some medical breakthrough that the Cubans would want back, and the feds obviously want to make sure that that doesn't happen."

"I certainly understand," Seth said. "That's why we stopped by, to let you know about the letter."

Machado glanced at the sheet of paper again. "So Vasquez tells you that he left you copies of his research. Did you go to this self-storage place?"

"Yes." Seth pulled the three original thumb drives from his jacket and handed them to the detective.

"It's all on these?" Machado asked.

Seth nodded. "As far as I know."

"You haven't looked at them?"

Seth shook his head, and I knew he was relieved to be telling the truth.

"What else is in that storage place?"

"Nothing," I answered, "just a small table and the box in which these were housed."

"You take the box and table from there?"

"No," Seth said. "We left them."

Machado exhaled a long, poignant stream of air and stood. "Let's go," he said.

"Where?"

"The storage place."

"Is it really necessary for us to go with you?" I asked.

"Can't make you, but I'd appreciate it."

A half hour later we were walking down the hallway toward space number sixty-one, whose door was wide-open.

"You locked it when you left?" Machado asked.

"Ayuh, I'm sure I did," Seth said.

We stepped inside. The smoked plastic box was gone; only the table remained.

Machado abruptly turned and left the room, with us following. We went to the lobby, where Machado flashed his TPD badge to a young woman at the desk. "I need to speak with the manager," the detective said. A few minutes later, a man appeared and introduced himself, checked Machado's badge, and said, "Not again."

"What do you mean by that?" Machado asked.

"You're the second cop—law enforcement officer—who's been here this afternoon."

"Who was the other one?"

"FBI."

"FBI? You're sure?"

"He had his credentials. He wanted us to open one of the lockers."

"Number sixty-one," I said.

"That's right. He said that the renter was deceased— Dr. Vasquez. I'd read that the doctor had died, hit by lightning, so I opened the locker and this FBI agent took what was in there, not much, just a table and a box on it. He took the box."

The manager accompanied us back to the open storage space, and Machado looked around. There was nothing to see aside from the table, which he dismissed with a cursory running of his hand over it. He thanked the manager and we retreated to Machado's unmarked car.

"Looks like you were right about the FBI being interested," Seth said as we drove back to police headquarters.

"The agent must have been after what Dr. Vasquez wanted Seth to have, the thumb drives he gave you," I said.

Machado grunted and drove the last few blocks in silence.

"Appreciate you coming in," he said to us as we prepared to get into our yellow rental car.

"What will you do with those thumb drives we gave you?" I asked. "They contain what could be very valuable information about Dr. Vasquez's medical research."

"We have experts to check them. I want to know whether he names names or says anything about fearing for his life. There's probably nothing, but then again . . . Anyway, thanks again for your cooperation. You can still be reached at the hotel?"

"Ayuh," Seth responded.

"How long do you plan on staying in Tampa?"

"Hard to say," Seth said.

"I'll stay in touch," Machado said, and walked away.

When we'd gotten in the car I said, "Either someone other than Dr. Vasquez knew that he'd rented that storage space, or—"

"Or what, Jessica?"

"Or someone followed us there, and that someone is involved with the government."

We drove a little farther before I asked, "Just how long *do* you plan on staying, Seth?"

He ran his tongue over his lips before answering. "As long as it takes to find out what really *did* happen to Al."

Chapter Fourteen

Seth was eager to get back to the hotel to read what was on the thumb drives, but I suggested that we first stop at Carlos Cespedes's cigar shop and factory. "He said that he wanted to discuss something about Dr. Vasquez's death," I said. "As long as you're committed to getting to the bottom of it, we should follow up on every possible source of information."

"Is that what you'd have people do if you were writing this as a novel?" he asked.

"Yes, I suppose I would," I said.

"Makes sense," he said.

I retrieved Cespedes's business card and read off the address to him, then consulted the street map that came with the rental car and gave directions.

Cespedes Fine Cigars was located in downtown Ybor City. The owner's business card billed it as a cigar factory and shop, although from the looks of it the use of the term "factory" was a misnomer. In reality, it was no more than a storefront with two small tables and a few chairs on the sidewalk in front. A sign next to the door offered coffee, cold drinks, and "Authentic Cuban Pastries." An older woman and a younger man occupied one of the tables. Both had large white mugs in front of them, and both were drawing on cigars.

We found a parking space in a lot across the street. As we got out and waited for traffic to clear before crossing, a family of four, mother, father, and two youngsters, emerged from Cespedes's shop, each carrying a small plastic shopping bag.

"You don't figure they bought cigars for the kids, do you?" Seth mused.

"Only chocolate ones, I hope," I said as we took advantage of a break in traffic and walked across.

The door to the shop was open, and we entered. A long counter to the left held a cash register and clear plastic boxes containing an assortment of cigars. Stacks of colorful cigar boxes filled shelves mounted on the wall. A young woman sat on a stool browsing through a magazine.

"*Buenos días,*" she said.

"*Buenos días,*" I replied. "Is Mr. Cespedes in?"

She pointed to the rear of the shop and went back to reading.

Our view of the back of the shop was obscured by a row of large barrels in which tropical plants bloomed. Once we reached them, we could see beyond to where two older men sat at wooden tables rolling cigars. They looked up for a moment before returning to their tasks, and I recognized one as Adelmo, who had been making cigars at Alvaro Vasquez's party. I was about to ask for Mr. Cespedes when he appeared through a slit in a red curtain.

"Ah," he said, smiling and coming to us, his hand outstretched, "you came, you came. I am so pleased."

"Thank you for the invitation," Seth said. "So this is your cigar shop."

I judged Cespedes to be in his late sixties or early seventies. A short, balding man with a sizable paunch, he wore a red-and-white checkered shirt and tan slacks and had a malleable face on which he adopted a hang-dog look. "It used to be much more, I am afraid. I once owned a whole building here in Ybor City, a real factory. I even had lectors."

My puzzled expression prompted him to explain.

"Lectors," he said. "Readers. While my *tabaqueros* and *tabaqueras*, the cigar rollers, do their work, the readers sit high above them and read aloud from the newspapers, or short stories. It is a very Cuban thing, very educational, yes?"

"I saw and heard the lectors when I was in Havana," Seth said.

"Ah, Havana," Cespedes sighed. "I miss it."

"You never go back?" I asked.

"Once—no, twice—many years ago. It is very different now that the *imbécil* Castro is there. I would go shoot him myself if I could."

My attention drifted to what the men were doing at their tables.

"Ah," Cespedes said, "too much from me about Castro, huh? You're interested in how my cigars are made."

One of the rollers, or *tabaqueros*, as I now knew,

picked up a small rounded knife and banged it on his table. Adelmo did likewise.

Cespedes laughed. "They welcome you with their banging, a Cuban custom."

I remembered that Adelmo had rapped his knife on the table when I'd said hello at the party. At the time, I hadn't realized he was responding to my greeting.

"That is the *chaveta*," Cespedes continued, "the knife used to smooth and cut the tobacco leaves, smooth the filler tobacco, cut the tips. They say they circumcise the tips, like a baby. See? He rolls the tobacco into a tube that goes into the wooden mold. Then he takes the solid cylinder—we call it the 'bunch'—and lays it on the wrapper and uses a tiny bit of vegetable glue to secure the second wrapper. Then he glues the cap into place and trims any excess tobacco."

"How many can he roll in a day?" I asked.

"For those medium-sized cigars, maybe one hundred, maybe a little more. For the bigger, fatter cigars, not so many." He gave out a plaintive sigh. "Everything is so different now in Ybor City. Once there were a hundred and fifty factories rolling a quarter of a million cigars every year. Now, for me, there is only this." He took in his shop with a wave of his hand. "It is a shame that you weren't here last month for the cigar festival. A team rolled the world's longest cigar, a hundred feet long. You can check it in that Guinness book."

I laughed as I envisioned a hundred-foot-long cigar.

Seth broke in with, "You said that you wanted to talk to us about Al Vasquez's death, Mr. Cespedes."

"Yes, I do."

A family of tourists came through the front door.

"Please, come with me," Cespedes said as he parted the red curtains. "We can talk better in here."

Behind the curtains was a small office. Large posters of famous cigar labels of the past dominated the walls. A calculator surrounded by piles of papers sat on a desk. Family photographs in silver frames were lined up on a table behind the desk.

"You were Alvaro's good friend," he said as Seth and I sat in director's chairs with floral-patterned canvas seats and backs, while he perched on a stool.

"That's right," Seth said. "I assume that you were a close friend, too."

"'Close friend'? We were friends, acquaintances, and I suppose you could say business partners."

"What sort of business were you and Al in?" Seth asked.

"He never told you? It is hard to explain. As you can see from my shop, what I once had is no longer. Now I make ends meet. But it wasn't long ago that there was plenty of money from when I sold my factory building. The company that bought it turned it into a handsome social club. You can see it on Avenida Republica de Cuba. Once my father had a hundred *tabaqueros* and *tabaqueras* rolling cigars in our factory, and the best lectors reading the latest news, and short stories, too, by your Papa Hemingway and Agatha Christie and other great writers. We treated everyone well. Our cigars were among the best in the world. Now members of the club drink and eat and dance and hold their meetings in what was our building. It is a good place, the club, but I am sad every time I drive by."

It was obvious to Seth and me that Cespedes would get around to addressing Vasquez's death only after he was finished lamenting what had happened to Ybor City and his family's cigar factory. We listened patiently until Seth again asked, "What sort of business were you and Dr. Vasquez in?"

Cespedes didn't hesitate. "His research, of course," he said.

Seth and I looked at each other before Seth said, "The research? How were you and Dr. Vasquez involved together in his research?"

"I invested in it, five hundred thousand dollars, what I received from the sale of my building."

Seth shook his head as though to clear it. "Let me get this straight," he said. "You invested in the research that Dr. Vasquez was doing to find a cure for Alzheimer's disease?"

"Yes."

"But what about—?" I started to say.

Seth finished the sentence for me. "Bernard Peters."

"Oh," said Cespedes, "Mr. Peters is also an investor."

"Does he know about *your* investment in the research?" I asked.

"No, no," Cespedes said. "It was very important to Alvaro that my investment be kept a secret from everyone, anyone. I have never even told my wife."

"Do you know if there were other independent investors like you?" I asked.

Cespedes shrugged. "Probably. Alvaro, he needed the money. He liked the high life, you know? The boats, the women, the good food. He liked to entertain his friends. Peters only gave him so much, and he expected it to go toward the laboratory."

"What were you to receive for the half million dollars you invested?" I asked.

"Ten percent. I wasn't sure whether to make the investment. Those savings were all I had. But to be on the ground floor, as you say, of a cure for that terrible disease, was a privilege I could not pass up. Alvaro told me that he was only allowing very few people to invest in his work."

"I assume you had a good written agreement with him," Seth said.

"Yes. Alvaro gave me a letter saying that when he found a cure, I would receive ten percent of all the money it would make. He told me never to show the letter to anyone."

"Just a letter?" I said, unable to keep incredulity from my voice. "And you trusted him that much?"

"Yes, of course," Cespedes replied. "He was my countryman—he was a man of great reputation, a man whose character was above reproach. He was—he was Cuban, my friend."

"This is what you wanted to talk to us about?" Seth said.

"Yes. You are a medical doctor and Alvaro's close friend. I asked Dr. Sardina about the research and whether Alvaro had found the cure."

"And what did he tell you?" I asked.

"He said that it would be some time before the results could be evaluated. Yes, that is what he told me. I thought that maybe you could tell me more."

Seth grappled for an answer, finally saying, "I don't

have anything to tell you at the moment, but I might have information later. I'll get in touch with you when I do."

"*Gracias, gracias,*" Cespedes said. "Alvaro told me that you are a fine and upstanding man and medical doctor."

"And I appreciate his kind words about me. We really should be going."

"Of course, of course. Before you do, may I ask you a question?"

"Go right ahead."

"There is the rumor in Ybor City, with some of my Cuban friends, that Alvaro might have been—how shall I say it?—that he might have been killed by an *asesinato,* not by the lightning."

"*Asesinato?*" Seth said. "Assassination?"

"Yes, yes."

"Who would assassinate him?" I asked.

Cespedes sighed deeply and shrugged. "The DI," he said, "Castro's intelligence agency. They have agents in Florida, many here in Tampa. They want to destroy our CAFA."

"Which is?" I asked.

"Our Cuban American Freedom Alliance."

"Al told me about that," Seth said to me. "It's sort of the Cuban government in exile here in Florida, groups that want to topple Castro and return to Cuba."

"Do you have any proof?" I asked Cespedes.

"Proof?" His laugh was cynical. "No, no proof, but there are the rumors, many rumors."

"Well," Seth said, "there are always rumors. Like I said, Mr. Cespedes, I'll let you know if I find out anything about Alvaro's research. Thanks for letting us drop in. It was—interesting."

Seth was silent as we got in the car and headed back to the hotel.

"What did you think?" I asked as he joined the flow of traffic.

"Gorry, I don't know what to think. I think I'd like to know who *else* invested in Al's research. I'm beginnin' to think that my good friend might not have been as much on the up-and-up as I thought."

Chapter Fifteen

Once settled in Seth's hotel room, I plugged in my laptop and inserted the first of three thumb drives, and we settled back to read the words on the screen. One of the first files we opened simply contained a short list of names. Carlos Cespedes was among them.

"Do you suppose these are the others who invested in Dr. Vasquez's research without Bernie Peters's knowledge?"

"Mebbe." Seth's expression was worried. He wrote down the names on a lined legal pad.

There were numerous separate documents, most of them containing a lot of long medical and scientific terms that I didn't understand but knew that Seth did. We read in silence; Seth made an occasional note on his pad.

After a half hour he said, "Stop it there, Jessica."

He rubbed his eyes and paced the room.

"Have you learned anything so far?" I asked.

"Not much, except that one of Al's earlier experiments didn't pan out the way he'd expected."

"It must be frustrating doing medical research," I said. "I imagine there are lots of dead ends."

"That's for sure. Hungry?"

"As a matter of fact, I am."

"Let's order up," he said.

I consulted the room service menu and read off items to Seth, who opted for onion soup and a Crab Louie salad. I was in a mood where making choices was difficult and simply ordered the same.

"I can't make sense out of this," Seth said as he sat on a small couch and massaged his temples. "It doesn't compute for me that Al would sell a stake in his research to someone like Cespedes. How could he do that? Bernie Peters is the one who bankrolled the research once Al came to the States. I'd understand it if Bernie approved having Cespedes provide additional funding, but to do it in secret?"

I had been thinking a great deal about what Seth had said in the car, that maybe his friend wasn't as honest and straightforward as he'd thought—as he'd *hoped*. I didn't want to rub it in by reinforcing that possibility, but Seth spared my having to mention it.

"How could Al do such a thing? Sounds to me like he was selling Bernie out from under." Seth brought his fist down hard on the couch's armrest. "There's got to be a reasonable answer to this, Jessica, because I will not accept that Al was conning people."

"Mr. Cespedes willingly and blindly entered into a business deal with Vasquez that wiped out what savings he'd accumulated from the sale of his building," I said. "He wouldn't be the first person to have been enticed to invest in something fraudulent."

"Well," Seth said, "Al was . . ." His words trailed off.

I knew what he was about to say.

Alvaro Vasquez had defected from Cuba amid much fanfare. His reputation in Cuba was that of a pioneering medical researcher who was on the verge of conquering a particularly devastating disease. He'd settled in Tampa, Florida, and opened a laboratory in which he could continue his much ballyhooed work. It didn't surprise me that Cespedes, and others like him, would have succumbed not only to Vasquez's reputation, but to the Cuban physician's personal charisma as well.

One of many questions I had was whether Vasquez had approached Cespedes, or Cespedes had approached him seeking to invest in his research. And would it have made any difference? The great showman P. T. Barnum once said, "There's a sucker born every minute and one to take him." The movie *The Producers* also came to mind. Zero Mostel plays a shady theatrical producer who sells fifty percent shares in a play to multiple wealthy widows, convinced that the play would flop and none of the duped investors would have to be accounted to.

Had Vasquez played that same con game, selling pieces of his research in the hope that . . . what? What could he have hoped for?

I told Seth what had occurred to me.

His silence said that his thinking was along the same lines.

Our dinners arrived and we watched the news as we

ate. It was toward the end of the newscast that a local anchor reported:

Breaking news in the death of Dr. Alvaro Vasquez. A credible but anonymous source in Tampa law enforcement has told this station that the police are now treating the esteemed physician's death as a possible homicide, based upon a report they received from the Tampa medical examiner. Dr. Vasquez, who was originally thought to have been struck by lightning, was a prominent medical researcher who'd defected from his native Cuba and settled in Tampa. The investigation is ongoing.

"Detective Machado was certainly right about there being leaks from the ME's office and his own department," I commented after we'd turned off the television.

"Seems that way," said Seth. "Let's get back to seeing what was on the laptop."

We spent hours more reading Vasquez's entries, and I had to fight to maintain interest. The words became a blur at times, and I excused myself now and then to go splash cold water on my face. When the final entry had been read, and Seth had finished making notes, he sat back, rubbed his eyes, and said flatly and wearily, "He failed."

"What do you mean?"

"Al failed, Jessica. According to what he's written— and he's written plenty, as you can see—every effort he made to find a breakthrough in definitively linking sugar and insulin resistance to Alzheimer's was unsuccessful. He outlines several more research pathways to follow up on, but to date, he's got nothing."

I didn't know what I had expected to learn from reading Vasquez's notes, but it certainly wasn't what Seth had just announced.

"You're sure?" I asked. I was well aware that Seth was highly knowledgeable when it came to medicine, but maybe—just maybe—there were aspects of Vasquez's research that were beyond his expertise.

He nodded glumly. "Yes, I'm sure," he said, "unless there were trials he ran that aren't represented on these thumb drives. But I don't think so. His last entry was the day before he died."

"He knew that his research had failed when he hosted the party at his house and wrote you that letter. But it sounded from what he wrote that he still felt that what he had achieved might be worthwhile in the hands of others."

"Ayuh, he did indicate that, Jessica. And it's not unreasonable. Knowing what blind alleys a researcher has gone down can save other researchers a lot of pointless planning, not to mention time and money. But that's not what's on my mind at the moment."

"What is?"

"Whoever killed him—and I'm assuming that the ME and the police are right in considering his death a homicide—did that person know that Al was engaged in these financial shenanigans, and even more important, did that person know that Al's research didn't pan out?"

"You mean, if someone like Cespedes suspected the money he gave Al was squandered, and that he wasn't going to share in the profits from the lab's research, that would give him a strong motive for murder?"

"It's something to think about," Seth said.

"Well, Cespedes may have had an inkling something was wrong, but evidently he didn't know for sure," I said. "He was hoping to learn more information from you. We should look up the other people on that list we found in the file and find out if any of them will admit to giving Al money on the side."

"I have their names," Seth said, drawing a circle around them on his legal pad. "But there's another scenario to consider."

"What's that?"

"We may be the *only* ones who know that Al was unsuccessful. Maybe the person who killed him thought the key to a cure was in here." He bounced one of the thumb drives up and down on his palm. "That person could have wanted Al out of the way, in order to benefit from the research."

"Bernie Peters?" I blurted out.

"Maybe. All I know is that I'm not leaving Tampa until I find out the answer."

I looked at my friend of many years. He looked weary. His color was gray, and his voice had lost some energy. But I also saw in his eyes a steely determination.

I didn't know what was in store for me over the coming days in Tampa, but I was sure that it would be nothing like the idyllic life I usually led back in Cabot Cove. And I also knew that I'd be there for Seth no matter where his investigations led us.

That's what friends are for.

Chapter Sixteen

"Sleep well?" I asked Seth the following morning when we met for breakfast.

"You always did have a sense of humor, Jessica," he said in a voice deepened by a lack of sleep.

"I withdraw the question," I said. "I didn't sleep well either."

"No reason you should if I didn't. Seen this?"

He handed me that morning's edition of the *Tampa Tribune*, opened to an inside page. I read the headline: "Intrigue on Davis Island: Dr. Alvaro Vasquez a Murder Victim? Police Think So."

The article took up the full page and was accompanied by a photograph of Vasquez.

It was written by Peggy Lohman, the reporter who'd come to our table at the hotel a few days earlier.

"No need to read it," Seth said. "Nothing new in it, plenty of background on Al's career and his defection from Cuba, lots of quotes from anonymous sources in the police department. She did interview Sardina."

"So he's back," I said. "What did he have to say?"

"Not much. The reporter asked him how Al's research was going, and Sardina said that it was going fine but that he wasn't in a position to discuss it."

"Spoken like a politician," I said. "Did he say anything else?"

"Only that Al was a wonderful man and mentor and that he missed him and expressed his condolences to the family."

"Not exactly what he told us."

"We weren't the press."

"I'm concerned about these leaks from the police. Have you heard more from Dr. San Martín?"

"As a matter of fact, I have. Had a strange call from him first thing this morning. He wants to meet with us today."

"Did he say why?"

"No, but he doesn't want us to come to his office. We're meeting him at some restaurant outside of downtown called the West Tampa Sandwich Shop. One o'clock. I have the directions."

"That *is* strange," I said.

"Everything about Al's death is strange. I'm concerned about the set of thumb drives that I gave to Detective Machado. Seems like the police department is a sieve. Nothing's secure. Maybe I shouldn't have left them with him."

"You didn't have any choice once he read about them in the letter."

Seth grunted his agreement.

"So," I said, "what's on our schedule today?"

"I called Al's house. We're going there at ten."

"Why so soon again?"

"I want to talk with Ivelisse, see if she knows anything helpful."

"Whom did you speak with?"

"Al's son, Xavier. He just returned from Key West."

"How did he sound?"

"Fine. I thought he might balk at having us come by. He actually sounded pleased. Hard to read him."

I glanced at my watch; eight o'clock.

"Feel up to a walk after breakfast?" I asked. "I need a little exercise."

" 'Fraid not, Jessica. Between my aching back and bad knee, I'd be lucky to make it a block, especially with the pace you like to set. Zach Shippee tells me I'm his annuity." Shippee was Seth's chiropractor in Cabot Cove.

I couldn't help laughing.

"Nothing to laugh at, Jessica. You'll get there one day, too."

"I wasn't laughing at you, Seth. It's just that what Zach said was—"

"Might be funny to you, but not to me. Eat your breakfast and take your walk. We'll meet up in the lobby at nine thirty."

I didn't make any further mention of Seth's aches and pains. He was clearly not in one of his better moods, and I'd learned years ago to back off when that was the case. We finished breakfast in relative silence. He headed for his room, and I winced as I saw him walk in obvious pain across the restaurant.

I ventured outside and took some deep breaths. It was a lovely beginning to the day in Tampa, sunny, a clear blue sky, and a refreshing breeze setting the palm trees in motion. I wondered what the weather was like back in Cabot Cove and reminded myself to place a few calls to catch up with friends.

I had forty-five minutes before I'd need to meet Seth and chose to take a short stroll through a wooded wetland adjacent to the hotel. I found a narrow dirt path leading into the undeveloped land and hesitated. While the wooded area was appealing, I wasn't sure whether it was wise to venture into unfamiliar territory. Were the paths all marked? How large was this plot of land anyway? Naturally, I thought of alligators—you can't be in Florida and *not* think about them. What was the possibility of coming across one? Highly unlikely, I decided. Alligators liked to be around bodies of water, and from what I could see from my vantage point, there didn't seem to be any ponds or lakes in this densely packed patch of land.

I progressed slowly, stopping every now and then to admire the variety of palm trees that lined my path, and clumps of flowers that would suddenly appear from behind a tree, vivid splashes of color in what was otherwise a monochromatic landscape. I moved through an area of trees on which someone had affixed a handwritten sign—*gumbo limbo*—which I assumed was to identify the species of those particular trees, their smooth bark peeling off in broad sheets to reveal red trunks beneath. Beyond was a swath of tall grass that looked like hay. It intruded on both sides of the path, narrowing my passage, and as I walked past it, my bare leg brushed against some of the strands. "Ouch," I said as I looked down to see a thin red line on my calf. I examined the grass more closely and saw that the strands had sawlike teeth, sharp enough to have broken the skin.

My leg stung, and a single, tiny drop of blood appeared at the end of the scratch. I considered returning to the hotel but noticed up ahead a clearing in which a wooden bench was situated next to a small pond. *Perfect*, I thought as I approached the clearing. I sat on the bench and used a tissue from my purse to blot the drop of blood.

A shaft of sunlight through the palm fronds reached where I sat, and I closed my eyes and tilted my face up to catch the warm rays. I was enjoying this moment of peace when I heard what sounded like muffled footsteps. I opened my eyes and looked back at the path I'd just taken. The sounds stopped. I glanced at the pond, hoping I hadn't awakened a sleeping alligator. I was wondering if climbing on top of the bench would provide any protection when I heard the sounds again. This time, I stood, straightened my skirt, and tensed. A moment later the source of the footsteps appeared—Karl Westerkoch. I was both surprised to see him and relieved that it was a familiar face.

"Good morning," I said.

"Good morning, Mrs. Fletcher. Communing with nature this morning?" he said in his pinched, British-tinged voice.

"I guess I am. The vegetation in Florida is so different from what we have in Maine."

"A very different climate."

"Yes. I'm surprised to see you here."

"Oh? Did you consider this your private domain?"

The man was seemingly incapable of being pleasant.

"I wasn't suggesting that it was," I said.

He came to the bench, sat, crossed his long legs, and looked up into the sun coming through the trees. "In the interest of full disclosure," he said, "I came because I saw you walk in here."

"You followed me?"

"You might say that, although it does sound terribly cloak-and-dagger, doesn't it?"

"To you, perhaps."

"Come, sit," he said, patting the bench beside him. "I'm really quite harmless."

"Mr. Westerkoch," I said, "since you've admitted to following me into this lovely grove of trees, I'd like to know why."

He ran his fingers over the crease in his slacks, moved them to his neck to adjust a tie that wasn't there, and said, "Please, sit down. I have a crick in my neck this morning and it's painful to have to look up at you while we talk."

My first inclination was to bid him a good day and walk away—he was that disagreeable—but of course I was curious as to what he had to say. I'd suggested to Seth that we take every opportunity to speak with anyone involved in Alvaro Vasquez's life, and Karl Westerkoch fell into that category, although I had no idea in what way they'd been connected. His name had not appeared on the possible list of investors Seth had copied from Al's file. I took a seat on the bench, leaving as much space as possible between us, and waited for him to explain his presence. When he did, what he said surprised me.

"You and your companion, the good Dr. Hazlitt, have ended up involved in a rather nasty business."

" 'Nasty business'? I haven't the slightest idea what you're talking about."

"Oh, I think that you do, madam. I can't imagine that someone whose brain is fertile enough to craft murder mysteries—and I understand that you've done quite well with your novels—would miss what's been going on over the past few days."

"If you mean Dr. Vasquez's death, I'm well aware of it. Dr. Hazlitt and I were there when he died, as were you. Remember?"

"How could I ever forget? But you see, dear lady, there is more to it than his unfortunate passing. There is, as you also know, the fruits of his efforts in the laboratory."

Where is he going with this? I wondered, and decided to offer nothing. Let him set the agenda for this unexpected conversation in an equally unexpected setting.

"You've spoken with Oona," he said flatly, a statement, not a question. He pulled a long, slender cigar from his sport jacket—or is it called a cigarillo?—lit it, blew the smoke up in the air so it curled over my head, and looked at me while waiting for an answer.

I didn't provide him with one.

"And I'm sure that Oona made it clear to you that Dr. Vasquez's untimely demise has potential ramifications far beyond the death of one individual," he continued.

I thought back to my meeting with Oona and tried

to recollect what she'd said. "She did indicate that there was interest on the part of the government in seeing that Dr. Vasquez's research not fall into Cuban hands."

"And she was absolutely correct," he said. "Oona has a way of being direct, much to her credit."

"That's always an admirable trait," I said, "and I would appreciate it if you would exhibit the same directness."

Westerkoch gave me a crooked smile before taking puffs and exhaling the smoke into the air, a satisfied expression on his gaunt face. I checked my watch.

"Oh, yes," he said as though his wandering mind had suddenly been brought back to the present moment, "being direct. Frankly, I thought I was."

"How about this for a starting point, Mr. Westerkoch? Seth Hazlitt and I have nothing to do with Dr. Vasquez's research. He and Seth had struck up a friendship, nothing more than that. I was in Florida on a book tour and decided to extend my stay and spend time with Seth here in Tampa. I certainly understand why the government would be interested in where Dr. Vasquez's research ends up, in whose hands it falls, but that has nothing to do with Dr. Hazlitt or me."

"Under ordinary circumstances I would agree with you, Mrs. Fletcher, just a small-town physician and his mystery-writing friend enjoying the good weather here in Tampa. But you see, there is a complication."

"I'd like to know what that is," I said, even though I suspected he was about to bring up Vasquez's missing laptop.

He was.

"Dr. Vasquez's approach to medical research was

unusual at best. He built an outsized reputation in his native Cuba, which traveled with him to Florida, where he established himself as an important citizen, albeit a controversial one."

"Controversial? Why?"

"Because of the way he conducted his research. Don't you find it strange that he worked in almost total secrecy, only one assistant, with progress reports on his work nonexistent? That's hardly the protocol one expects from a medical researcher whose work promises— and I stress 'promises'—such great results."

He was right. I had found Vasquez's methods to be strange, and I had voiced that to Seth. Then again, I could claim to know nothing of how medical research worked, which would have been the truth. Because Seth had become such an unabashed champion of Vasquez's work, it served to temper any doubts I had, at least initially.

"Of course," he said, "his methods aren't the most important thing." He cackled. "The mad scientist at work, hey? No, his methods aren't at issue here, Mrs. Fletcher. What *does* interest the government is what he managed to achieve in his laboratory."

"Again, what does that have to do with Dr. Hazlitt and me?"

"You asked me to be direct, and I will be. But I expect the same from you. No one seems to know what he achieved through his research, and we would like to know."

"Just who is 'we'?" I responded. "You? The government? I'd like to know what role you play in all of this, Mr. Westerkoch."

"Let me just say that I have a vested interest."

"A financial interest?" *Perhaps that list we'd found was incomplete,* I thought.

"Do I strike you as being that crass, Mrs. Fletcher?"

"Protecting one's financial interests isn't crass unless the gains are ill-gotten."

It was obvious that Vasquez's missing laptop was at the core of Westerkoch's interest, and that posed a dilemma for me. As far as I was aware, only Seth and I knew what had been on that laptop. Unless, of course, Detective Machado had attempted to decipher the material on the thumb drives we'd turned over to him. My hunch was that the detective had probably dumped them in an evidence locker until he could find an expert to interpret them. Nevertheless, before releasing them, Seth and I had transferred every word from the drives to my computer and then put them on the three new thumb drives, which now rested in the safe in Seth's hotel room. Then again, the information was still on the hard drive of the computer in my room, which was sitting out in plain sight. I had a sudden urge to return to the hotel.

"I have to be getting back," I said.

"To meet with your Dr. Hazlitt?"

"I don't see how that's your concern."

"Plans for the day?"

"I would say it was nice to see you again, Mr. Westerkoch, but I'm not sure that's true," I said, standing.

"A word of advice, Mrs. Fletcher?"

"I'm listening."

"Don't discount the seriousness of the matter in which you and Dr. Hazlitt find yourselves enmeshed. The stakes are high, *very* high."

"I'll keep that in mind."

He looked down at my leg and cooed, "You have a boo-boo."

"A plant with sharp leaves."

"Saw grass," he said. "Nasty things, those leaves."

"It's nothing," I said.

"We'll have to continue this little chat another time," he said, rising and stamping out his cigar on the dirt.

I started up the path out of the wooded wetland but was struck with a thought. "Are you responsible for having people follow me and Dr. Hazlitt?" I asked.

"Me? I'm simply concerned with your well-being, Mrs. Fletcher."

"That may be true, but I assure you we don't need someone watching after us."

He ignored my comment and said, "Careful walking back to the hotel, Mrs. Fletcher. Avoid the saw grass, and keep a sharp eye out for alligators. They have a voracious appetite."

I had to work at steadying my nerves on my way back to the hotel, not because he'd been threatening, but because I disliked him so.

Why had he bothered seeking me out that morning? All he'd done was to corroborate what Oona Mendez had said, that the United States government was interested in Vasquez's research and in seeing that it not fall into Cuban hands.

I'd had the feeling after my conversation with Oona that she was aware that the laptop on which Vazquez's notes were stored was missing, although she hadn't said as much.

But if Seth was correct, it was all moot anyway. His

reading of Al's notes said that Vasquez had failed to come up with any conclusions that might lead to a cure for Alzheimer's. The problem seemed to be that neither Oona nor Westerkoch, nor other governmental types, knew what Seth and I knew, and that begged the question: Was it incumbent upon us to let it be known?

I wasn't the one to answer that. It would be Seth's call, and his alone.

I filled Seth in about my conversation with Westerkoch during the ride to the Vasquez home on Davis Island.

"I don't like it," Seth said. "I don't like this fellow trailing behind you."

"I'd prefer that he didn't, too. Do you have an agenda this morning?"

"Nothing specific, but I think it's time I asked some direct questions."

I was pleased to hear him say that because I had a few direct questions of my own.

Chapter Seventeen

The Vasquez daughter, Maritza, answered the door.

"How is your mother today?" Seth asked once we were inside the house.

Maritza twisted her hand from side to side, a non-verbal "so-so" reply. "She's asked for you, Mrs. Fletcher."

"Oh? I'd enjoy very much seeing her."

Maritza's brother, Xavier, joined us.

"How was your trip to Key West?" I asked.

He lifted his brows, apparently surprised that I knew he'd been away. "Great," he replied pleasantly. "Smooth flight both ways. How have you been?"

"We've been fine," I said, aware of the change in his demeanor. During our first meeting, he'd been sullen, perhaps even rude, but on this day he seemed more relaxed and there was warmth in his voice.

Maritza, who'd left us, returned with her mother as

Xavier disappeared into another part of the house. Mrs. Vasquez looked stronger than she had the last time we'd seen her. She'd abandoned the blanket and was now stylishly dressed in a taupe skirt, teal blouse, and sandals.

"Hello, Mrs. Vasquez," I said. "I'm Jessica Fletcher."

"Of course," she said. "How good of you to come. Please won't you join me in some coffee or tea?" She sank gracefully into a chair in front of a small table and waved at her daughter.

"Coffee would be fine," I said, and Seth opted for the same.

We settled on a love seat across from Ivelisse as Maritza gave instructions to the housekeeper to fetch "*café con leche*" as Mrs. Vasquez had requested.

"Have you seen the newspapers?" I ventured, deciding to be direct.

"I never read those scandal sheets," Ivelisse said placidly, smoothing her hair with one hand.

"Mami," her daughter said. "I read the story about Papi to you this morning, don't you remember?"

Ivelisse looked momentarily confused. Then she closed her eyes and slowly shook her head. "How could they even think such a thing? To say that Alvaro was murdered upsets me. The American press, with all its liberties, abuses them at times, don't they?"

"I'm afraid they do sometimes," I said. "It's a price we pay for freedom of the press."

"There is no free press in Cuba. The government controls what is written and broadcast. But when I hear what your reporters say about Alvaro, I wonder whether it isn't better in Cuba."

Seth joined the discussion. "Government-controlled press is never better," he said with gravity.

Ivelisse cocked her head at him. "I suppose you're right, Mr. . . . ?"

"Seth Hazlitt," Seth answered.

"Yes, yes, you were a friend of Alvaro's."

"That's right. I'm a physician."

"Like Alvaro."

"He was a great physician and a fine gentleman," Seth said.

Her smile was part agreement but somewhat cynical. "Alvaro was a handsome man, yes?" she said to me.

"Yes, he was very handsome," I replied, a vision of him flashing in front of me.

"So many women," she said, as though casually commenting on the weather or a pretty flower.

Seth and I looked at each other as Maritza said, "I don't think we need to talk about that, Mami."

Ivelisse's face was blank, serene, and a tiny smile came to her lips and stayed there while the housekeeper set out a tray with cups of strong Cuban coffee, sugar cubes, and a pitcher of hot milk.

"Have the police been in contact with you again?" Seth asked, adding sugar to his cup and stirring.

"The police?" she said in a startled voice. "Oh, them," she said. "The police. Why would they be here?"

"I thought they might want to talk with you about their suspicion"—Seth hesitated before continuing—"that Al was murdered."

Her serenity morphed into a hard mask. "Murdered? I will not stand to hear that. No, there will be no talk of murder in my house."

"Maybe you'd better rest again, Mami," Maritza said.

"I do not want to rest," she said. "I want to talk with Mrs. Fletcher. She is a writer."

"That's right," I said, "although I have to admit that I do write *about* murder."

"Murder in books is all right," she said.

Xavier returned and gave his sister a piercing look.

"I'm afraid Mami is getting tired," said Maritza, rising.

"I am not," Ivelisse said sternly.

Maritza motioned to Xavier and they walked from the room.

"My daughter is studying medicine," Ivelisse said.

"You must be very proud of her," Seth said.

"What sort of doctor are you?" she asked Seth.

"General practice."

"Alvaro was a respected research scientist," she said.

"Yes, I know," said Seth. "Did he talk to you about his research?"

"Oh, no, and I didn't want to know about it. He was trying to find a cure for . . ." She trailed off.

"For Alzheimer's disease," I filled in.

"That's right, for Alzheimer's disease," she said. "For the brain."

"For the brain," Seth concurred.

"Alvaro liked women," she said.

"Did he?" Seth said. "I do, too."

"Do you cheat on your wife?"

Seth sat back on the couch as though having been shoved. "I'm not married," he said.

"You, Mrs. Fletcher? Do you see other men?" she asked.

"Other than my husband? I'm widowed, Mrs. Vasquez, have been for a number of years. But my husband, Frank, and I had a wonderful marriage. We were devoted to each other."

"That's nice," she said dreamily. She looked at Seth and her brow furrowed. "I'm sorry, but you are?"

"Dr. Seth Hazlitt, Alvaro's friend."

"Of course, yes, yes, yes, I know that. What do they call it when you get older and forget?"

"A senior moment?" I suggested, although the term "Alzheimer's" was at the front of my thoughts. "I have those senior moments myself now and then."

She didn't respond to my comment. She adopted a dreamy expression as she said, "Alvaro was such a handsome man, a Cuban Casanova. He was proud of that. Cuban men are hot-blooded, Mrs. Fletcher. We accept that when we marry them."

Seth cleared his throat and asked, "Did Al ever share with you what was on the laptop he brought home with him every night from his laboratory?"

"No," she said sharply. "I already told you that. He never told me about his work."

"I'm sorry," Seth said. "You did tell me that."

"Where is Maritza?" she asked, swiveling her head left and right.

Her daughter immediately reappeared as though she'd been poised to be summoned.

"Is it time?" Ivelisse asked.

"Yes."

Maritza explained to us, "My mother likes the Spanish soap opera *La Casa de al Lado*. She never misses it."

"What does that mean in English?" I asked.

" 'The house next door,' " she replied. "Please excuse us."

After they'd left the room, Xavier returned and took his mother's place, sitting in the chair she had vacated and pouring himself a cup of coffee.

"Your mother is a lovely woman," I said, adding, "and a proud woman."

"Yes, she is both of those things, and more."

"How is she handling your father's death?"

"She is very strong and doesn't show her emotions easily," Xavier said, sipping his coffee, "certainly not to strangers."

I had thought she was open in expressing her opinions, but I wondered how much her memory problems affected her understanding of the current circumstances.

"Behind her closed door," Xavier continued, "my mother is able to express herself to her family. She is very sad, of course. She and my father were married a long time."

"There are a lot of questions about your father's research," Seth said.

"Yes. I've heard about the missing laptop," Xavier said flatly.

"That's right, his missing laptop. I was told that he brought it home with him every night from the lab, but it doesn't seem to have shown up. Got to be an answer for that."

"You aren't suggesting that I might have done something with it, are you, Dr. Hazlitt?"

"I'm not suggesting anything, Xavier, but it is strange that something as visible—and important—as that laptop would go missing."

"Well," Xavier said mildly, "maybe it'll show up one of these days." He turned to me. "So," he said, "you told me at the party that you have a pilot's license. I love to fly. I received my license in Cuba." He laughed. "My father was supportive, but my mother was certain it would mean an early death for me. So far, she's been wrong."

"Thank goodness for that," I said. "What sort of certificate do you have?"

"I am instrument rated and have started working on my instructor's license."

"What's your goal?" Seth injected. "To fly big commercial planes?"

"Yes, I would like that someday. When I am in my plane, I feel free, more free than at any other time in my life. Do you feel that way, too, Mrs. Fletcher?"

"Yes, I do," I said. "There's something liberating about being up there all alone, looking down at the earth, seeing your town from the air. I'm sorry that I'll never get much further beyond my basic private pilot's license, although I never intended to."

"Mrs. Fletcher doesn't have a driver's license," Seth said, chuckling, "but she can fly a plane."

Xavier smiled broadly. "That is funny," he said.

I returned his smile. "That's what all my friends say."

"Which includes me," said Seth. "Frankly, I thought

she was crazy when she said she was going to take flying lessons."

"I thought for a while that maybe I *was* crazy," I said, "but once I started I knew I'd made the right decision."

"How about going up for a spin with me, Mrs. Fletcher?"

"That sounds appealing," I said.

Seth fixed me with a hard look.

"Maybe we can do that one of these days," I said, keeping it vague for Seth's sake.

"You know," Xavier said, changing the subject, "my father surprised everyone when he welcomed your friendship, Dr. Hazlitt. He didn't have many close friends."

"Then I'm proud to have been among the few."

"I'm thinking maybe we don't even need my father's laptop to know how his research was going."

"Meaning?"

"Well, it's just that since you became one of his close confidants, I figure you'd know a lot about his progress."

"'Fraid I can't help you there," Seth said, slapping his knees and standing. He put a hand out to help me up.

I thought of the three thumb drives back at the hotel, and that not only did Seth know everything that Vasquez had noted about the research, but I did, too, although without the medical background to truly understand it.

Xavier said that it was good of us to have stopped by and repeated his invitation for me to go flying with him.

"Before we go," Seth said, "I wanted to ask you about Ms. Mendez and Mr. Westerkoch."

"What about them?"

"They were friends of your father's, too, and I wonder what the basis of the friendship was."

Xavier shrugged. "The 'basis'? He liked them."

"I know that Ms. Mendez works for the Cuban American Freedom Foundation here in Tampa," Seth said. "Was she helpful in your father's defection and application for asylum?"

He thought before answering. "Oona Mendez has her own agenda where my father was concerned. Sure, she was involved in those things, but she also had a more personal interest in dear old Dad."

Maybe I'd been right when I speculated that Oona might have lost a lover in Dr. Alvaro Vasquez. I also found Xavier's expression "dear old Dad" to be disparaging. I'd sensed tension between father and son during the party and now wondered about the extent of their animosity toward each other. Ivelisse may have been in mourning, but was Xavier also sad to have lost his father?

"And Mr. Westerkoch?" Seth asked. "He seems to be—well, he's demonstrated a keen interest in your father's research."

"Did he?"

"What does he do?" I asked. "He says he's a consultant, but he never said what company he consults for."

"He's—look, I really don't care about Westerkoch." He flashed me an engaging smile. "Last chance, Mrs. Fletcher. I'm flying to Key West first thing in the morning."

"So soon again?"

"The weather report is good," he said, ignoring my question, "so it should be nice flying weather. You can get in some flying time, and you can meet my girl-friend. You, too, Dr. Hazlitt. It's a four-seater, a really nice plane. Game?"

"Can I think about it and call you later?" I said.

"Sure. I'll be around all day. Now, if you'll excuse me, I'll go see how my mother is."

When Seth and I were alone, he said, "You aren't really considering going flying with him, are you?"

"It's tempting," I said. "He invited you, too."

"It's not tempting to me."

"It would give us a chance to spend some uninter-rupted time with him, Seth. I know that you're not a fan of flying, especially in small planes, but he sounds like a responsible pilot. He has his instrument rating and is going for his instructor's license. That means he's a serious pilot. Besides, you've flown with Jed back home in his small planes and you made it out alive."

He curtailed that topic of conversation by making a show of looking at his watch. "Let's go get lunch," he said, "and meet up with Dr. San Martín. I'm eager to find out why he wants to see us."

I found Maritza and told her that we were leaving.

"My mother was happy to see you, Mrs. Fletcher. She admires authors. Are you sure you wouldn't like to stay awhile?"

"I'd love to," I said, "but we're meeting someone for lunch at a place called the . . . What is it, Seth?"

"The West Tampa Sandwich Shop."

"Oh," Maritza said, "everybody raves about the Cuban food there—very authentic, I'm told. Xavier goes there a lot."

"I'm ready for some good Cuban food," Seth said.

"Enjoy it," Maritza said, "and please come back anytime."

We managed to find the West Tampa Sandwich Shop, a small, nondescript former house on the busy North Armenia Avenue, across from a large church. Seth had to circle the block a few times to find a parking space, and we ended up two blocks from the restaurant.

"Doesn't look much like a place to find good food," Seth said as we approached the building.

"Looks can be deceiving," I said. "Time to enjoy real Cuban food."

"We'll see," he said as we came upon what looked like a run-down carport attached to the house. There were a few tables beneath the canopy, and a group of six older men, dressed in colorfully patterned shirts and Cuban guayaberas, sat at a long table smoking cigars and talking.

"Is this the entrance?" I asked Seth.

"Beats me," he replied.

Conversation stopped when we entered the sheltered space, but we saw that there was a door leading inside.

"*Hola!*" one of the men said to us.

I returned his greeting as we passed their table and pulled open the door to a small room where a dozen tables were covered in lacy white cloths with clear plastic sheets over them. A short counter with a few backless stools occupied one side of the restaurant opposite a TV set. The white walls were covered with hundreds of photographs collected inside large black frames, presumably pictures of regular customers. Above the collages were individually framed portraits of those I gathered were especially honored guests. Two waitresses, well familiar with the routine, scurried among the tables, all of which were occupied, pushing carts that were transporting diners' meals. All in all, there was a sense of controlled frenzy.

Dr. San Martín sat at a table only slightly removed from the next, where five gray-haired men engaged in a loud, friendly argument on the benefits of vitamin supplements. I was surprised to see that the ME was with another man, considerably younger, who looked out of place with his dark suit, shirt, and tie. San Martín saw us and waved.

"Good to see you," he said as we joined the table. "Welcome to Tampa's best-kept secret."

I looked around and laughed. "Judging from the business they're doing," I said, "I think the secret's gotten out."

"Much to the chagrin of the owners," said San Martín. "There are so many regular customers, they don't want to fill the place up with tourists." He turned to his companion. "Mrs. Jessica Fletcher and Dr. Seth Hazlitt, this is Harry Guterez."

"A pleasure to meet you," Guterez said as we shook hands. "I'm certainly aware of your books, Mrs. Fletcher, although I admit I haven't read one."

"We'll have to rectify that," I said pleasantly.

"Are you with the medical examiner's office?" Seth asked.

"No," Guterez replied. "I'm FBI."

His simple statement had the effect of silencing Seth and me.

"Agent Guterez has something he'd like to discuss with you," San Martín said, "but I suggest that we enjoy a good Cuban lunch before we get into that conversation."

I knew that Seth shared my thought at the moment—we'd rather not have to wait to hear what was on his mind. But that wasn't the way Dr. San Martín had choreographed the meeting. So lunch it was.

"Everything is good here," San Martín said, "and the portions are large. They make a superb Cuban sandwich, although it's misnamed. What people today call a Cuban sandwich was actually born in Tampa in the late eighteen hundreds. Cigar workers, who settled here from many parts of the world, brought their own favorite foods, some of which went into the sandwich. The Spaniards contributed the ham, the Italians the Genoa salami, the Cubans *mojo*-marinated pork, and the Germans and Jews added the pickles, mustard, and Swiss cheese. Of course, without good Cuban bread, it falls flat. Cuban bread is the best. When you make the sandwich, you butter the outsides of the bread and brown it up in a pan or press, like a grilled-cheese sandwich, only better." He pressed his fingertips to his lips and blew a kiss into the air.

"What is *mojo*?" Seth asked.

"It's a Cuban concoction used to marinate pork. When I make it, I use garlic cloves, salt, black peppercorns, oregano, and sour orange juice."

"Never heard of sour orange juice," Seth said.

"Not easy to find," said San Martín. "There are lots of sour orange trees in Cuba. You can substitute regular orange juice and add a little lemon or lime."

"Sounds like you know your way around the kitchen," Seth said.

"I love to cook," San Martín said. "I did all the cooking when my wife was alive and still find fixing myself supper to be relaxing after spending the day probing dead bodies."

I made a face and he apologized for inappropriate table talk.

I was willing to order anything as long as it came quickly and allowed us to get to what Agent Guterez wanted to say. After San Martín's enthusiastic description, we all settled on Cuban sandwiches, and he insisted that I try a mango milk shake.

Guterez didn't have much to add to the conversation, and once the food came, we all stopped talking anyway. I found myself, as I often do, studying the scene in the restaurant, a habit I imagine a lot of writers—and probably just as many nonwriters—have. Frequent people watching gives me insights into human behavior—at least I hope it does—and many an unwary diner has ended up as a character in one of my novels.

At the neighboring table, the group's loud discussion about a variety of health topics paused for a moment while one man told a joke: "So I went to the VA hospital and this nurse at the desk says to me, 'I already called your name. Didn't you hear me?' And I said to her, 'If I could hear you, I wouldn't be here.'" The story brought forth hearty laughs from his companions and made me smile, too.

The men were momentarily distracted by a shapely young blonde who sashayed through the room wearing tight jeans and a low-cut sweater. At the table next to ours, a middle-aged woman with jet-black hair also eyed the new arrival and registered her opinion of the blonde to her tablemate by pushing out her lower lip and rolling her eyes.

While all of this captured my interest, my main thought was that I wanted lunch to end so we could get to the reason for having gotten together. The sandwich was good, the mango shake sweet, but the combination was too filling. The waitress asked if I'd like to take home the other half of my sandwich and I declined.

Finally, Dr. San Martín paid the bill and suggested that we leave. Seth and I looked at each other in surprise.

San Martín caught our exchange and said, "It's a little too crowded in here for privacy."

Once outside, Agent Guterez led us to the church's parking lot, where a black limousine stood, engine running. A man dressed like Guterez got out on the driver's side when he saw us approach, and opened the rear door.

"I thought a little ride after lunch might be in order," said Guterez.

"A ride?" Seth said. "We have our car parked a coupla blocks from here."

"We'll bring you back, Dr. Hazlitt; just a short drive for us to talk."

Seth and I climbed into the rear of the car and sat on the bench seat. There were two fold-down seats, which Guterez and San Martín took, allowing them to face us.

The driver exited the parking lot and drove slowly down North Armenia Avenue, destination unknown to us. Dr. San Martín provided nonstop conversation during the trip, commenting on his love of cooking, the political situation in Tampa and its relationship to what was happening in his native Cuba, and his love of the city's own national league football team, the Buccaneers. It was almost as though he was attempting to head off any questions we might have about where we were going and why.

Twenty frustrating minutes later we arrived in a suburban area, its sign announcing that we were in Citrus Park. The driver parked beneath a tree, turned off the ignition, and got out of the car. San Martín and Guterez made no move to leave their seats.

"Are we getting out and taking a stroll?" Seth asked, not bothering to mask the annoyance in his voice.

Guterez smiled as he said, "No, Dr. Hazlitt, but we will have a chat if it's okay with you and Mrs. Fletcher."

"Do we have a choice?" I asked.

"Probably not," Guterez said. "Why don't you begin, Dr. San Martín."

San Martín came forward on his seat and said, "I know this is confusing, and I must admit that I was against hijacking you this way. But Agent Guterez and his colleagues decided that making it a bit of a social event would be more conducive to accomplishing what it is they *wish* to accomplish. The truth is that the two of you have placed yourselves in an awkward situation."

"Really?" I said. "How so?"

San Martín crossed his legs and thought before continuing. "Let me start by congratulating you, Mrs. Fletcher, for being astute. I suppose that writing murder mysteries has sharpened your powers of observation."

I cocked my head. "I appreciate your kind words, Dr. San Martín, but I have no idea what you're referring to."

"Cigars," he said.

"Cigars?"

"Yes, the one you picked up on the day that Dr. Vasquez died."

"I'd forgotten about that," I said, not entirely truthfully. It simply hadn't been on my mind that day.

"I almost did, too," he said. "You left it in my office and I ignored it for a few days. I'm surprised I didn't toss it away. At any rate, I was looking at it one day and got to thinking about whether it might shed any light on Vasquez's death. It had been beaten up a bit and was still a little soggy since I'd left it in the plastic bag, but I ran it through some preliminary tests to see what it contained. The usual chemicals were present; a cigar contains thousands of poisons, like nitrosamines, ammonia, cadmium, hydrogen cyanide, carbon monoxide, and, of course, nicotine. I expected to find those elements along with others, and I did."

"Are you suggesting that one of those poisons found in cigars killed Dr. Vasquez?" I asked.

He smiled like a kindly uncle correcting an honest misunderstanding. "No," he said, "none of those are capable of killing someone, at least not from one cigar. A lifetime of smoking them might do you in, but none

of those poisons are found in sufficient quantity in one
cigar to be lethal."

"So did you find something else that might have
contributed to Dr. Vasquez's death?" Seth asked.

"I certainly did," said San Martín. "The neurotoxin
botulin."

"Is that related to botulism caused by spoiled
foods?" I asked.

"That's correct, Mrs. Fletcher. One and the same."

"Is it possible he'd eaten something that contained
that toxin?"

"No. As I said, I found it in that cigar you left at my
office."

"I take it that botulin isn't usually found in cigars,"
Seth said.

"Not in my experience," San Martín replied.

"Now, wait a minute," Seth said, holding up his
hand. "I've treated my share of patients who ended up
with botulism either through something they ate or an
infected wound. I've had a few babies who came down
with botulism poisoning because of honey their mothers gave them during their first year. I tell every new
mother to not give their babies honey until they're
older."

"I'm aware of the problem with honey and new-
borns, too," San Martín said.

"But I've never lost a patient who had botulism poisoning," Seth said. "I had one young fella who waited
too long to come in to see me and ended up in the hospital on a breathing machine for a few weeks, and I had
another patient who worked for a dermatologist who

breathed in too much Botox. But as you know, it takes a few days for the symptoms to show up. With Al Vasquez, his death was pretty darn fast, almost instantaneous. Doesn't figure that inhaling smoke from a single cigar would do him in like that."

"You're right," San Martín said, "provided that what he'd inhaled was common, run-of-the-mill botulin. It wasn't!"

He had our full attention. Alvaro Vasquez had offered his cigar to Seth that night, and when Seth declined, he'd offered it to me. If either of us had accepted—I shuddered at the mental picture it brought up—Seth or I could be dead right now.

Next to me, I felt Seth stiffen, and I was certain his line of thinking followed mine. Both of us had suspected Vasquez had been murdered, but we never realized how close to our own deaths we might have come.

San Martín spoke, breaking into my horrified thoughts. "I took it upon myself to personally deliver that soggy cigar to the lab at the Institutes of Health in Washington, D.C., and waited until they'd analyzed it. Didn't take long. That cigar was full of *C. botulinum*, one of the most powerful known bacteria to secrete toxins. A single microgram is lethal to humans. It acts by blocking nerve function and leads to respiratory and musculoskeletal paralysis. Still, it would not have killed Dr. Vasquez that quickly."

"Then what?" I asked.

"It had been chemically enhanced, no easy trick. It would take a highly sophisticated lab to accomplish that."

Agent Guterez, who'd said nothing during San Martín's explanation, now entered the conversation.

"You might wonder why the FBI is now involved," he said. "Initially this was considered a local matter, something for the Tampa police to handle. But what Dr. San Martín has uncovered changes the landscape. Obviously, someone injected the botulin into the cigar that Alvaro Vasquez was smoking when he died. We believe Dr. Vasquez was the intended victim. Because the toxic substance is, as Dr. San Martín has explained, highly sophisticated, we're going on the assumption that a government could be involved."

Seth and I said in unison, "The Cuban government?"

"Or someone in our own," Guterez said grimly.

Dr. San Martín spent the next ten minutes further explaining what he'd found in the cigar, and the nature of the chemical enhancement that had turned Dr. Vasquez's favorite pastime into a lethal weapon. When the ME was finished, Seth asked, "This is all fascinating, but what does it have to do with us?"

"A good question, Doctor," said Guterez. "The fact is that we feel it would be better if you and Mrs. Fletcher returned to your home in Maine."

"Do you mind if I ask why?" I said.

"I can't be too specific," said Guterez. "National security. Just let me say that Dr. Vasquez's murder and the missing results of his research have spawned a budding problem between our government and that of Cuba. It has the makings of an international incident."

"National security," Seth muttered. "Always a good excuse to not be straightforward."

Guterez said, "I'll be direct. The agency insists that you leave Tampa by tomorrow."

"Is that an order?" Seth asked.

"If you'd prefer to view it that way," Guterez said, his heretofore pleasant, noncombative demeanor replaced by a steely tone and expression.

We were driven back to where Seth had parked the car a few blocks from the West Tampa Sandwich Shop.

"I assure you that the bureau appreciates your cooperation," Guterez said.

Seth was furious that he'd been ordered to leave Tampa by the agent, but I didn't necessarily share his anger. While my mind was swirling with questions—and I knew they would bedevil me for some time to come—I was actually relieved that we'd be leaving.

Cabot Cove had never been so appealing.

Chapter Eighteen

"National security my foot," Seth grumbled as he started the rental car and pulled away from the parking spot.

"It doesn't matter," I said. "Agent Guterez and his people know a lot more than we do. Maybe it's best that we give up trying to make sense out of your friend's death and go back to what we know and where we're comfortable."

"I never thought I'd hear you give up on something, Jessica."

"I'm not giving up on anything, Seth. We've been spinning our wheels trying to find answers. Maybe if it were just a local matter, a homicide without international repercussions, we'd be successful. But that's not reality."

His mood was glum and tinged with irritation as we headed back toward the hotel.

"Let's pack, have a nice dinner at that restaurant I've been dying to visit, the Columbia, and get on a plane tomorrow," I said. "Frankly, I can't wait."

"I suppose you're right, Jessica, but it's gravel in my craw. I want to go back to Al's house first. The least I can do is say good-bye. I also think I should level with Xavier about his father's research notes."

"Tell him what?"

"Tell him that I've read Al's notes and intend to bring those thumb drives back with me to Maine. Al asked me in his letter to show them to the researchers I know up north, and that's what I intend to do."

"But you said that from what you read, he hadn't made much progress in finding a cure for Alzheimer's."

"Ayuh, that's right. But it's not up to me to make that decision. As I told you, they may find his mistakes useful, save them from following an unproductive path. Or even suggest a different way to go."

"But don't you think that if Xavier knows you have those thumb drives, he'll want to read his father's notes?"

"He can get them from the police and Detective Machado. Besides, Al's laptop has to be someplace. It's bound to show up one of these days. I'd just feel better being straightforward with Xavier."

"I hope he'll appreciate it," I said.

Xavier answered the door. "Didn't expect to see you again so soon," he said.

"We've had a change of plans," Seth said, "and wanted to see your mother one last time before we leave Tampa."

"She's resting right now, but she should be up soon. When are you leaving?"

"Tomorrow. I'd like to have a few minutes with you, too, Xavier."

"A problem?"

"No, but there's something you should know. Can we go to your dad's study?"

"Sure. Let me get Maritza."

He returned with his sister, who invited us to have coffee with her on the deck until Ivelisse awakened.

"Dr. Hazlitt and I have something to discuss," Xavier said.

"Only be a few minutes," Seth assured her.

I wasn't certain that what Seth intended to tell Xavier was the right thing to do, but it was, after all, his decision. I walked outside to the deck—not far from where Alvaro had collapsed after smoking the poisoned cigar—and waited for Maritza to bring us small cups of strong Cuban coffee and sugar cookies.

"My mother has become very upset that people are saying that my father was murdered," she said after we'd settled in comfortable cushioned white chairs at a white round table, a red umbrella providing a bit of shade.

"I can understand that," I said. "Hopefully the police will do their job and identify who might have done it."

"That Detective Machado came by earlier," she said.

"What did he have to say?" I asked.

"He just wanted us to know that he and his department are working on the case."

"Did he mention anything else?" I asked, thinking of what we'd just been told by Agent Guterez, and that

Detective Machado had a set of the thumb drives from Dr. Vasquez's laptop.

"No," Maritza said. "Is there something else we *should* know?"

"I don't know," I said. "We'll give him a call before we leave."

We passed the next fifteen minutes with small talk until Xavier and Seth reappeared. Both men seemed in good spirits. If what Seth had confided in Xavier had upset the young man, it didn't show.

"Bad news on flights," Seth said. "All the flights out of Tampa tomorrow are booked solid. There's a big convention that ends tonight. That's probably the problem."

"What about flights from other cities?" I asked.

"That's the good news," Xavier said. "I can get you on a flight from Fort Lauderdale to Boston tomorrow afternoon if I book it right away. This is high season in Florida, but the airlines have cut back on the number of flights. If you want, I'll book the last two remaining seats for you."

"That's good of you, Xavier," I said, "but what about getting from here to Fort Lauderdale? It's a long drive."

"Easy," he said, grinning. "I told you I'm heading for the Keys tomorrow morning. No problem dropping you off in Lauderdale on my way."

I looked to Seth for his reaction. His initial expression was one of dismay, but it soon morphed into reluctant acceptance.

"Here," Seth said, handing his credit card to Xavier, "use this to pay for the tickets."

Xavier returned ten minutes later with our printed

boarding passes. "How about we leave at eight in the morning?" he said.

"Sounds fine," I said.

Ivelisse Vasquez joined us just as we were about to leave. We again expressed our condolences, wished her well, and thanked her for her hospitality.

"You are welcome in my home anytime," she said.

"I hope we see you again soon," I told her, though I suspected that we never would.

Once in the car, Seth used his cell phone to call Detective Machado.

"Thought we might have a chance to see you again before we leave Tampa," Seth said, and went on to tell him of our plans for the next morning.

"I'd enjoy that," he told Seth. "Free for dinner?"

We were, and Seth arranged to meet him at seven at the famed Columbia Restaurant in Ybor City.

We spent time at the hotel packing and—in my case—napping before heading out for dinner. Knowing that we'd be leaving had siphoned away some of my adrenaline, and I'd felt a wave of fatigue roll over me. I awoke groggy and in need of a shower to wake me up. Refreshed, I met Seth in the lobby.

"How do you feel?" I asked. He'd looked drained, too, when we'd parted a few hours earlier.

"Fair to middlin'," he said. "I suppose what I'm really feeling is disappointment at having to leave without the answers I wanted about Al's murder."

"I understand, Seth, but it's beyond us. You meant well and tried, but sometimes we have to accept what we can't change."

He agreed, and we left the hotel and went to the car.

"Look," I said, pointing across the small parking lot to where a young man wearing a hoodie stood next to a car, smoking a cigarette. "That's the same person who was following us before."

Without saying a word, Seth walked in the young man's direction.

"Seth," I called after him.

He ignored me and picked up his pace, actually breaking into a labored trot. The young man saw him, dropped his cigarette, and started to walk away.

"Hey, young fella," Seth called. "I want to talk to you."

The man paused before darting out of the lot and up the street.

I came to Seth's side.

"Just wanted to know who he was and why he's been following us," Seth said, out of breath.

"It doesn't matter now," I said.

"Matters to me," he said. "People've got no right to be following other people."

"Forget it," I said. "Let's go to dinner. I've been looking forward to an evening at the Columbia. Everyone we've met has raved about it. Besides, I'm eager to hear what Detective Machado has to say. As far as we know, he didn't have much to offer when he visited the Vasquez house today. Maybe he'll open up more to us."

The Columbia restaurant on East Seventh Avenue takes up a city block in Ybor City, between Sixth and Seventh avenues and Twenty-first and Twenty-second streets. We parked in a lot across the street and stood admiring the elaborate facade, hundreds of Moorish-style tiles in a wild variety of colors. A larger tile sign spelled out the restaurant's name and included the date it had been established, 1905. An ornate white overhang spanned the entire length of the building, reaching from one corner to the next, where the Columbia Gift Shop was situated.

"Some fancy building," Seth commented.

"Makes me feel like I'm in Spain," I said.

"Or Havana," Seth said. "I read that Cubans founded the restaurant."

"Does it look like buildings in Havana?" I asked as we crossed the street.

"Like they used to be, I suppose. Everything seems to be falling down there these days."

A young woman greeted us in the opulent entrance-way, also a colorful mosaic of tiles punctuated with heavy chairs and myriad works of art covering the walls.

"We're meeting Detective Machado," Seth told her.

"Oh, yes, he's already here waiting for you in the Café Room. Follow me."

Machado, dressed in suit and tie, sat at a table in a corner of the handsomely furnished and appointed room, which was both dining room and bar. He kissed me on the cheek like an old friend, shook Seth's hand, and waved for the waitress. A pitcher of sangria sat in the middle of the table; the glass in front of him was half-consumed.

"Welcome to the Columbia," he said. "Been here before?"

"No, we haven't," said Seth, "but Mrs. Fletcher has been dying to come."

"Oldest restaurant in Florida, oldest Spanish restaurant in the U.S. This is the original room built in 1905. There're fifteen rooms now, seats almost eighteen hundred people. What are you drinking?"

"That sangria looks appealing," I told the waitress, who delivered glasses for Seth and me.

"Best sangria in all of Tampa," Machado said. With our glasses full, he raised his in a toast. "Here's to you two," he said. "Not often I get to have dinner with a famous author."

"I wish we'd met for a different reason," I said, touching my glass to his.

"That's the problem with being a homicide detective," he said, grinning. "I get to meet interesting people, but only because somebody's been murdered."

"I don't always get to meet people under the best of circumstances either," Seth said. "Too many times it's because someone got sick and is dying."

Their comparison of the grimmer aspects of their professions was interrupted when a man came to the table. "I see that our favorite detective is taking good care of you," he said. "I'm Richard Gonzmart, manager of the Columbia."

"It's a spectacularly beautiful restaurant," I said.

"Thank you. It's been in my family for more than a hundred years. Casimiro Hernandez, my greatgrandfather, opened the room you're sitting in back in 1905 to serve fellow immigrants who worked in the cigar factories. He kept adding rooms, including the first air-conditioned dining room in Tampa."

"Do you have time to join us?" I asked.

"Only for a moment. Carlos told me that he was

having dinner with the famous writer Jessica Fletcher. I am honored to have you here this evening. We've had many celebrities dine with us," he said. "We had a strip steak on the menu, 'The Bambino,' named after Mr. Babe Ruth, who came here often back in the twenties and thirties." He laughed. "I've been told that he would eat two fourteen-ounce steaks at a single sitting."

Seth made a face. "Hate to see *his* arteries," he said.

"So many of your baseball greats made the Columbia their home when in Tampa," he continued proudly. "Baseball is the Cuban national pastime, just as it is in America. Joe DiMaggio and his wife, the beautiful Marilyn Monroe, also used to come here." He became conspiratorial. "One night they had quite a row at the table, and Ms. Monroe went to the restroom and confided in the attendant there. Word has it that she returned to the table a much happier woman."

He went on like that for another ten minutes, telling tales of the famous who'd dined at the Columbia. I was impressed with the obvious pride he demonstrated, not only in the restaurant, but in his family as well.

"Enjoy your dinners," he said as he stood to leave. "I have reserved a special place for you in the Patio Room. Nalda will show you to your table when you are ready to eat. *¡Buen provecho!*"

"What a charming man," I said.

"I've been coming here for years," Machado said. "I feel like a member of the family." He sat back, a satisfied smile on his face. "So, how has your stay in Tampa been so far?"

"Frustrating, to say the least," Seth answered. "We're leaving in the morning."

"So you said when you called. A last-minute decision?"

"Yes," I replied without elaborating. "We understand that you stopped by the Vasquez house today."

"That's right."

"Maritza Vasquez said that you told her that you were continuing the investigation into her father's death."

Machado sighed and slowly shook his head. "It seemed to be the right thing to say," he said.

Seth and I looked at him quizzically.

"I'll be honest with you," Machado said, "because you've been honest with me. You didn't have to bring me that letter the doctor wrote to you, or the flash drives you gave me. To put it simply, the investigation is out of my hands now."

"I'm sorry to hear that," I said. "Someone new has taken over?" I asked, knowing the answer.

"You might say that," Machado said.

"The FBI," Seth said flatly.

"That's right," Machado said, shaking his head. "We're not completely out of the picture," he added. "Whether they admit it or not, they still need our local expertise. But I'd say there are several more layers of authority above us, and I don't see wasting the department's money and the time of our detectives investigating a murder if the federal government is pushing us out of the way."

Seth looked at me questioningly, and I knew what he was thinking. "We'd like to give you something else we found," I said in a low voice. "We're not sure if it's relevant to Dr. Vasquez's death, but since we can't follow up on it, perhaps you'll find it useful."

Machado looked from me to Seth. "What's that?"

Seth pulled out the lined paper on which he'd written the list of names we'd found on Al's thumb drive. "We think these people may have invested money with Dr. Vasquez without the knowledge of K-Dex and Bernard Peters," he told Machado as he handed over the page.

"It's just a hunch we have," I added. "We know that Carlos Cespedes gave Al a considerable sum in expectation of sharing in the profits when Al's research bore fruit. His name is on this list. The others here may have done the same thing."

Machado scanned the list and smiled. "I recognize some of these names. They're among our wealthier citizens." He pocketed the paper Seth had given him. "Thanks. I'll check it out. It'll be nice to have another piece of information the feds don't know about. By the way, how did you know they'd taken over the case?"

"That's why we're leaving Tampa," Seth said.

That got Machado's attention. "Can you talk about it?" he asked.

"I suppose I'm not telling tales out of school," Seth said, "when I say that we've been asked to leave Tampa by the FBI."

"Is that so? They tell you why?"

"National security," Seth said disgustedly.

"I'm not sure that's what it is, although that's the excuse they used," I said. "I think they feel that our being here gets in their way. Since Dr. Vasquez's death seems to have moved from a local homicide to something with international consequences involving our government and the Castro regime, I also wonder whether they feel that we might be in some sort of danger."

Machado's smile was small but telling. "Who've you been talking to?" he asked. "An agent named Guterez?"

I looked at Seth before saying, "Yes."

Machado lowered his voice. "You know," he said, "the CIA's involved, too."

I didn't hesitate to say what immediately came to mind. "Would that be Karl Westerkoch?"

Another smile from the detective. "Our resident spook," he said. "He's hardly the sort of invisible spy who stays undercover."

Seth chimed in. "I still don't understand why they're sending us home to Cabot Cove," he said. "Seems to me that . . . Wait a minute, you say that Westerkoch works for the CIA?"

Machado leaned close to Seth and said sarcastically, and with mirth in his voice, "Not so loud. You'll blow his cover. More sangria?"

For dinner we were seated in the absolutely spectacular Patio Dining Room. A huge glass ceiling that could be opened covered the large space patterned after classic outdoor patios found in Andalucía in the south of Spain. Machado ordered a wide variety of tapas for us, including scallops, lobster, crab cakes, shrimp, stuffed peppers, and chicken. It was a veritable feast, accompanied by another pitcher of sangria.

"This was wonderful," I said as one of two attentive waiters cleared our table. "I don't think I'll eat another thing for a week."

"You must have dessert," Machado insisted, and so he ordered a flan and key lime pie and three spoons. It was over cups of powerful Cuban coffee that the conversation came back to the death of Dr. Alvaro Vasquez and the multiple law enforcement agencies that were now involved.

"What have you done with those thumb drives we gave you?" Seth asked.

"They're under lock and key," said Machado.

Seth's doubtful expression prompted the detective to add, "And I mean locked away. You're aware of the leaks from our department, but I assure you that those devices will be handed over to the appropriate people."

"Other medical researchers?" Seth asked. "Al—Dr. Vasquez specifically asked me to show his notes to other physicians engaged in Alzheimer's research, and that's what I intend to do."

"Then I assume you made a copy before giving the originals to me."

"As a matter of fact, I did."

"And you will carry out the doctor's wishes?"

"You bet I will. I know some top-flight researchers in Boston who'll make good use of what's on those thumb drives."

I understood why Seth didn't want to share with Machado his belief that what was on the thumb drives wasn't especially promising. As he'd told me, he didn't feel it was his place to make such judgments. But I wasn't sure it was wise not only to have copied evidence, but also to admit his actions to a police detective. It was an evening for candid exchanges, however. I was surprised at how forthcoming Detective Machado had been. Perhaps our pending departure made him feel free to discuss the Vasquez case and others. Up until that point, he had dominated the conversation, telling amusing, interesting stories about fighting crime in Tampa. "Actually," he'd said, "we have a pretty solid record in lowering the crime rate. Of course there's always drugs and gangs, but Tampa is a relatively safe city." Then he shifted the conversation to what I assumed he had been planning to talk about all evening. "We do have occasional problems with some of the zealots in the Cuban American Freedom Foundation."

"I've heard they're a group of Cuban exiles who are against the Cuban government," I said.

"Right you are. On the other side are Castro loyalists in Tampa and Miami who get their marching orders from the Cuban Comités de Defensa de la Revolución. That's the organization inside Cuba that recruits and runs the CDRs, neighborhood spies. It's a very active and wide-sweeping organization that reports to the Cuban national police, who work for the Ministry of the Interior. We know that they have agents in Florida who report back on what the members of the Freedom Foundation are up to. That's why we work with the CIA and FBI on occasion. Real cloak-and-dagger stuff. I was wondering if you two have learned anything about the Cuban exile group while you've been in Tampa."

"I don't think we can help you there," I said. "The closest we've come to cloak-and-dagger stuff, as you put it, is that we've been followed almost every day. I thought it might be one of your men."

Machado laughed. "No, not us. We'd have no reason to follow you. Maybe it was Westerkoch. I get the feeling that he enjoys following people. Makes him feel like James Bond."

We parted on the sidewalk outside the Columbia.

"Travel safe tomorrow," Machado said.

"We intend to," I said, checking Seth's reaction, which was noncommittal.

In the car on the way back to the hotel, I caught Seth smiling.

"What are you thinking?" I asked.

"I'm thinking that what we need in Cabot Cove is good Cuban food. What do you think if I ask Ed Kim whether he'd be interested in opening a Cuban restaurant?"

Kim was a Chinese American entrepreneur who'd recently opened two small eating places in Cabot Cove, one specializing in Thai food, and the other a Spanish tapas place.

I hesitated before saying, "The problem, Seth, is that we don't have a Cuban population in Cabot Cove to support it."

"Doesn't matter," he said. "Not sure we have many Thai or Spanish people there either."

"True."

"Once people taste authentic Cuban cuisine, they'll flock to it. Besides, it's healthier than lobster chowder and whoopie pies."

I laughed. "What made you think of whoopie pies?"

"You can't be a true Down-Easter and not think of whoopie pies every now and then," he said. "I could go for one right now."

"Even after flan and key lime pie?" I asked.

Seth didn't answer, but he looked a little embarrassed.

I've never developed a taste for whoopie pies, but they are a quintessential Maine dessert staple. I teased Seth. "Then I guess you won't be unhappy about going home tomorrow if you have a package of whoopie pies in your cupboard."

"I do."

As Seth and I parted in the hotel lobby, I said, "What a wonderful evening, a perfect final farewell to Tampa. The restaurant is superb."

"Ayuh, it certainly is. Well, I'd better get some shut-eye before we take off tomorrow, provided I can get visions of a small plane out of my head."

"The flight will be fine," I assured him. "I have plenty of faith in Xavier Vasquez."

Chapter Nineteen

We were up early the following morning and in the dining room by six thirty, our packed bags checked with the concierge. Seth had turned in the rental car at the hotel when we returned from dinner; we would take a taxi to the Vasquez house on Davis Island to meet up with Xavier.

I'd picked up a copy of the *Tampa Tribune* on my way in to breakfast and showed it to Seth. Peggy Lohman had written an article about the Vasquez case in which she reported that "people inside the investigation who wish to remain anonymous" told her that the FBI was now an active participant in the investigation and that Dr. Vasquez's death had been officially labeled a homicide, the method of death poison, the cause of death acute respiratory failure.

"Keeping a secret seems to be out of the question

with the police here in Tampa," Seth commented after reading the piece.

"I wouldn't blame the police," I said. "With so many agencies involved—the medical examiner's office, the FBI, and even the CIA—the sources of the leaks could be anyone, even the family."

Seth pondered that for a few moments before saying, "Dr. San Martín said that the sort of *C. botulinum* they found in Al's cigar had to have come from a very sophisticated laboratory. Remember that story about how the CIA developed a virulent strain and used it in cigars to try to assassinate Fidel Castro?"

"I do remember. But it didn't work. He'd stopped smoking by the time the CIA tried it."

"The point is, Jessica, Dr. San Martín and Agent Guterez suggested that the laboratory might have been a government-run one."

"But why would our government want to kill him?" I asked.

"Maybe it wasn't *our* government," Seth replied. "Al told me Mr. Castro and his government were pretty upset when Al defected with all the research he'd conducted there."

"Do you think those Castro agents here in Florida might be responsible?"

"Could be. Let's get over to the house before I lose my nerve about flying in that stupid little plane."

I smiled but didn't say anything. All I hoped was that Xavier would take into account that he had a white-knuckle flier onboard and would make all his maneuvers slow and easy.

Xavier appeared to be angry when he greeted us at the door.

"Bernard Peters is suing us," he said without prompting. "I never liked him, never trusted him."

"He's basing his suit on having financially supported your father's research?" I asked.

"That among other things. I don't know what he's complaining about. He had some sort of insurance policy that paid him off in the event my father died."

Which could have provided a strong motive to kill Alvaro Vasquez, I thought, *especially if Peters somehow learned that the research had hit a dead end.*

"You ready to fly?" Xavier asked.

"Ready as I'll ever be," Seth said.

Maritza appeared carrying a small suitcase.

"You're leaving, too?" I asked.

"I'm going with you," she said. "I'm spending a few days with Xavier in the Keys before going back to Havana."

"Will you have trouble going back?" Seth asked as we gathered up our luggage and headed for the taxi that would take us to the Peter O. Knight Airport at the tip of Davis Island, where Xavier housed his plane.

"No," she answered without elaborating.

Xavier's Cessna 172 aircraft was a more recent model of the popular aircraft. It sat shiny and bright in the morning sun, its red and white paint glistening.

"It's a beauty," I told Xavier.

"My baby, Mrs. Fletcher. It's the R model, with a Lycoming fuel-injected engine and a Garmin avionics package, top-of-the-line, ADF, GPS, transponder. It's even got added fuel capacity in the wingtips and extra baggage compartments."

"There are four of us with our luggage," I said, aware from my days as a student pilot how critical weight was with a smaller aircraft.

Xavier grinned and asked how much Seth and I weighed.

I told him but Seth hesitated, finally admitting his heft. Xavier did a fast mental calculation, taking into account the luggage. "We should be fine," he said. "It's got a gross takeoff weight of over twenty-five hundred pounds. We'll be below limits, though it may slow us down a little."

Seth, who'd been listening, said, "If there's a weight problem, I'll be happy to volunteer to stay back and find another way to Fort Lauderdale."

"Seth," I chided.

"Just bein' generous," he said.

Xavier carefully loaded our luggage into the baggage holds and wedged a few small pieces behind the two rear seats. "Let's see," he said. "Mrs. Fletcher will want to do some of the flying, so she'll sit up front with me. Maritza, you and Dr. Hazlitt sit in back."

"I'd love to fly," I said, "but I think Seth would be more comfortable up front. There's more leg room."

Seth eyed the cramped rear seats and said, "If you wouldn't mind, Jessica."

"I wouldn't mind at all," I said, slightly disappointed that I wouldn't be taking the yoke and flying the plane, but more concerned with my friend's comfort.

The plane's leather seats were comfortable, and

there was more room in the rear than I'd anticipated. I settled in next to Maritza, fastened my seat belt, and observed as Xavier walked around the plane to visually check its condition. He climbed into the pilot's left-hand front seat, ran down a printed checklist, cracked open his window and yelled "Clear!" to inform anyone nearby that he was about to start the engine, and set the propeller into motion.

Seth sat ramrod straight, as though to move would in some way cause the plane to blow up. He watched everything Xavier did, including using another checklist to run down various engine settings. He handed Seth a set of earphones attached to a tiny microphone. "Thought you might like to listen in," he said. Seth reluctantly put it on, and I was glad that Xavier had thought to offer the set to Seth. It would occupy his thoughts and take his mind off his anxiety. Or so I hoped.

Xavier donned his own microphone and earphones and informed the tower that he was starting his taxi to the runway. He was cleared and slowly moved down a taxiway until reaching the runway in use that morning, its designation based upon the wind's direction. Planes take off and land into the wind whenever possible. After some more chatter with the tower, he turned onto the runway, advanced the throttle to the firewall, released the toe brakes, and started his takeoff roll. I was concerned at how long it took us to become airborne, but I chalked up the extended takeoff to the weight of the plane. Eventually we lifted off. Xavier banked, affording us a view of downtown Tampa. From my seat behind the pilot, I could see Seth squeeze his eyes shut when the plane tilted in the air.

Xavier continued his climb until he'd reached his desired cruising altitude. He adjusted the controls and looked back over his shoulder. "There's a sectional chart in the pocket behind my seat," he said. "We'll be heading down the west coast until we reach the Naples beacon, then fly due east to Lauderdale."

Xavier's plane was considerably quieter than the older model in which I'd taken my flying lessons in Cabot Cove from Jed Richardson, and its smooth flight through the air at five thousand feet was almost hypnotic. I noticed that Seth nodded off a few times, snapping his head up when he realized that he had. I, too, had to fight dozing off despite Xavier's occasional commentary pointing out sights along the coast and on the ground. Maritza didn't contribute to the conversation during the trip. She'd barely said a word from the time we'd taken off until we reached Naples, where Xavier was to alter his course.

In order to head for Fort Lauderdale, we would have to fly due east, which was what Xavier had said he intended to do. But as I followed our course on the aeronautical chart, I was aware that we were now flying southeast, which would take us south of Miami. I debated asking Xavier about it but held back. This was, after all, his plane, and he was the pilot in command. He'd probably changed course because of the weather forecast for east of Naples, or perhaps he'd been instructed to alter his flight plan by air traffic control.

But as we continued in the southeasterly direction, I decided to ask why we'd changed course.

"Weren't we supposed to fly east when we reached Naples?"

He didn't answer my question.

"Xavier, I'm just curious why the change in our course," I said louder.

When there was still no reply, I leaned forward and tapped him on the shoulder. That was when Maritza tapped *me* on the shoulder.

I turned to see her pretty face set in a scowl. Then I noticed the small handgun she held. It was pointed directly at me.

Chapter Twenty

"What are you doing?" I said in a loud voice to Maritza.

Seth heard me, turned, and peered through the space between the front seats. "What's the matter, Jessica?"

I started to explain, but the words wouldn't come. I pointed to the gun in Maritza's hand.

It was difficult for Seth to see, but when he did, he said, "Gorry, what in the world is going on?"

"I'd suggest you both be quiet," Maritza said coolly and calmly. "I won't hesitate killing you."

"This is . . . this is outrageous," I said, realizing as I did that it was a pathetically weak response to a powder-keg situation.

"Just what do you think you're doing?" Seth asked Xavier.

The young pilot turned to Seth, and I could see the

traces of a smile on his face. "Righting a wrong," he said.

"*What* wrong?" Seth demanded.

"You'll know soon enough," he said.

I looked out my window in search of a landmark below but saw nothing distinguishable that would indicate where we were.

"Xavier," I said loud enough to be heard over the engine's noise, "where are you taking us?"

When he didn't answer, I asked the same question of Maritza.

"Just shut up, Mrs. Fletcher, and enjoy the ride."

"No, that's not good enough," I said. "This is kidnapping. Don't you realize that you're engaging in a criminal act?"

She laughed and said, "The only criminal act was taking my father's research away from the people it belongs to, the Cuban people."

"What does that have to do with us?" I asked.

She guffawed. "You and your doctor friend got a lot closer to my father than anyone else. If anybody knows what stage my father was at in his research, it's you two."

"That's absurd," I said. "I'd just met your father before he died."

She waved her gun at Seth. "But your friend was in Tampa a lot and spent plenty of time with my father, reading his notes, hearing about the research."

Seth, who'd undone his seat belt and was trying to twist around, was admonished by Xavier in no uncertain terms. "Sit still! I don't need you wiggling around while I'm flying this plane. Do you want to end up in the water? My sister means business. She'll blow your brains out before we land if you don't cooperate. Now, put your seat belt back on."

Seth and I fell silent until I said, "You're taking us to Cuba, aren't you?"

"How did you ever guess?" Xavier said as he banked sharply, pushing Seth against his door and exerting g-forces on everyone. Seth quickly buckled his seat belt. We looked at each other and simultaneously came to the same unstated conclusion. There was nothing to be gained by fighting the situation, not at five thousand feet above the ground, and with someone holding a lethal weapon in her hand. We settled back in silence as Xavier continued en route to Cuba.

When he'd reached a point over the ocean off the Florida coast, he communicated with Cuban air traffic control. I knew from having read about others who'd violated Cuban air space without permission that the result could be deadly. Xavier obviously knew the system, complete with language that would allow him to approach the island without fear of being intercepted by Cuban military aircraft.

We could do nothing but sit stoically and watch the island of Cuba come into view. I was aware that the José Martí International Airport, Cuba's main aviation hub, was located close to Havana, and that many international airlines scheduled flights into it on a daily basis. Xavier continued radio contact with Cuban air traffic controllers in Spanish, although English is the universally accepted aeronautical language throughout the world. Maybe the sort of special dispensation he had with Cuban authorities called for all communication to be in his native tongue.

I saw a Virgin Atlantic jet approaching for a landing, and a KLM jet turning to enter the pattern. Xavier was in a holding pattern, waiting for his landing instructions, which would come once the jets had landed and had cleared the runway. Getting too close to the jet blast from a large aircraft could flip a smaller plane like the Cessna.

Finally, Xavier banked sharply, and the runway appeared ahead. It looked to be very long; our plane would take up only a fraction of its length. We touched down, bounced up, then settled on the asphalt runway and stayed there. Xavier turned off the runway at the first available exit and taxied for what seemed an eternity to a large building on which a sign said TERMINAL 2. He headed for an isolated area at the far end, where a half dozen armed men wearing drab green pants and shirts, and with wide belts over their shirts, stood. Five of them wore black berets; the sixth's hat had a visor, and I assumed that he was an officer. All had automatic weapons slung over their shoulders.

"So," Seth growled at Xavier, "what are we supposed to do now?"

"Just do as you are told," he replied. "Do not try anything foolish."

"You realize that kidnapping us will kick back on you," I said. "I called people back home to tell them of our travel plans. Once they haven't heard from us, they'll want to know why."

Neither Xavier nor his sister said anything in response as he brought the Cessna to a stop, shut off the engine, opened his door, and hopped down. He was approached by the soldier who I assumed was in charge and they had a spirited conversation, with Xavier frequently pointing back at the plane. The officer issued a command to the five soldiers, and they surrounded us. One opened Seth's door and ordered him to get out. Maritza said to me, "You're next," and waved the handgun for emphasis. I pushed Seth's seat forward and managed to slide past it, then step down on a foothold and to the ground.

The officer barked an order in Spanish, but because we didn't understand what he said, we didn't move.

"That way," Xavier said, pointing to a doorway at the end of the terminal.

With the soldiers flanking us, Seth and I followed Xavier and Maritza to the door. Another uniformed man opened it, and we entered a large gray cinderblock room with a table and four chairs, the only furniture in the room. We were told to sit, which we did, of course, and waited for what would come next. Maritza had disappeared, but Xavier took one of the chairs. After five minutes of silence, I decided to take a stand.

"I insist on seeing someone from the United States embassy," I said in as strong a voice as I could muster.

"You have no embassy here in Cuba," Xavier said.

"But we have offices under the auspices of the Swiss embassy, as I understand it."

"You have nothing to talk to them about," he said.

"We're American citizens who've been taken hostage. We've been hijacked to Cuba."

"Look, Mrs. Fletcher," Xavier said, "we've brought you here for a good reason. All you have to do is cooperate and everything will be all right. No one wants to see you or Dr. Hazlitt hurt. Just do what you're told, tell the officials here what they want to know, and everything will be fine."

Seth, who'd said nothing during my exchange with Xavier, now spoke up. "Your father must be turning in his grave the way his only son has turned out."

"My father knew how I turned out, Dr. Hazlitt, and frankly I couldn't care less what he thought. He was a traitor and deserved what he got."

"A traitor?" Seth barked. "A traitor to what?"

"His people."

"And just who are they?"

"The people of Cuba, *my* people. My esteemed father abandoned them while he went looking for money. The Cuban government financed his research here, and what did Papi do? He ran away with the results, defected, sold out to Yankee imperialism, to that fraud Peters."

"But you defected, too," I said.

"In preparation."

Seth and I were about to ask him to explain, but it was obvious that none was needed. He'd been sent to Tampa by the Cuban government to spy on anti-Castro people and to sabotage any actions they might contemplate against the Castro regime.

Seth and I asked a few more questions without receiving answers. The next ten minutes seemed like hours as we sat in our uncomfortable chairs, eyes nervously going to the armed soldiers standing in each corner of the room. What could they possibly have in mind for us?

While Seth knew something about Alvaro Vasquez's research, it hardly represented the sort of knowledge that would be of help to someone in Cuba. Besides, Seth had come to the conclusion that Vasquez's research efforts hadn't led to anything tangible or useful in the fight against Alzheimer's disease. Would they believe Seth if he told them that? And if they didn't believe him, to what extent would they pursue it? Torture?

Would I ever have thought it possible that Seth and I would end up being kidnapped and brought to Cuba? The more I pondered the situation, the colder the room seemed to get, and I wrapped my arms about myself.

I was deep in those thoughts when the door opened and a middle-aged man entered. He wore a gray suit, white shirt, and tie and carried a briefcase. Xavier jumped up, greeted him, and pointed to his chair, which the man took. He opened his briefcase, laid a stack of papers on the table, smiled at me, and said in good English tinged with his Cuban accent, "Welcome to the People's Republic of Cuba, Mrs. Fletcher." He said the same thing to Seth, referring to him as Dr. Hazlitt.

"Who are you?" Seth asked.

"I represent the Ministry of the Interior," he said matter-of-factly.

"No, what's your name?" Seth insisted.

"That is of little interest," he countered. "I am authorized to welcome you and to see that your stay is a pleasant one."

"Our *stay*?" Seth erupted. "Mrs. Fletcher and I are not staying here one more minute. I demand that you either see to it that we are delivered back to the United States or put us in touch with U.S. officials here in Cuba."

The man listened impassively. When Seth was finished with his demands, the Cuban official said in the same flat, low-key voice, "All in due time, all in due time—provided that we have your cooperation."

"Cooperation in what?" I asked, buoyed by Seth's spark. "Why have we been brought here? Who ordered that we be brought here?"

The man sighed, slipped the papers back into his briefcase, and stood. "You obviously do not intend to make this easy for yourselves. Surrender your cell phones to the officers. Enjoy your stay in Havana. I will see you again this evening." He barked an order at Xavier, who jumped up and followed him.

"You have no right to take our phones," I called out as they walked from the room, to be replaced by two other men wearing army uniforms. They were older than the soldiers we'd first encountered. One of them repeated the order that we turn over our phones. Seth balked, but the menacing look on the soldiers' faces, fortified by the weapons in the hands of the others, won out, and we handed them over.

"Get up!" one of them ordered us.

"Now, look," Seth said, "I won't tolerate this. I demand to know under what authority we've been brought here."

The men came to either side of Seth and placed their hands on his arms. Seth tried to shake them off, but they tightened their grip.

"Seth," I said, "don't argue. I'm sure that they'll see that this has been a big mistake and let us go."

My advice calmed him, and he allowed the men to escort him from the room. I followed, flanked by two of the younger soldiers, though they refrained from touching me. We went down a dank concrete corridor and out a different door from the one we'd previously entered. Waiting was a gray Mercedes limousine with blackened windows.

We were instructed to get inside the car. We followed their orders and settled in the backseat, with two of the soldiers facing us on jump seats, another in the front passenger seat. The doors were closed and locked, and the driver sped off, destination unknown.

It was a bumpy ride that lasted twenty minutes. I was certain we were in the city because of the sounds heard outside the limo: music, laughter, cars with loud, damaged mufflers, and even a few loud reports that might have been gunshots. Eventually we came to a stop, the doors were opened, and we got out, blinking in the glaring sunshine. One of the men popped open the trunk and I was relieved to see that our luggage had been transported with us. However, I noted that a piece of red tape had been affixed to each of our bags, suggesting to me that they had probably been searched before being put in the trunk.

We stood in front of a small cabin with a porch situated on a lovely stretch of pebbly beach. I looked around in search of others, but Seth and I and our handlers—if that's the right word—were the only people there.

The door to the cabin opened, and a tall man wearing a bright yellow guayabera, tan slacks, and sandals sans socks emerged. He walked down the two steps leading to the porch, came directly to me, and extended his hand. "Mrs. Fletcher, welcome to Havana."

Seth came to us and said, "I want you to know, whoever you are, that I'll report this outrageous situation to our State Department."

"I hope there won't be any need for that," the man said in perfect English. "My name is Dr. Eduardo Rodriguez of the Health Ministry. I will be your host while you are here."

"Host?" Seth said. "You make it sound like we're on a vacation."

Rodriguez's laugh was gentle. "I would hope that you would consider it a vacation of sorts," he said. "You have been here before, Dr. Hazlitt, and can appreciate our country. And once you have satisfied the authorities with answers to their questions, I am authorized to extend to both of you some days of sun and relaxation, at the expense of our government, of course."

At that moment, I was dazzled with confusion. We'd been forcibly kidnapped and brought to Cuba by Xavier and Maritza Vasquez, who said that their father's research on Alzheimer's disease had to be returned to the Cuban people. We'd been greeted by armed soldiers, made to sit in a stark concrete room, threatened if we didn't cooperate, piled into a car and driven to a cabin on a beach, and now offered an all-expenses-paid vacation in sunny Cuba.

I could do nothing but laugh, which seemed to please Rodriguez, who laughed along with me.

"You say you're a doctor?" Seth said. "So am I. This is one heck of a way for a physician to act."

"I am sure that after a good night's sleep, you and your charming companion will be in better spirits, Dr.

Hazlitt. You'll find that your accommodations are satisfactory, and that the meals provided for you will be likewise. A car will pick you up here this evening at six. In the meantime, I suggest that you relax, freshen up, perhaps nap. *Buenas tardes.*"

He walked to where the officer stood with his men and issued instructions in Spanish. Two of the soldiers came to us and indicated through hand gestures and a smattering of English that we were to go into the cabin.

"Let's do as they say, Seth," I said.

The cabin consisted of one room, a pair of twin beds with colorful bedspreads, a small desk and chair, a brown vinyl easy chair that had seen better days, and a tiny bathroom lighted by a single wall lamp, in which towels and a bar of soap were provided. There was a window at the front. I looked out and saw that the soldiers had taken up positions thirty feet away. They sat on a low stone wall, their weapons resting on the ground, their faces mirroring their boredom.

Seth plopped himself in the easy chair and I sat at the desk.

"Are you all right?" I asked.

"Tired, that's all. You?"

"I'm fine. I'm just wondering whether there's a way for us to escape."

"Don't be foolish, Jessica," he said. "We're on an island. Where would we escape to? More of Cuba?"

"Can we get word out to someone that we're being held prisoner?"

"I don't see how. They took our phones."

"It's stuffy in here," I said. "I'm going out on the porch."

As Seth followed me through the door, two soldiers picked up their weapons and approached. They shouted orders, presumably for us to return to the cabin, but I said to Seth, "Ignore them."

We defiantly sat in two green-and-white webbed chairs and stared at the soldiers, who continued to issue orders and used their weapons to indicate that we were to go inside.

"Ignore them," I repeated. "We're here because someone up the chain of command wants something from us. They won't dare hurt us."

I wasn't sure that my bravado was appropriate, but it seemed to work. The soldiers muttered under their breath and returned to their colleagues. They must have found the situation humorous, because they all laughed at something one of them said.

"The way I figure it, Jessica, there's one good thing to come out of this," Seth said.

"What is that?"

"The question of Al's death and why he died. I keep thinking about what Dr. San Martín said about the strain of *C. botulinum* that was in that cigar Al smoked just before he died, that it had to have been concocted in a sophisticated lab, most likely a government lab. Seems to me that it had to have come from here in Cuba."

"That makes sense to me," I said.

"And if that's true, the next question is, who gave Al that cigar?"

"He said it was a gift from someone special."

"He also said it was Cuban," Seth said.

I knew where he was taking this and didn't want to acknowledge it.

"Had to be one of his children," he said grimly.

I started to respond, but he cut me off.

"That's not a pleasant thought to have," he said, "that a son would kill his own father."

"Or a daughter," I said. "But we don't know whether that's true."

"How else could it have happened? They obviously resented their father defecting with the research he'd started in Cuba, research that was paid for by the Castro government. Xavier said it himself, that the research belongs to the Cuban people. The cigar was Cuban. He must have had his sister get it for him. Who else would have easy access to Cuban cigars? The way I see it, Xavier and Maritza murdered their father to get hold of his research and return it to his native land. I'll bet you all the moose in Maine that Xavier also ended up with Al's laptop."

"Then why bring us here?" I asked. "If they have the laptop, they have the research."

"I don't have an answer for that, Jessica, but I suppose we'll find out tonight when they come get us. Meantime, I'm going back inside and catch me a nap. I suggest you do the same. We'll need our wits about us this evening."

I was too keyed up to nap. I stayed on the porch for an hour before returning inside, where Seth was snoring loudly on one of the beds. I curled up on the other and tried to fall asleep but to no avail. The afternoon passed slowly, but eventually it was time to get ready for whatever the next step would be. We walked out on the porch just as the gray limousine arrived. Dr. Rodriguez came to us, a wide smile on his face. "Did you rest?" he asked.

"No," I said.

"I am sorry that you didn't. I imagine that you and the doctor are hungry."

"As a matter of fact, I am," said Seth. "Hungry and damn mad."

"I assure you that we will feed you well," Rodriguez said. "Come. Time to go."

After another bumpy half-hour drive, we came to a stop in a sprawling square, where an intimidating eight-story building stood, its drab front dominated by a soaring black metal mural bearing the unmistakable face of Fidel Castro's revolutionary colleague Che Guevara. The mural dwarfed the building, and the setting sun gave the picture an eerie three-dimensional look.

"Where are we?" I asked Rodriguez.

"The Plaza de la Revolución," he answered pleasantly as two of the soldiers took up positions on either side of Seth and me. Back home in the United States, the sight of two obvious foreigners being escorted across a wide plaza by armed soldiers would have aroused the interest of onlookers, but no one—and I judged there to be a couple of hundred Cubans milling about—paid us any notice.

"Why are we being taken here?" Seth asked, indicating the building.

"We are not going there," Rodriguez replied. "That is the Ministerio del Interior building. We are going to *that* building." He pointed to an equally uninspired gray building across the square. "It is where our Maximum Leader, Prime Minister Castro, and his brother have their offices. It is also headquarters for the Central Committee of the Communist Party." He laughed.

"See?" he said. "We treat you especially well. Few tourists see the inside of our most important buildings."

"I don't care whether we see the inside of your buildings or not," Seth said. "I already saw this square when I visited Havana as part of a tour. Now I wish I'd never come."

"Follow me," Rodriguez said. "Just a few questions to be asked."

"And what if we don't want to answer them?" Seth asked, sticking out his jaw for emphasis.

Rodriguez's reply was a noncommittal shrug.

We were propelled toward the gray building, where armed guards checked papers that Rodriguez carried before allowing us entry. He led us down a long hallway past dozens of closed doors until reaching an elevator manned by an armed guard. It carried us up two floors, where we exited and walked across the hall into an office's anteroom. An open door led to a conference room with a small black-and-white marble table and six comfortable yellow swivel armchairs. A large color photograph of Fidel Castro dominated one wall. The other walls contained smaller framed photographs of Havana scenes intermingled with pictures of Castro posing with foreign dignitaries. There was only one person in the room when we entered, the gentleman from the Ministry of the Interior who'd spoken with us at the airport. While Rodriguez was congenial and treated us politely, this man had the look of someone who'd been absent when genes of sympathy and sensitivity had been handed out. He sat ramrod straight at the head of the table, small, rimless eyeglasses catching the light from overhead fixtures.

"Please take a seat," Rodriguez said. "I will be back in a moment."

As Seth and I took chairs, our eyes went back and forth between the interior ministry representative and the only item on the table, a laptop computer. I was about to whisper something to Seth when the door opened and Rodriguez entered, followed by Dr. Pedro Sardina.

"I believe that you know Dr. Sardina," said Rodriguez.

"Yes, we do," I said, "and I must admit, I'm shocked to see him."

Sardina said nothing as Rodriguez took a chair, opened the laptop, and sat back as though expecting us to comment on what it revealed.

"Is that Alvaro Vasquez's laptop?" Seth asked.

"It is," replied Rodriguez.

I looked at Sardina, who sat stoically, his eyes fixed on the tabletop.

"How did you get it?" I asked.

"That really doesn't matter, Mrs. Fletcher," Rodriguez said. "What's important is what is not on it."

"*Not* on it?" I said.

"Yes. Unfortunately someone—and I must assume it was Dr. Vasquez—saw fit to remove the hard drive from the computer. There is nothing on the computer. Absolutely nothing."

I addressed my next question to Sardina. "Did you bring the laptop here to Cuba? Or was it Xavier?"

Sardina looked at Rodriguez, who told him, "You can answer her, Pedro."

"We brought it here together," Sardina said.

"Even though there was nothing on it?"

"We didn't know that. The night Dr. Vasquez died, Xavier hid it away until we left for Havana. We assumed it had all the notes."

"You can imagine how disappointed we were when we turned it on and nothing worked," Rodriguez said. "We had been awaiting its arrival with great expectations. Needless to say, it was a very unpleasant discovery."

"So why have you brought us here?" Seth asked. "You've broken the law, United States law and international law, too. Believe me, sir, someone will pay for this."

Rodriguez told Sardina to bring Xavier to the room. They returned a moment later and joined us at the table.

"Dr. Hazlitt wishes to know why we have invited him and his lovely friend to join us," the Cuban doctor said to Xavier. "Perhaps you are the one to explain."

"I'd like to wipe that smirk off your face," Seth said to Xavier.

"Big, tough talk from you," Xavier said. "You're just like my father, lots of talk, always talk."

"And your father is dead," Seth said, "murdered by the son he loved."

I felt a wave of disgust come over me, and I knew that Seth was feeling the same thing.

"I don't care what you think of me," Xavier said, the nasty smile still on his lips. "What is important is that my father's research benefits the Cuban people."

"And if it doesn't do that," I said, not trying to hide my anger, "was it still worth murdering your father?"

"It wasn't murder," Xavier said. "It was a political assassination. If he hadn't defected, he'd still be alive. But no, he was greedy, and he and my mother abandoned everything good that was given to them and done for them here in Cuba, to sell out for a fancy home and a boat. You know what we call Cubans who defect to the United States? We call them *escoria*. Scum. Worms."

"You are a despicable young man," Seth said. He turned to Dr. Rodriguez. "And you would sanction a murder in order to get your hands on Alvaro Vasquez's research?"

"It was not my decision," Rodriguez said, casting a glance at the Ministry of the Interior's representative. "While I agreed that Alvaro Vasquez's work belonged here, I would never have suggested that he be killed in order to accomplish that. There are always other ways of recovering what has been lost. Alvaro was a friend and colleague. Whenever he mentioned defecting, I always tried to talk him out of it, but I never took him seriously. When he actually did leave for the United States, I was shocked and dismayed."

He looked again at the other official at the table, and I had the feeling that Rodriguez was concerned that he might be viewed as having cooperated with Vasquez's defection. I believed him when he said that he would not have wanted Vasquez assassinated and had tried to talk him out of defecting. Whether the Ministry of the Interior official also believed him was something Rodriguez would have to deal with.

Rodriguez picked up where he'd left off.

"But this has all resulted in a blind alley, I am afraid.

That Alvaro's laptop has been dismantled leaves us in a quandary, Dr. Hazlitt, one that we hope that you will resolve."

I hadn't seen Seth smile since we left Tampa, but now he shook his head in response to the situation, an ironic smile playing on his lips.

"I can't believe how wrong you people could be," he said. "You assumed that because Al Vasquez and I became friends, and because we spent time together over the past few years discussing his research, that I would know anything about his results. Want the truth?" Seth stood and leaned on the table. "Here's the truth. Al never told me anything that could be used by anyone else because every avenue he explored in his research resulted in a dead end. There were no advances toward finding a cure for Alzheimer's. Every test failed. Every hypothesis proved a waste of time."

"You lie!" Xavier snapped. "He was paid millions by Bernie Peters. You think Peters paid that money for nothing?"

"That's exactly what I think," said Seth. "No one liked and admired your father more than I did. I treasured the friendship that developed between us, was thrilled that such a great man would call me—an insignificant country doctor—his friend. But since his death, I've also come to realize that he was not the man I thought he was. Maybe I even suspected it before then—or at least I should have."

"Meaning what, Dr. Hazlitt?"

Seth drew a deep breath before continuing. "From what Mrs. Fletcher and I have learned, Alvaro might not have been completely honest when it came to his business dealings. I believe that even though his research wasn't getting anywhere, he continued to claim that he was on the verge of a breakthrough, encouraging his backer, Bernard Peters at the pharmaceutical company K-Dex, to keep funding his laboratory. Despite his failures, he manipulated Peters—and maybe others, too—into giving him more and more money without any hope of a return."

"That's quite an accusation," Rodriguez said.

"And I hate making it."

"But why should we believe you?" Rodriguez asked. "Everything that Alvaro ever told me, and based upon information we've received from friends in Tampa, he was making progress."

"Friends in Tampa?" I said. "You mean those spies your government has in Florida who report back on Cuban American citizens living there?"

The man from the Ministry of the Interior cleared his throat but said nothing.

"Please sit down, Dr. Hazlitt," Rodriguez said.

"No, I won't sit down," Seth said. "You've brought Mrs. Fletcher and me here under false pretenses in order to satisfy your government's need to benefit from Alvaro's work. Let me tell you something, Dr. Rodriguez. I've always had mixed emotions about where Alvaro's research should end up. On the one hand, I was pleased that a cure for Alzheimer's would come out of the work of someone in America. At the same time, I felt sympathy for Cuba, where Alvaro's work started and was supported for years. But the truth is that neither of our countries will benefit from his research because it didn't lead anywhere, not to a deeper understanding of the disease, nor to a cure. In other words, Dr. Alvaro Vasquez was murdered by his son for no good reason."

"That's not true!" Xavier shouted, pounding the table with his fist. "My father told me he'd already made significant progress." He looked at the official from the Ministry of the Interior, who was scowling at him. "He did. He even said that he had developed an outline of the next steps in his research that would lead to discovering a cure. Everything was in place. He just had to follow his outline."

"He lied to you," Seth said. "There was no outline."

"Perhaps he simply wanted you to have faith in him," I added.

"No! It's true. It must be true."

Rodriguez turned his mild gaze on Vasquez's son. "That's enough, Xavier. We will talk later," he said. To Seth, he said, "I would like to believe that you have told us the truth about Alvaro's research results, Dr. Hazlitt, but I have only your word for it. That is not enough for our government."

"Then maybe these will convince you."

Seth reached into his sport jacket pocket, withdrew the three thumb drives, and slapped them down on the table with such force that everyone jumped.

Chapter Twenty-one

"What are those?" Rodriguez asked once the initial surprise had dissipated.

"*These,*" Seth said, "are what was on Alvaro's laptop, all his notes on his research."

I felt myself release a sigh of relief. When I'd seen the red tape on our luggage, I'd feared that our captors had found the thumb drives and confiscated them. I hadn't said anything to Seth. Our situation was upsetting enough. But he had been wise enough to keep such valuable items on his person, and we'd been fortunate not to be searched personally.

"Where did you get those?" Dr. Rodriguez asked.

"Dr. Vasquez left these thumb drives to me in a letter he wrote."

Rodriguez asked Xavier, "Did you know about these?"

"Yes," Xavier replied. "*He* told me about them yesterday. My father must have transferred his notes to them before he destroyed the laptop."

"You have the letter?" Rodriguez asked.

"No," Seth said. "I left it with the Tampa Police Department, along with a set of the thumb drives."

"The police?" Xavier said. "You never mentioned them."

"That's right," said Seth, "the same police who'll see that you pay for your father's murder."

Xavier's smile grew wide. "Don't count on it, Dr. Hazlitt. Your police don't have jurisdiction here in Havana."

Rodriguez had picked up the thumb drives and held them as though weighing their contents. "You say that Alvaro's research led to nothing?" he said.

"That's right, Doctor. As much as I hate to admit it, Dr. Vasquez's work didn't cast any new light on Alzheimer's disease. I wish it weren't so."

"Don't believe him," Xavier said. "I bet that when you see what's on those thumb drives, you'll know that he's lying."

Rodriguez said to the Ministry of the Interior's representative, "I'll look at what these devices contain overnight, sir, and report to you in the morning."

"What about us?" I asked.

The ministry official answered, "You must remain overnight until Dr. Rodriguez completes his examination."

"In that case, I need to make some calls back home," I said.

"That will not be possible," the ministry official said

in a voice that warned arguing with him would be a waste of time.

Nevertheless, I tried. "There are people who are expecting us to arrive home today," I said. "They'll be worried when we don't show up."

"Depending upon what Dr. Rodriguez reports, you may be allowed to use your phone tomorrow. For now, this meeting is ended." He stood and picked up his briefcase from the floor. "I will expect to hear from you, Dr. Rodriguez, no later than eight o'clock in the morning."

Rodriguez was visibly relieved to see the ministry official leave. There was little doubt who was in charge, and I had the sense that the doctor was feeling pressure to come up with something that would please the taciturn government bigwig. "Well," he said, "there is nothing more to do here except to see that you have a satisfactory dinner and a good night's sleep."

When the limousine pulled up in front of the cabin on the beach, a small white panel truck was also there. A young man wearing a wide-brimmed straw hat and smoking a big cigar hopped out and came to where Seth and I stood with Dr. Rodriguez and our military escorts.

"Your dinner is here," Rodriguez said. "I took the liberty of ordering for you."

The young man removed an insulated box from the truck.

Rodriguez spoke to him in Spanish, and the driver carried our dinner into the cabin.

"A hot meal and a bed," I said with a laugh. "I suppose we should be grateful we're not in a jail cell."

"You have a water view, too," Rodriguez said, smiling. "I trust the accommodations are satisfactory."

"And if they weren't?" I said half seriously. "Would we be given suites in your best hotel?"

"I am afraid not," he replied. "Please, go inside and enjoy your dinner before it gets cold."

Seth, who by this time had calmed down, trudged to the cabin.

"I assume, Mrs. Fletcher, that I needn't underscore the importance of you and Dr. Hazlitt remaining here for the night," Rodriguez said. "We will not take it well if you decide to go for a stroll on the beach."

He needn't have bothered to remind me. I was hardly going to plan an escape, not with the armed soldiers in attendance. Even if we had been able to evade their notice, where would we go? We had no access to a vehicle by land, sea, or air. And while we knew we were close to Havana, the nearest American refuge was all the way on the other side of Cuba at the Guantanamo Bay Naval Base.

"Good night, Dr. Rodriguez," I said.

He leaned close to my ear and said, "Believe me, Mrs. Fletcher, this is not how I would have arranged for your visit. Have a good night's sleep. Tomorrow the sun will shine. It always does in Cuba."

Seth had his suitcase open on the bed when I came into the cabin. He grunted. "Nothing seems to be missing." He turned to me. "Pretty clever of me to keep the thumb drives in my pocket, don't you think?"

"I do," I said. "Thank goodness, too, because they're our only proof of what took place in Dr. Vasquez's laboratory. Without them, the Cubans wouldn't have believed you. I'm sorry to say, though, I doubt if the man from the Ministry of the Interior will let Dr. Rodriguez return them to you after he's examined them."

Seth heaved a great sigh. "You're probably right. Shame I can't follow up with my plan to give them to the researchers in Boston. At least Al's work might have saved someone else from following a wrong turn in the future."

I set our dinner out on the desk—slices of pork in a marinade, served over black beans and white rice, lettuce drenched in a tart dressing, and two loaves of bread with olive butter. Also in the box were two slices of key lime pie, and napkins and utensils. The big surprise was a bottle of red wine and two plastic glasses.

"I suppose we should count our blessings for little things," I said. "It's a nice meal."

"The least they could do for us."

I uncorked the wine, filled the glasses, and held mine up in a toast. "Here's to our visit to the People's Republic of Cuba," I said.

"Not funny, Jessica."

"Better than wallowing in the situation we're in," I said. "Come eat. The pork looks good."

After dinner I settled in the easy chair and got back to a novel I'd started in Tampa. I'd resolved to try to maintain a sense of humor and to keep things in perspective. There was nothing we could do about our situation, at least not until morning, and that wonderful Serenity Prayer popular with members of sobriety groups came to mind: "Grant me the strength to accept things I cannot change, the courage to change the things I can, and the wisdom to know the difference."

Seth had moved outside to sit on the porch. When my eyes started to close, I dog-eared the page I was on in the book and joined him. "I'm going to bed," I said.

"Seems like a sensible decision," he said. Then he started laughing.

"What's so funny, Seth?"

He waved his arm at the door. "Here we are about to share a cozy little cabin in Cuba. Can you imagine what those nosey parkers back in Cabot Cove would have to say about that? Mara's Luncheonette would be buzzing."

"It would certainly give them something to gossip about."

"Don't want to give 'em any ammunition. I'll sleep out here on the porch if you'd like."

"Don't be ridiculous," I said. "We both need a good night's sleep. Let's just not tell them about this part of our adventure. I'll go inside and wash up, change, climb into bed."

"And I'll be along shortly."

I was almost asleep when I heard him come in, use the bathroom, and get into his bed, and I realized how fortunate I was to be in this predicament with someone like Seth Hazlitt. That was my final thought as I drifted off.

To my surprise, I awoke refreshed, having slept solidly. I'd heard Seth get up and shower, and he was on the porch when I emerged dressed and ready for what the day would bring.

"Good sleep?" he asked.

"As a matter of fact, yes. You?"

"Not bad, not bad. Wonder what kind of sleep *they* had." He tipped his head toward the guards who were sitting on the ground under a tree. "When do you think they'll be by to get us?"

"I have no idea." My watch said eight thirty.

"Could use some breakfast," he said, patting his stomach.

"Blueberry pancakes at Mara's?"

"Don't be cruel, Jessica."

The limousine came up the road and pulled to a stop.

"You both look rested," Dr. Rodriguez said.

"Dinner was good," I said.

"Speaking of that, how about breakfast?" Seth said. "Expect breakfast at a five-star resort like this."

"I don't blame you for being irritable," Rodriguez said. "Please pack your suitcases and come with me. We have a stop to make, and then we will make sure you don't go hungry."

Seth and I looked at each other. *Did packing our bags mean we would be leaving Cuba?*

I asked.

"Yes, but we have things to do before you go."

Since we'd never really unpacked, we were back on the porch within ten minutes. Two soldiers took our luggage and put it in the limo's trunk as Seth and I got in the back along with Rodriguez. A solitary armed soldier shared the front with the driver.

"Where are we going?" I asked.

"To an interview."

Interview? I hoped it wasn't an interrogation.

"Could we roll down these darkened windows?" I asked.

"Yes, but why?"

"So I can at least see something of Havana."

"Of course," he said, and the rear windows were lowered halfway.

As we drove slowly through the streets, Havana came alive to me. I saw the island's fabled vintage American automobiles, kept running by ingenious Cuban mechanics; stall after stall of vegetables, fruits, and cigars; uniformed police directing traffic with a flourish; horns blowing in a cacophony of sounds; men, women, and children walking with purpose; street musicians performing for donations; and fascinating buildings, most in desperate need of repair but painted in gaudy island colors, augmented by the strings of laundry drying on the balconies. I was filled with a sense of what a wonderful island this used to be before it fell to Fidel Castro and his Communist leanings. But even though its present-day plight was evident, the spirit of its people was palpable. I wanted to return of my own volition and soak it in.

Seth, too, responded to the vivid scenes outside our windows. "The Cubans are lovely, warm, and gracious people," he said. "They couldn't have been nicer to me and the other physicians that last time I was here. Mind you, I'm not talking about the officials we spent most of our time with, our so-called 'handlers.'" He glanced at Rodriguez. "No offense," he said.

"None taken," Rodriguez replied.

"I had a chance to mingle with some of the common folk on the island," Seth continued. "Despite the lousy situation they're in thanks to Mr. Castro, they're filled with pride and optimism that it'll change one day."

Rodriguez cleared his throat.

"No sense in contradictin' me," Seth told him. "That's what I believe, and you're not going to convince me otherwise."

"I wouldn't dream of it," Rodriguez said, "but I would suggest perhaps that you refrain from expressing such thoughts at our next meeting."

We pulled up in front of the building in the Plaza de la Revolución where we'd been taken the day before. The limousine doors were opened by soldiers, and we stepped out into the bright sunshine. Rodriguez led the way into the building, where we were met in the lobby by a half dozen people, including armed guards in different uniforms from those the soldiers wore, and the same somber representative from the interior ministry we'd met the day before. We were greeted in Spanish and led to a section of the building where security was especially tight; we had to pass through a gauntlet of armed men as we entered a spacious anteroom.

"Please wait," the interior ministry official said as he disappeared through a door. A minute later he reappeared and motioned for us to enter.

The office was huge. Seated behind a massive desk was a man wearing a white suit, white shirt, and white tie with narrow blue stripes. He'd been looking down at papers on his desk through half-glasses. We came to a halt in front of the desk. He looked up, removed his glasses, stood and said, *"Buenos días."*

Rodriguez said, "Dr. Hazlitt and Mrs. Fletcher, may I present to you Señor Raúl Castro, president of the Council of the State of Cuba, and first secretary of the Communist Party."

Seth and I were momentarily speechless. President Castro smiled and shook our hands.

"I have asked that I be allowed to meet you," he said through an interpreter, "and to address a mistake that has been made. My brother would also be here, but he is busy with other matters."

Or too ill to be here, I thought. News of Fidel Castro's failing health was widely reported, which had led to his brother Raúl taking over the reins of government.

"Please accept my apology for the inconvenience you have suffered," the interpreter said after waiting for the president to finish his speech in Spanish. "Sometimes such mistakes are made even when the motivation is pure. I trust that when you return to your United States, you will not look back with too much resentment at what has occurred." He sat down at his desk again. Our interview was over.

Seth and I were hurried out of the office and taken downstairs. Once we were back in the limo, Dr. Rodriguez told the driver, "The airport."

We stopped in front of Terminal 2, and Rodriguez escorted us inside the cavernous building, where he was greeted by two men in suits. After conferring for a few minutes, Rodriguez and the men led the way to a restaurant with a table far removed from others.

"Time for your breakfast, Dr. Hazlitt," Rodriguez said. "My apologies that you had to wait."

"You folks sure do things different here in Cuba," Seth told Rodriguez as he finished up a platter of eggs, bacon, and Cuban bread, which I'd grown to love. "You kidnap us, then you bring us to meet your leader and buy us a big breakfast."

"It is the least we can do," he said. "But as President Castro said, sometimes mistakes are made even with the best of intentions."

"That doesn't excuse the fact that—"

I nudged Seth under the table. This was no time to get into an argument.

Rodriguez gave us back our cell phones. "You are scheduled to leave in one hour," he said. "We have a plane reserved only for you, and all clearances have been obtained from your government and air traffic control to fly to Tampa."

"I hope it's bigger than that puddle jumper we flew in to get here," Seth grumbled.

"It is." Rodriguez's smile faded. "Before you go, I must take a moment to explain something to you. While I was charged with the assignment of learning what progress Dr. Alvaro Vasquez had made in his research, I never once considered that he would be killed. Xavier Vasquez is employed by the Ministry of the Interior, and I was told to use him as a means of determining the status of his father's work. Unfortunately, the young man had his own agenda. He had access to scientists in the interior ministry and was able to obtain the lethal poison he used to murder his father. He and Dr. Sardina conspired to steal his father's laptop, which, as you know, contained nothing."

"Al must have suspected something was up when he stripped the hard drive from his computer," Seth said.

"That's probably when he wrote you the letter saying where the thumb drives could be found," I put in.

"When you informed Xavier about the drives, he decided to bring the two of you to Havana at gunpoint," Rodriguez said. "He is a foolish, brash young man who does not represent me or the Cuban government. He took for granted that bringing you here would make him heroic in our eyes, that he was doing something good for the Cuban people. Instead, he has embarrassed me and all my people. Believe me, President Castro does not often apologize—to anyone!"

"Xavier is a murderer," Seth said. "He has to pay for his crime."

"I'm sure the Ministry of the Interior will have something to say to him."

"That's not enough!"

"What about his sister, Maritza?" I asked.

"I don't know who will undertake to discipline Maritza Vasquez." He looked at Seth. "You know she is a very talented medical student."

"So I've heard," Seth replied.

Rodriguez shook his head regretfully. "Her place in the university was in jeopardy when her parents defected. I often wondered if they realized the pressure put upon their children by their decision to leave."

"Is she still in medical school?" I asked.

"Oh, yes. She managed to convince the authorities that her loyalty lay with Cuba, not with her mother and father. I believe it is she who introduced her brother to the idea of using a powerful poison to take their father's life."

"What a calamity for the Vasquez family," I said. "The children conspire to kill their father and leave a mother struggling with the disease he was trying to cure. Poor woman."

"Perhaps Ivelisse will be fortunate enough not to comprehend all that has taken place," Rodriguez said. "But come. Your plane home is waiting."

The plane that would take us back to Tampa and the United States was, as Rodriguez had promised, larger than Xavier Vasquez's Cessna 172. It was a vintage Russian-built twin-engine piston-prop Ilyushin 11-14 that had probably been built in the 1950s to replace America's workhorse DC-3. A pilot and copilot greeted us from the cockpit as we boarded and took two of the eighteen vacant seats.

"You sure this thing will fly?" Seth asked Rodriguez.

He laughed. "It hasn't crashed yet," he replied. As he shook our hands, he said, "One last favor."

"Yes?"

"You will undoubtedly be asked by many about your unexpected stay here in Cuba. All I ask is that you report that you were treated with dignity while here as our accidental guests."

"Accidental?" Seth said. "I'd hardly call being kidnapped and threatened an 'accident.'"

I quickly said, "We will report that considering the circumstances, you did all you could to provide for us."

"*Buen viaje*," he said. "Spanish for have a good trip."

"*Gracias*," I said.

"Oh," he said, "please remember me to Ivelisse Vasquez. A lovely woman. I am afraid that her deteriorating condition was very much behind Alvaro's interest in Alzheimer's disease, and perhaps why he felt he needed to leave Cuba to continue his research in the United States. *Adiós*, my new *amigos*."

Chapter Twenty-two

The flight to Tampa in the vintage Russian-built aircraft was smooth and without incident. It was a strange feeling being in a plane with nothing but empty seats around us—except for those on which we'd piled our luggage—but we used the time to discuss everything that had happened to us over the past twenty-four hours.

"I only hope that Xavier gets what's coming to him, and not just some bureaucratic reprimand," Seth said. "His father may not have been the most honest man, but he certainly didn't deserve to be killed."

"When he introduced me to Xavier at the party, Al sounded so proud of him," I said.

"Al told me that their relationship suffered when he and Ivelisse defected, but he was still fond of his son and hoped they could patch things up. Too bad it's too late."

"It's too late for Alvaro Vasquez," I said, "but it's not too late for you to give those thumb drives to your research colleagues in Boston."

"What do you mean? I never got them back from Rodriguez."

"I know, but I've got this." I reached into my shoulder bag and pulled out my laptop. "We copied Al's files onto my computer before transferring them to the second set of thumb drives," I said. "All his notes are still in here."

"Jessica, you're a marvel!" Seth said, delight on his face. "But I wonder why the Cubans didn't confiscate your computer when they searched our luggage."

"I was wondering that myself," I said, "but I think I've figured it out. You're the one who was so close to Vasquez. They were probably more interested to find out which bag was yours, and when they opened mine and saw women's clothes, they just closed it up again. Besides, I had this buried in the bottom of the suitcase wrapped inside my robe."

"Talk about a cover-up," Seth said, chuckling at his own joke.

The pilot landed smoothly at Tampa airport and taxied to a remote corner of the field, far removed from the terminal and other commercial aircraft. We had naturally speculated about the behind-the-scenes machinations that had transpired before this flight from Cuba to Tampa could be arranged and had hoped that it wouldn't involve us in any official role. But we were to be disappointed.

I looked out my window and saw a dozen or so people awaiting our arrival. Included in the group were

Oona Mendez and Karl Westerkoch. I pointed them out to Seth, who muttered, "I could do without having to see them again."

The copilot came back and opened the door, and two members of the ground crew pushed a wheeled set of stairs to it.

"Thank you," I told the copilot.

"My pleasure," he said, smiling as he lowered our luggage down the stairs to waiting hands. *"Buenas tardes, señora."*

Seth preceded me down the staircase. Before going to the door, I poked my head into the cockpit and gave a final good-bye to the pilots, who wished me well. I stepped outside and looked to where Seth now stood speaking with Oona and Westerkoch. I carefully negotiated the narrow metal steps, holding on to the railings, and stepped onto the tarmac with a sense of overall relief. It was good to be back on U.S. soil.

"Come with us," Oona said and led us through the knot of people into a small hangar reserved for private aircraft. We were ushered into an office with a round wooden table and folding chairs. We'd no sooner been seated when two others arrived who were introduced as representatives of the U.S. State Department.

"We need to debrief you on your recent trip to Cuba," one said.

"Nothing to tell you," Seth said grumpily.

"Just a few questions," the fellow from State said. "We promise we won't take too much of your time."

"We're happy to cooperate," I said. "We're just glad to be home."

Our official debriefing took almost an hour, and I

was concerned that Seth's patience would wear thin and that he would rebel. But he maintained his composure and even made a few witty comments about Cuba and our meeting with Raúl Castro. The State Department officials were especially interested in our evaluation of President Castro's physical and mental health.

"He looked in good physical shape to me," Seth said.

"What did he say about his brother Fidel Castro?"

"Just that he was busy," I said.

"Nothing about his health?"

"No," I said. "That never came up."

We were asked about the other people with whom we met, including Dr. Rodriguez and the unnamed representative of the Cuban Ministry of the Interior. We told them everything we could think of, including that Dr. Rodriguez was especially solicitous and that we were treated with respect considering the circumstances.

Naturally, the questioners were also interested in how we were kidnapped by Xavier and his sister and what we knew of their life and connections in Cuba.

"One thing we do know," Seth said, "is that Xavier Vasquez murdered his father using a poison he'd gotten from someone in the Cuban government. You can find out more about it by talking to Dr. San Martín, the medical examiner here in Tampa."

"We'll be sure to do that. You say that Xavier Vasquez murdered his father. Is it your belief that he plans to remain in Cuba?"

"No doubt about that. Practically bragged to me that he was out of the range of our criminal jurisdiction."

"We'll see about that."

"Dr. Rodriguez led us to believe that the Ministry of the Interior would deal with him," I added. "I don't know whether they're concerned that he's a murderer, but he's obviously upset those he works for."

"We have ways of keeping track of what happens to him in Cuba," Westerkoch said.

I'm sure you do, I thought.

"What about the daughter?" we were asked.

"After her father's death, she was allowed out of Cuba to see her mother," I said. "She's still a student, so I imagine that she'll remain in Cuba, too. It's so sad."

"What is?"

"Dr. Vasquez's widow, Ivelisse. She's all alone. Aside from not being well, she has a son who murdered her husband and a daughter who may have abetted him. This entire affair defines the word 'tragedy.'"

The State representatives thanked us for our information and cautioned us to be careful about what we said about our experience.

"Staying in Tampa for a while?" Oona Mendez asked.

Seth was quick to answer. "No," he said, "we'll be leaving on the first available plane home."

Westerkoch chuckled, actually chuckled. "Intrigue not your cup of tea, Doctor?"

"No! It certainly is not," Seth said.

"There's a plane leaving for Hartford, Connecticut, in an hour and a half," Oona said.

"Do they have seats?"

"They have seats," she replied.

"Then we'll be on it," said Seth. "Right, Jessica?"

"Right," I said.

I called Jed Richardson at the Cabot Cove airport and arranged for him to meet us in Hartford and ferry us home, and Seth called his office and told his distraught nurse—"Where have you been? I've been frantic"—to tell her our plans.

We were waiting in the boarding area when the reporter from the *Tampa Tribune*, Peggy Lohman, breathless and talking as fast as ever, entered the lounge and came to where we sat. "I missed you before," she said, "but they told me you were leaving for home and—"

"Why don't you sit down, Ms. Lohman," Seth suggested, "and *slow* down."

"Thank you. I was afraid I'd be too late. Wow, what a twist to the Vasquez story. Is it true that you were hijacked to Cuba by Dr. Vasquez's son and daughter?"

I checked Seth before responding. "Actually, Ms. Lohman, I think that Dr. Hazlitt and I would prefer not to comment on what happened."

She looked horrified. "You can't say that," she said. "This is big news. My editor told me to tell you that if you stay in Tampa for a few days, we'll pick up all your expenses, every one of them, for an exclusive."

"I understand that you've a job to do, Ms. Lohman," Seth said, "but Mrs. Fletcher and I are anxious to get home and put this behind us."

"But what about your experiences in Cuba? We have a big Cuban American readership in Tampa. Would you at least comment on that?"

Seth gave me a look that said that I should answer the reporter.

"All we have to say about our experiences in Cuba—

and bear in mind they only lasted a day and a night—is that we were treated decently, were not abused in any way, and we found the Cuban people to be warm and friendly. As for the government, Dr. Hazlitt and I fervently wish that the Cuban people will be free one day, and we expect that will eventually happen. Other than that, Ms. Lohman, it was truly a pleasure meeting you. You'll have to excuse us. They're boarding our flight."

Chapter Twenty-three

We arrived in Cabot Cove that evening in Jed Richardson's twin-engine Cessna. Seth was so grateful to be going home, he refrained from commenting about the size of the plane. Jed kindly dropped us off at Seth's house before driving himself to town. Seth's office is in his home, and his nurse and receptionist had left him a sheaf of pink papers detailing calls to be returned. While I rustled up food from Seth's freezer—we'd never had any lunch—Seth excused himself to retrieve something from his office, returning a few minutes later with a big fat cigar.

I couldn't help but laugh. "Where did you get that?"

"Al gave it to me the first time I was in Cuba," he said pulling out a chair at his kitchen table.

"You're going to start smoking cigars?" I asked.

"I might," he said, sitting back and admiring the cigar he held in his fingers. "That's between you and me,

Jessica. Cuban cigars are illegal here in the States. This is a Hoyo de Monterrey Double Corona, one of the best, robust and full-bodied."

"You sound like an advertisement," I said. "If it's illegal, how did you get it into the country?"

"Slid it in one of my shoes that I packed and crossed my fingers that Customs wouldn't check my bag. Didn't want to end up a prisoner in Guantanamo."

"Or stateside," I added. "You know that won't go over big with those patients you're always urging to quit smoking."

He came forward in his chair and used the cigar the way Groucho Marx would, twirling it in front of me. "I'll just have to smoke it sub rosa," he said, "sneak a puff now and then the way I did as a teenager with cigarettes behind the barn."

"I never knew that about you, Seth Hazlitt," I said.

"Lots you don't know about me, Jessica," he said with a smirk.

He was joking, of course, about intending to smoke that cigar.

Or was he?

"We toured a cigar factory there," he said. "Amazing how many steps are needed to create a truly good cigar, a painstaking process. In fact, Castro once said—at least that's the story—that it's easier to produce a fine cognac than to produce a good cigar." He grinned.

"Sounds like a bit of Castro braggadocio to me," I said. "I'm surprised that a bunch of American physicians would end up visiting a cigar factory."

"All part of the experience," he said, his smile fading. "We spent most of the time meeting with Cuban doctors. Amazing, Jessica, how much good research was being conducted in that poor country, first-class medical research. That's when I met Al."

I put my hand on Seth's arm. "He was a good friend, even if he wasn't all he professed to be."

"That he was."

We ate at Seth's kitchen table. He insisted upon cleaning up since I'd prepared the meal. Afterward, he sat down again to go through the pink notices of all the calls he'd received while he'd been away. Some of them were from media, and one, of course, from Evelyn Phillips, editor of the *Cabot Cove Gazette*. "The last thing I want," he said, "is to have to deal with another jo-jeezly reporter."

"I share your feelings," I said, "but I'm afraid that we won't have much of a choice. Our little adventure is bound to be big news. After all, it wasn't a PTA bake sale or a cat rescued from a tree. Maybe it won't be as bad as we're anticipating. How about giving me a ride home? I'm ready to fall on my nose."

As it turned out, it *was* as bad as we'd anticipated. Once word got out, we were bombarded with calls from media, local, regional, and national. Even the British Broadcasting Corporation got in touch and requested an interview. We turned to a friend, Sanford Teller, who had a public relations agency in town, and he urged us to hold a press conference and get it over with in one fell swoop. It was a standing-room-only event held in our city hall's meeting room. Seth and I answered the questions as best we could, careful not to stray into editorializing or venturing into the political arena. Everyone seemed satisfied as the room cleared, and Teller congratulated us on putting on a good performance. I didn't consider that we'd *performed*; I was just glad that it was over and we could get back to our normal lives. The only positive thing that came out of all the attention was that the sales of my latest book increased dramatically, which pleased my publisher, Vaughan Buckley, and my agent, Matt Miller.

Thankfully, media interest in our Cuban experience soon faded, replaced in newspapers and on television by more pressing issues of the day, which didn't mean that either Seth or I would ever forget it. What stayed with us most was the exasperation that Xavier Vasquez had murdered his father and was getting away with it by living in Cuba.

I copied Dr. Alvaro Vasquez's research notes from my laptop to a set of thumb drives, which Seth delivered to a colleague in Boston, who confirmed that Alvaro Vasquez's research on the mysteries of Alzheimer's disease hadn't led to anything medically useful. We both maintained occasional contact with Dr. San Martín, and with Detective Machado, who informed us that Tampa PD had charged Xavier Vasquez with his father's murder and had listed him as a fugitive. Seth telephoned Ivelisse Vasquez a few times and reported that a full-time caregiver had been hired. Our hearts went out to her. She'd not only seen her husband murdered; she had to live with the knowledge that her son had been his killer. If her advancing disease allowed her to forget, it was a blessing.

I had a few things to remind me of the adventure Seth and I had been on. I used the cigar lighter I'd purchased from the peddler in Ybor City to light kindling in my fireplace, and I'd framed a photo of the Columbia Restaurant and hung it over my desk, along with other photos from past trips. But in time our forced visit to Cuba receded in our memories, replaced by the activities of our day-to-day lives.

Then, six months after we'd returned to Cabot Cove, I received a phone call from Tampa.

"Oona Mendez," the caller said. "Remember me?"

"Of course. How are you?"

"Doing splendidly. I'm calling with a bit of news. As you know, Xavier Vasquez has been charged with his father's murder."

"Dr. Hazlitt and I were pleased to see that those charges had been filed, not that anything will come of it."

"That's where you might be wrong."

"Oh? Tell me more."

"A remarkable thing has happened. I don't know if you're aware that we have an extradition treaty with Cuba."

"We do? I had assumed the opposite."

"And for good reason. The original treaty was signed back in 1904 but rescinded in 1926. Then, in 1959, a new extradition treaty was signed. Of course, because of the frayed state of relations between Washington and Havana, that more recent treaty hasn't been used since it was signed into law. However—"

"Are you saying that it's about to be put to use where Xavier Vasquez is concerned?"

"That's exactly what I'm saying. It's been a long, tough process to bring it to this point, a lot of strings being pulled, and a real diplomatic push by the State Department among others, but it looks like it's worked. The Cuban government has agreed to extradite Xavier to the United States."

"That's wonderful! Justice will be served."

"Believe me, I share your enthusiasm. Yes, justice will be served, but there's a much larger meaning to all this. Raúl Castro, who now runs the government, is less hard-line than his brother Fidel. We've learned through diplomatic channels and intelligence agencies that he's leaning toward opening up new lines of communication with us. It's the opinion of those in State and the other agencies that his acceptance of extradition might be a signal that he's serious about making those changes."

"Well," I said, "I'm pleased to hear that. I know that Dr. Hazlitt will be delighted to know that Xavier might soon be facing trial for murder."

"I knew that you'd be interested," Oona said. "I get the feeling that your unexpected and unwelcome visit to Cuba might have helped pave the way for this to happen. Maybe you charmed Raúl Castro."

"I don't see how," I said. "I don't think I said two words to the man, but thank you for sharing this news. I can't wait to tell Seth."

Seth and I celebrated that night with friends. Toward the end of the evening, our travel agent, Susan Shevlin, said that she was putting together a State Department–approved person-to-person trip to Havana. "How about you two signing up?" she said.

Seth looked at Susan quizzically and said, "You can't be serious."

"Oh, but I am," she said. "How about you, Jessica?"

"I don't think so," I said, but I felt doubts creeping in.

What little I'd seen of Cuba had been as a reluctant visitor. Experiencing it as a willing tourist was appealing. I tucked that thought away, but in my heart I knew: One day I would return.

Read on for a peek at another
Murder, She Wrote Mystery

ALOHA BETRAYED

Available now from
Obsidian.

***Aloha*—Hawaiian greeting that can mean "hello"**

"Look at the enemy. It looks beautiful, doesn't it? But it, like the shiny red apple handed to Snow White, is poisonous. Touch the sap, and it will burn you. Ingest it, and its cardiac glycosides will impede your heart function. Breathe in the powdery fumes of the dry, dead vine, and it will induce a violent cough. Yet some gardeners still insist on planting *Cryptostegia grandiflora* as an ornamental."

Mala Kapule tapped a key on her laptop and the image of the flower projected on the wall disappeared. "So, this is your assignment for the weekend. Take your camera, your cell phone, your tablet, and look into your neighbors' yards. Don't tell them I said so."

I laughed along with the rest of the class.

"You're looking for *Cryptostegia grandiflora*, also

known as Malay rubber vine. Look for pink buds and white flowers with a pink throat. Look for the glossy leaves set opposite one another on the stem. But do not touch it! Just fill out the report for the Maui Invasive Species Committee, the same as you did for the Madagascan ragwort or fireweed. See the handout for more instructions."

A buzzer sounded and Mala's students gathered their papers and filed out of the room. One tall young man lingered near her desk, perhaps hoping for a moment of private attention. He stooped over so that his head was closer to hers.

"Not now, Dale," I heard her say. "We can discuss it on Monday."

Dale scowled at her. "You're always putting me off."

"Perhaps you should think about why that is," his young professor replied, stuffing her briefcase with the extra handouts left on her desk. "Now, please excuse me."

She aimed a wide smile in my direction and came forward with her right arm extended. "Mrs. Fletcher, I'd know you anywhere. What a surprise to see you here. I heard you were coming, but I didn't expect you to slip into the back of my classroom." She pumped my hand.

"I hope I didn't disturb the lesson," I said, returning her smile.

"Not at all. How is Dr. Hazlitt? Charming as ever?"

"He would blush to hear you say that," I replied.

Mala chuckled. "Uncle Barrett said that Seth Hazlitt was the crabbiest fellow in their class at medical school, but also the best diagnostician."

"I don't doubt it," I said, "about being a superb diagnostician. But Seth really isn't crabby. He just doesn't suffer fools easily."

"Uncle Barrett was the same way."

"I was sorry to hear about your uncle," I said.

Mala's expression turned wistful. "He was a marvelous man. I think I disappointed him in choosing botany over medicine, but he always graciously included me when he boasted about the *scientists* in the family."

"As well he should. I understand that you're in line for chair of the department."

"That was Uncle Barrett's idea, not mine." Mala walked with me down the hallway of the one-story building. "It's never going to happen. Even forgetting my political views—which they won't—there's a lot of competition in the college's horticultural department. The landscaping specialists have an edge. My specialty, invasive species, doesn't have the snob appeal of aquaponics and xeriscaping."

"I'll take your word for it," I said through a laugh, "but you're speaking a different language."

"Aquaponics is a fancy term for a kind of agriculture that grows fish and plants in the same pond, and xeriscaping is simply landscaping with drought-resistant plants," she said, pulling a pair of sunglasses from her handbag and putting them on. "The climate on Maui varies depending upon where you are on the island. It's a challenge for landscapers to match plants to the conditions, which gives them a chance to show off."

"But such variety must be rewarding for botanists, too." We pushed through the doors to the outside, where I also donned sunglasses.

"There's certainly a lot to keep us busy," she replied. "Do you have time for a cup of coffee? They're featuring Kona at the café today."

"I'd love it."

I had arrived in Hawaii the day before, a guest of the Maui Police Department, to teach a class on community involvement in criminal investigations. My coteacher was a retired Maui detective and local legend. Since it is the rare government that will pay for a mystery writer's opinion, my expenses had been defrayed by a foundation dedicated to bringing in speakers "to broaden the vision of police recruits and encourage the application of creative thinking to solving crime." At least that's what the invitation letter had stated as its goal.

I was hesitant at first, not certain what I could contribute to the education of future police officers since the field had changed so drastically with the integration of technology into forensics. Besides, it had been a good many years since I'd taught criminology in Manhattan. But Seth Hazlitt, my dear friend and Cabot Cove's favorite physician, had convinced me to accept.

"Anyone wants to give me a free trip to Hawaii, I'd be a fool not to take it," he'd said with the lack of subtlety for which he's renowned.

Since I was between books, and with the added incentive of Seth's insistence that I look up his medical school buddy, I had accepted the challenge to conduct a class on community involvement in police investigations. Unfortunately, Barrett Kapule, Mala's uncle and Seth's old friend, had died the month before my arrival, and Seth had asked me to deliver a condolence letter he'd written to the family. I hadn't done it yet, wanting to wait for the appropriate time.

Mala and I entered the bustling campus café and found an unoccupied table. She insisted on getting the coffee and I gratefully accepted. The trip to Honolulu from New York's John F. Kennedy International Airport was catching up to me—a ten-and-a-half-hour flight, not counting the travel time it had taken me to get to New York from my home in Cabot Cove, Maine, on one end of the trip, and the connecting flight to Maui from the Hawaiian capital on the other. Although I'd slept well the night I arrived, my body wasn't certain what time zone it was in, nor was my brain.

"Is this your first trip to Hawaii?" Mala asked when she'd returned to our table carrying a tray with two mugs.

"Ooh, that smells wonderful," I said, taking one of them. "I've been to Hawaii a couple of times, but not in recent years. The last time, I was returning to the States from a book tour in Japan and stopped off in Honolulu for a vacation. This time it's a working trip, but I'm looking forward to exploring the island between classes. May I count on you for suggestions of special places to see?"

Mala laughed. "Try to stop me. There are so many beautiful and interesting things to see here. Do you have a car?"

I smiled at her over the rim of my mug. "I'm afraid I don't drive."

"Really?"

"I've never gotten around to it, which never fails to

amuse my friends back home. I do have a pilot's license, though, but that won't do me much good."

"Not driving may prove a little tricky, but I'm sure we can fix you up with some form of transportation. I have a cousin who drives a cab."

"I can ride a bike," I said. "In fact, I biked over here from the resort where I'm staying."

She looked me up and down.

"What is it?"

"I don't want to offend you."

"How can you offend me?"

"There is a famous bike excursion, but it's not for the faint of heart."

"I'm listening."

"Tour companies host a sunrise trip up the Haleakala volcano and offer bicycles to those brave enough to ride down. It's pretty harrowing to bike on those twisting roads. Think you might be up for that?"

I took a sip of the aromatic coffee and stifled a yawn. "Not today or tomorrow," I said with a wink, "but maybe later in the week."

Mala's silvery laugh had several students turning to see whom it belonged to.

She was a beautiful woman with thick black hair pulled back into a low ponytail, and deep brown eyes that tilted up when she smiled, which was often. I estimated her to be in her mid-thirties, but with her smooth skin and delicate build, she could have passed for a student instead of a teacher. It was her manner, however, that gave her age away. She held herself confidently and ignored the appreciative glances sent her way. She assumed that people were interested in her because of what she had to say rather than her looks, which only enhanced her attraction. To be fair to her admirers, perhaps it was a little bit of both.

Seth had shown me some of Barrett's e-mails to him extolling Mala's intelligence and the contributions she made, not only to the college but also to the community, through her activism on the ecological front. While she'd rattled a few commercial cages—nurseries that insisted on selling plants she considered a threat to the native vegetation—her latest project, and the one that raised the most controversy, was her opposition to a new telescope being built atop Haleakala.

With the University of Hawaii firmly in the "pro" column for the telescope, Mala had offended the powers that be by siding with a group of Hawaiians who argued that the construction not only jeopardized the ecological balance of the mountain, but also threatened to have a devastating impact on the dormant volcano, a *wahi pana*, or sacred site, a cultural touchstone for the Hawaiian people. Mala's contrary stance notwithstanding, her uncle Barrett was certain the university would recognize and reward her brilliance.

"Speaking of Haleakala," I said, "is that controversial telescope project still going forward?"

"Unfortunately, yes. I have a meeting next week on what our next steps should be. What do you know about it?"

"Not very much—only what your uncle Barrett passed along to Seth Hazlitt."

"Are you interested? Maybe you'd like to join us," she said eagerly. "We can always use an extra voice, especially one as articulate as yours."

"It's nice of you to say, but I don't see what help I could provide, not being knowledgeable about the topic or its history. You certainly wouldn't want this voice to say the wrong thing."

"No, I wouldn't. But somehow I don't think you would expound about a subject you don't know. You're not opposed to the idea of learning more about it, are you?"

"No, of course not. I'm always interested in new things."

"I hope you won't be sorry you said that," Mala said, laughing as she pulled her briefcase back onto her lap. "I get furious e-mails from people who object to what I'm doing. Next thing you know, there'll be death threats."

"Oh, my, is it as bad as that?"

"I'm afraid so. It's an emotional issue." She opened a side pocket and withdrew a large envelope containing a sheaf of papers. "This is your basic course in Haleakala's Science City." She handed me the envelope. "If nothing else, it should help you get to sleep at night."

"I don't think getting to sleep is going to be a problem," I said. "Staying awake is another matter altogether."

"When you're well rested," Mala said, "I'll give you a list of things you might like to do while you're here, other than tag along with me to meetings. You certainly want to attend a luau."

"I'm going to one tonight."

"In Wailea?"

"I believe so."

"Wonderful! Another cousin is one of the dancers. Perhaps I'll see you there. It depends on the outcome of my next meeting." She looked at her watch.

"Am I holding you up?"

"Not at all. I have a little time yet, but if I get there early, I may be able to sneak in ahead of the appointment before mine. My competition for the department chair wants to meet with me." She made a face. "Dreadful man. It should be interesting."

We left the café and walked back toward the horticulture building.

"Where will you be teaching?" Mala asked.

"The college has given us a classroom in one of the buildings near the police station," I replied. "We start tomorrow. I stopped there today to introduce myself to the other instructor who'll be teaching with me."

"Oh, and who is that?"

"Detective Mike Kane. When I told him I was going to look for your class, he said he'd heard great things about you. Do you know his name?"

"Of course," Mala said with a grin. "It's a small island. Everyone knows everyone."

"How is that possible? There must be more than a hundred thousand people living here, not counting the tourists."

"I think it's closer to a hundred fifty thousand now," she said. "And maybe saying everyone knows everyone is a bit of an exaggeration. We don't know the seasonal workers, of course. Not many of the kids who come to work in hotels and restaurants stay long enough or interact with the locals enough to become familiar. And I couldn't say we know all the retirees who've decided to live out the rest of their lives on our golf courses. But for those of us whose families have been here for generations, we all know or at least know *of* each other."

"Detective Kane is a Native Hawaiian?"

"We don't use the word 'native.' His father was, or at least has Hawaiian in his background, but Mike is also a *kahuna*, a big shot. I don't know how many times he's been written up in the local paper. But I thought he was retired."

"He's retired from the police department," I said. "Now he works in hotel security, but he calls it something else."

"Loss prevention," she said, chuckling and shaking her head. "The hotels in the islands don't want you to think there's any crime here, so they renamed their security offices. It's still the place you go to report if anything's missing."

"Yes, that's the term. But I understand he also consults for the police department."

"I'm sure he does. He's famous. Probably every young police officer with a puzzling case shows up on his doorstep looking for advice."

"Well, now they'll get a chance to pick his brain in a formal setting," I said. "I'm looking forward to what I can learn from him as well."

"And he must be thrilled to have a famous writer to work with."

We had stopped outside an impressive concrete and steel building with a turquoise roof, on top of which were solar panels and small white wind turbines rotating in the breeze. A sign outside read 'IKE LE'A, which I later learned means "to see clearly."

"This is the new science building," Mala said. "My appointment is in here." She smiled softly. "I'm so happy you're here. Uncle Barrett would have loved to meet you."

"And I would have loved to meet him, too."

She sighed. "I hope I get to see you later."

"Let's plan on it."

"Well, the Wailea luau draws several hundred people. It may be hard to locate one person in that crowd."

"You look for me and I'll look for you," I said. "I'm sure we'll find each other."

But I was wrong.

FROM THE MYSTERY SERIES
MURDER, SHE WROTE

by Jessica Fletcher & Donald Bain

Based on the Universal television series
Created by Peter S. Fischer, Richard Levinson & William Link

**Available wherever books are sold or at
penguin.com**

S0013